For Jan and Stan
who taught us that the best Friday nights are spent at the library

Baker's Magic is published by Capstone Young Readers
A Capstone Imprint
1710 Roe Crest Drive
North Mankato, MN 56003
www.mycapstone.com

Text copyright © 2016 by Diane Zahler

Library of Congress Cataloging-in-Publication Data
Zahler, Diane, author.
Baker's magic / Diane Zahler.
pages cm
Summary: Bee is an orphan in the poor kingdom of Aradyn, and when she is caught stealing a bun from a bakery, the lonely baker offers to take her on as an apprentice—but when she meets Princess Anika, and the evil mage Joris who is her "guardian," she embarks on a journey to save Anika, and restore the kingdom to its rightful ruler.
ISBN 978-1-4965-2724-0 (library binding) — ISBN 978-1-62370-642-5 (paper over board) — ISBN 978-1-62370-643-2 (paperback) — ISBN 978-1-4965-2726-4 (eBook PDF)
1. Baking—Juvenile fiction. 2. Orphans—Juvenile fiction. 3. Magic—Juvenile fiction. 4. Quests (Expeditions)—Juvenile fiction. 5. Wizards—Juvenile fiction. 6. Princesses—Juvenile fiction. [1. Fantasy. 2. Orphans—Fiction.] I. Title.
PZ7.Z246Bak 2016
813.54—dc23
[Fic]   2015026868

Editor: Kristen Mohn
Designer: Tracy McCabe

Design elements: Capstone: Mina Price; Shutterstock: Daniela Barreto, fluidworkshop, OK-SANA, Potapov Alexander, Vertyr

Printed and bound in China.
009971S17

BAKER'S MAGIC

DIANE ZAHLER

capstone

CHAPTER 1

Bee had never been so hungry in her life.

Oh, she'd been hungry plenty of times. Stomach-growling, eat-a-big-meal hungry. But this was different. This hunger clawed at her insides, making her legs weak and her vision blurry. She couldn't remember the last time she'd eaten. Was it yesterday morning, or the morning before? It didn't matter. She had to keep walking. One foot in front of the other, the way she'd been doing for hours. For days. For weeks.

She kept her gray eyes trained on the ground, watching her feet move along the dirt road. She'd passed only two travelers since dawn. The first had been a hedge wizard, his green robes flapping as he strode past her, muttering to himself. The second was a merchant traveling back toward the coast, his cart piled high with nets to sell to the fishermen in the little coastal villages. If he'd been heading inland toward Zeewal, she would have asked for a ride, but luck hadn't been with her.

At least it was flat, as the whole countryside of Aradyn was flat—waving grasses for miles with nothing taller than a bush or a windmill to break the horizon. A hill would have been too much for her. The road ran alongside a canal, its slow-moving water green with algae. The banks of the canal were worn away, eroded by the fierce autumn storms that came sweeping up from the sea. Bee knew there were fish in there, and the thought of them made her mouth water. Roasted fish, fried fish, fish baked in a crust with fragrant steam rising . . . *Stop it. Just walk,* she told herself. *Just keep walking.*

A sudden flash of red made her raise her head. Her jaw dropped in amazement, the pain in her stomach momentarily forgotten. Off to the side, opposite the canal, a crimson stripe of field stretched into the distance, as far as she could see. Bordering it was a long swath of bright pink, and next to that a band of brilliant orange. She moved to the edge of the road and tried to bring the field into focus.

Flowers. It was flowers! Hundreds, no, thousands upon thousands of flowers, red, pink, and orange. She'd reached the tulip fields outside Zeewal at last. She'd seen tulips before, of course, but only small patches of them, and rarely in colors other than red or yellow. They didn't grow very well in the sandy soil at the coast, where Bee had lived. For years she'd heard about these fields, and she'd never quite believed the reports. Like the biggest carpet in the world, with the brightest colors, all made of flowers, people had said. How ridiculous it had sounded! But that was exactly what it looked like—only the description didn't really express how astonishing, how incredibly beautiful it was.

Bee stood and stared for a few minutes, entranced. In the distance, there were other colors—yellow, white, a deep purple so dark it almost looked black. The vivid stripes wavered in the sunlight. It was dizzying, and she turned away. Up the road, she saw stone walls rising high. Above them soared spires and turrets. *It must be Zeewal,* she thought. It was hard to tell how far away it was, but just seeing the walls of the town gave her the strength to start moving again. One foot, then the other. Faster now, because food was near.

Finally Bee reached the town gate. It was open, and she trudged through unnoticed, just a skinny, raggedy child like any other in the kingdom. She passed a cobbler's shop, and a bookbinder, a fishmonger's, a silversmith's. Her nose guided her. There was a scent of something wonderfully sweet that grew stronger and stronger as she walked.

And then, at last, she saw a bakery. The sign over the door showed a beautifully painted cake and a loaf of bread; just the picture was enough to make Bee clutch her middle.

She peered in through the front window and was glad to see that the shop was crowded with buyers. When she pushed open the front door, a little bell at the top rang and she winced—she hadn't wanted to be noticed. But the customers were all too intent on their purchases to pay her any mind. The shop smelled even better inside. There were loaves of bread, brown, white, and embedded with rye seeds. There were a few little tarts with red berries nested in custard. And there, sitting alone on a plate on a metal shelf near the front window, was one perfect sweet roll.

It was the most beautiful sweet roll Bee had ever seen. A flawless circle, puffy from rising, it was studded with raisins and drizzled with pink icing. She could feel the hunger rake its claws along her stomach lining as she gazed at it. Without thinking, she reached out and grabbed the sticky pastry, then turned and shoved her way back through the crowd.

She pushed against the door, relieved when it swung open. But then, behind her, she heard someone shout, "You! Stop, you!"

Shocked, Bee turned her head. Everyone in the bakery

stared at her as the voice continued to yell, "Thief! Stop that thief!" It took a moment for Bee to realize that she was the thief. But hunger gnawed in her stomach, and so she spun and sprinted out of the shop.

Bee dodged across the street, around a carriage and past a cart to the other side. Then her foot caught on something, and all at once she was airborne. She landed on the hard stones with a bone-jarring thump. To her horror, the bun flew out of her grasp and rolled slowly across the cobblestones until it came to rest on a fresh pile of horse dung.

"Gotcha!" A hand grabbed her by the ear and pulled her up. It was the baker. For a big man, he had moved fast. He stood, one hand holding her by the ear in a painfully tight grip, the other on his hip. His white apron strained over a round belly, and his face was just as round. He had a little halo of white curls, and his cheeks were strawberry-red with rage.

"Do you know what we do with thieves in Zeewal?" the baker demanded.

Bee stared at her feet. Her toes showed through her right boot, where she'd had to cut it open when that foot grew too big. Her left foot was a little smaller. Her trousers were ripped at the knee from her fall, and her hand was scraped. She hurt all over, but the worst pain was her stomach when she looked at that roll sitting in the horse manure.

A crowd had gathered around Bee—the customers from the bakery and all the people who'd been passing by when she ran out. She couldn't bear to look at them. She'd never stolen anything before. She was no thief. Except . . . now it seemed she was.

"Why, you're a girl," someone observed. She looked up. It was a boy who'd spoken, one of the scruffy children of Zeewal. He was older than Bee, maybe sixteen or seventeen, and he was even dirtier than she was. His face and apron were streaked with black, and his nails were filthy.

"So you can tell the difference!" she said, the scorn in her voice living up to the sting in her name. The crowd snickered. But Bee could understand the confusion. Her hair was short and uneven; she'd chopped it off herself when she caught it on fire trying to cook porridge in her foster home. And then there were the trousers. It was just too hard to work in skirts.

"It doesn't matter if she's a she or a he," the baker said, irate. "She stole from me, that she did."

"Sorry I tripped you," the boy said. "It was a reflex."

"You tripped me?" Bee said, outraged, as the baker yanked again on her ear. "Ouch!"

"The child is hungry," a woman said. "Look at her. She's half starved." Bee felt herself turning red as the crowd stared. It was mortifying. She breathed deeply, determined not to cry, and tried to look down again, but the baker's grip on her ear kept her head up. So she glared at the boy who'd tripped her.

"Let her go, Master Bouts," the woman said. "She didn't mean any harm."

"Let her go? But look what she did to my bun!"

"I'll pay for it," the boy said. Bee blinked in surprise. "And I'll pay for another as well, so she can eat it."

The baker snorted, but slowly he released Bee's ear. "There's no need for that," he said. His tone was grumpy, but the anger was fading from his face. "You come on in my shop, girl," he said to Bee. "I'll give you a bun, and then you'll tell me where your parents are and why you stole from me."

Bee looked at the people standing in a circle around her. She was trapped. There was no place to go but back into the bakery. At least there she might have something to eat. And she could escape the knowing gazes of all those who'd seen her steal—who thought she was nothing more than a thief. The boy who'd tripped her gave her a small nod as she turned to follow the baker.

Back inside the fragrant shop, the baker, Master Bouts, introduced himself. He shooed out the few people left waiting to buy their bread and buns. There was much grumbling.

"I'll be open again in five minutes," he promised them, clicking the lock behind the last, an elderly woman who refused to let go of the loaf she clutched to her chest like a baby. "You can pay me later, Mistress de Vos," Master Bouts told her. Then he turned to Bee.

"So," he said thoughtfully. Bee was glad to see that he was no longer frowning. "So, who are you, girl? Where do you come from? No, wait." Master Bouts interrupted himself, reaching behind the counter and pulling out another sweet roll. It was very nearly as beautiful as the one that had come to such a tragic end. He held it out to Bee, and she snatched it from him, appalled at her own behavior but unable to stop. In an instant she'd wolfed down half of it. She was so ravenous that she hardly had time to taste it.

"Slowly!" the baker cautioned. "You'll make yourself sick, that you will."

Bee forced herself to chew the next bite. Oh, but it

was good! The tender raisins, the sweet icing, the soft dough . . . just delicious.

"S'good," she mumbled, her mouth full.

"I should think so!" the baker huffed. "It's my specialty. The Bouts Bun, I call it. Can't keep them in stock." He went into the back room and returned with a glass of water. "Wash it down, girl," he instructed. "I'd hate to have you choke to death still owing me for a bun."

Bee chewed and swallowed, chewed and swallowed, biding her time. "I don't have any money," she admitted finally, licking the last crumbs off her fingers.

"You don't say." The baker pursed his lips. "What's your name, girl?"

"Bee."

"That's not a name, that's a bug."

Bee scowled, ready to be offended, but the baker raised an eyebrow, as if daring her to get angry. She wouldn't give him the satisfaction. "Beatrix," she said reluctantly.

"Well," Master Bouts mused, "Bee suits you better. I can tell you have a sting. And where are you from? I haven't seen you in town before."

Bee looked down at the floor. "From the coast. A small place. You wouldn't know it."

"And where are your parents?"

"I've no parents."

There was a silence. Then the baker said, more gently, "Can you sweep, Bee?"

"Sweep?" Bee looked up. "You mean, with a broom? Of course I can. Anyone can sweep."

"Can you wash dishes?"

Bee nodded.

"Can you bake?"

"I can bake," she said. It wasn't a lie. Bee never lied. But she didn't mention that her baked goods never seemed to go over very well. People grew unhappy eating them, or even angry, though usually pastries were a cheering food. Bee didn't think there was anything wrong with her breads and tarts, but others, it seemed, did not agree.

"Well, there you are," the baker said. "I'm short shifted and need a hand, and you need to pay me back. Work for me for a day or two, and you can earn a few more Bouts Buns."

"Can I have another one before I start?" Bee asked. She couldn't help herself.

Master Bouts shook his head in amazement. "You do have a nerve, girl—that you do!" But though his tone was stern, Bee saw a smile threaten to push up his round cheeks. And despite her still aching stomach, despite her sore feet and bloody knee and scraped palms, despite her shame and humiliation, she gave the baker a tiny smile back.

CHAPTER 2

Before he opened the shop again, Master Bouts brought Bee into the kitchen in the back and made her a sandwich. He smoothed soft butter across slabs of fresh bread, layered on a slice or two of ham and smoked cheese, and then cut the bread into triangles, which he placed on a blue flowered plate. Bee couldn't believe he would share his food with her. No one else she'd met on her travels had been willing—or able—to share.

"Eat, girl," Master Bouts commanded. "Then you can rest back here." He showed her a tiny room behind the kitchen range, big enough only for a small bed and a leather trunk at its foot.

"Isn't this where you live?" Bee asked.

Master Bouts shook his head. "I live next door. This is where I sleep sometimes while the bread is rising. I get up in the darkness to start the bread, then I sleep again while it rises."

Bee wasn't sure what he meant. She'd made bread before, but it had been flat and rather hard. But when she bit into Master Bouts's sandwich, she understood. His bread was lofty, light. If she didn't hold on to the sandwich tightly, she thought it might float away. Every bite was a revelation of smoky cheese, creamy butter, and salty-sweet ham.

She took her time savoring the sandwich as Master Bouts left to reopen the shop. "When you're finished, take a nap. You look worn to a frazzle. Come out to me after you wake," he ordered.

Bee could hear the jingle of the bell above the bakery door as patrons came and went. Many of them started to talk to the baker about her, but their voices hushed immediately. Bee pictured Master Bouts pointing back toward the kitchen and whispering, "She's right back there!" Their faces would tighten, their lips press together in disapproval, their questions break off.

The sandwich filled her shrunken stomach completely, and she sat back in her chair and looked around the kitchen. It was spotlessly clean and practically arranged, with an enormous range, two ovens along one wall, a double sink with a newfangled pump along another, and a marble-topped table down the center. Cabinets filled every empty space, and high windows let in light and air. Motes of flour danced in the sunlight that splashed across the walls. A cat slept in a basket in a corner.

Bee got up and tried to work the pump. Her hands and face were grimy, and she didn't want to dirty the bedding. But her arms had no strength; she couldn't get the water to come out. When a wave of exhaustion hit her, she gave up and staggered into the little room with its soft, feather-filled bed. She was asleep before she finished lying down.

When Bee woke, she had no idea where she was. Moonlight streamed in through a window above her, and a breeze pushed the lace curtains in and out. Oh yes— the bakery. The roll, the baker, the delicious sandwich— she remembered now. She could smell the scent of rain-washed cobblestones and was grateful that she hadn't been outside during the downpour.

She stretched blissfully on the fluffy mattress. Her boots were gone and a warm blanket lay over her. The sudden realization that the baker must have taken off her muddy, shredded boots made her flush hot with embarrassment. She pushed off the blanket and sat up. Oh dear. She was supposed to have helped the baker when she woke! Now, it was clear, the shop was closed for the day. Everyone had gone home.

She stepped tentatively into the kitchen, where the windows were so big that the moonlight made it almost as bright as day. On the marble tabletop was an upside-down bowl. When she lifted it, she gasped in pleasure to see another sandwich and a Bouts Bun nestled together on a plate. Hungry again, she ate slowly, enjoying every morsel.

Next to the plate of food, the baker had left a pile of clothing. Bee shook out a simple dress and undergarments, and placed a pair of leather shoes on the tile floor. They looked about her size and were far nicer than any shoes she'd ever owned. Then she tried the pump again, and this time she managed to get a stream of water flowing. She ducked her head under it and drank, and then took a bar of rough soap lying beside the sink and scrubbed herself, wincing at the chill of the water. It was painful, but it felt good to be clean, after so many weeks on the road.

She put on the neat, fresh clothes. The blue dress was too big but about the right length. She tucked the necklace she always wore into its collar. Then she slipped on the shoes. They were as soft as feathers. She walked around the table, trying them out, and danced a little step. Dresses were a bother, but she'd wear one if she could keep those shoes—even if just for a few days. She'd surely have to give them back when she'd worked off her debt.

She washed the plate that had held her sandwich and dried it carefully. Then she tried to figure out where it belonged, opening cupboards and drawers. The kitchen had a place for everything. There were whisks and spatulas, dozens of spoons, measuring cups, knives, rolling pins. There were bowls and more bowls, some of them big enough for Bee to nest inside. There were plates plain and fancy, some tiered, some with filigrees of silver and gilt, some painted with scenes of hunting or royal parties or mythological beasts. There were dishes and utensils Bee had never seen before that she held up and turned over and over, trying to decide how they might be used.

A sound came from behind her, and Bee spun around.

"That's a potato masher," Master Bouts said. A candle illuminated his round, pink face. He pointed to the implement Bee held.

"I've always used a fork to mash potatoes," she said, twirling the masher in her hand.

"That works too," Master Bouts agreed. "You look better, Mistress Bee. The dress suits you."

"I like trousers," Bee said.

"As do I. But in my shop, I think a dress is best. We don't want to alarm the old ladies, do we?"

Bee had to smile. She'd seen those old ladies, standing around her in the street. There was no need to make them gossip any more than they already did.

"Why are you here?" Bee asked then. "It's the middle of the night."

"And that is when we start the bread, my girl. Those selfsame old ladies would be powerfully angry if they didn't have their fresh loaves for breakfast. And then do you know what they would do?"

"No." Bee tried to imagine the old ladies storming the shop, threatening the baker.

"Why, they would go to another bakery, of course!" The baker chuckled at his own joke.

Bee pointed to a row of books on a shelf. "What are those?" she asked.

"My cookbooks."

Bee walked over and pulled off a dusty volume.

"Gently, girl," Master Bouts warned. "That one's a rarity. Very old."

The book cover was leather, darkened and stained by years of use. She could just make out the title, hand

21

lettered in gilt paint: *A Booke of Baking*. Carefully she looked through the pages. There were illustrations showing pastries the likes of which she'd never seen. There was a pie heaped with what looked like snow, in whorls and swirls of whiteness. There was a cake iced in a dark brown that looked like mud. She tried to read the recipes, but her reading was poor at best, and these recipes were handwritten in an elegant script that she couldn't make out at all.

"Can you read, girl?" Master Bouts asked gently.

Bee was immediately on the defensive. "Of course I can read! I went to school . . . for a while."

"Ah," Master Bouts said. "Well, this is hard reading even for a scholar. These recipes are from long, long ago. They have ingredients even I've never seen nor barely heard of. Look here." He pointed to the snow-heaped pie. "This is a lemon meringue pie."

"Lemon?" Bee asked. "What is that?"

Master Bouts shrugged. "Something that grows in a far-off land, I daresay. See, the lemon is the yellow under the meringue. We can't make lemon, but we can make meringue—when there's a customer who can pay for it."

They looked through the book for a few more minutes, and Master Bouts pointed out the other peculiarities of the recipes. Pecan tarts, chocolate fudge, coconut macaroons—what were these things? Bee had never heard the words *pecan, chocolate,* or *coconut* before. But the pictures nearly made her mouth water.

"Enough of this," Master Bouts said at last. "We can look more another time. Now we must bake!"

At Master Bouts's instruction, Bee shelved the book carefully and pulled out a very large bowl. Using a scoop as big as her head, she dug flour from a barrel and added a little salt and a little sugar. Then she lit the stove and heated water, testing it with her finger until the baker said it was just the right temperature, and added the yeast. "Too warm and it will cook the yeasts, that it will. Too cold and they will not come out to play," he said.

"But what does the yeast do?" Bee asked. The smell of it was odd—sour, sharp, with just a hint of dirty feet. It was hard to imagine that it had anything to do with something as delicious as bread.

"It makes the bread rise, of course! It is the great ingredient—the most important ingredient. Have you never used yeast before?"

Bee shook her head.

"Where *do* you come from, girl?" Master Bouts asked as he mixed. "Wait—look at this. See the bubbles?"

In the bowl where the yeast and warm water had mixed, little bubbles rose up, as if the yeast were breathing under the water.

"It lives!" Master Bouts crowed, then stirred the grayish yeast mixture into the flour. "Now the hard work—the kneading. The flour and yeast meet and create something new." He pushed and turned the sticky mass as it grew doughlike, pushed and turned it, pushed and turned it, growing quite red in the face from the effort. He let Bee try it, but she was barely able to move the large hunk of dough around on the floured tabletop.

"You'll get better," Master Bouts said. Then he oiled an even bigger bowl, dumped the ball of dough inside, and covered it with a cloth.

"Out of the draft," he instructed, placing the bowl on a small table beside the range. "Warm, but not too warm. And magic will happen."

"Magic?" Bee asked skeptically, and he nodded.

"Time for breakfast," the baker said. With no wasted movements, he brewed a pot of tea and uncovered a plate that held two Bouts Buns. "You've already had a bun today, but you may have a second, because you are nearly skin and bones. From now on, though, only one!" Bee reached greedily for the bun, and Master Bouts looked very satisfied to see how much she liked it.

"Now, tell me your story," Master Bouts said, pouring tea into porcelain cups.

Bee looked down at the table, tracing the veins of the marble with her finger. She had hoped he would forget to ask. "There isn't much to tell," she said.

"Tell it anyway."

"My parents are dead. I was raised by a family in Boomkin, a fisherman and his wife. I don't know who they were to me. They . . . they weren't very kind. After a time I couldn't bear to stay there anymore, so I left. I've been on the move since then."

There was a silence. "That's a hard tale," the baker said, his voice gentle.

Bee shrugged.

"How long were you on the move?"

"Since late winter."

"Well, you're here now," the baker said. "That room is empty, and I've no apprentice. You did well with the bread. You can stay on if you want. If you don't steal any more from me," he added with a raised eyebrow.

"I'm no thief," Bee said fiercely. Then, as Master Bouts gazed at her without speaking, she flushed and looked down at her feet in their soft leather shoes. "I'm sorry," she said, her voice barely audible.

"I know you are, girl," the baker said. "We'd all do things to stay alive that we would never do otherwise."

There were sudden tears on Bee's lashes, and she blinked them away furiously. Then she looked up at the baker and smiled, a little shakily. "If I stay," she said, "I have one condition."

"Conditions now!" Master Bouts exclaimed. "Well, what then?"

"You *have* to teach me how to make the Bouts Bun."

Both Master Bouts's eyebrows went up so high they nearly vanished into the fringe atop his head. "The Bouts Bun recipe is not a gift. You have to earn it," he said gravely. "First the bread and the pastries. *Then* the Bouts Bun."

Bee sighed dramatically, hiding her relief at the baker's invitation. "I'll have to stay awhile then," she said. "At least until I master that recipe!"

The magic of dough rising was clear to Bee before long. The giant ball of dough had swollen to twice its original size, threatening to overrun the bowl and engulf the whole kitchen. She loved punching it down, and she helped Master Bouts knead it again and then shape it into long loaves, which they set to rise a second time. Then the baker showed her how to make a buttery tart crust, and she made crust after crust while he filled them with custards and berries. It was hard work, but there was a rhythm to it, and Bee found that she enjoyed it much more than she had expected. She was happier than she could remember being in a long time.

They baked the sweets and the bread in the two ovens, and when the first batches came out, perfectly browned and smelling like heaven, they arranged them on the bakery shelves out front. Master Bouts let Bee choose the plates to hold each tart and batch of cookies, and she was surprised at how much fun it was to match the plate to its pastry. A plate decorated with leaves and vines held blackberry tarts. Star-shaped cookies graced a plate the color of the evening sky just before dark. When the bakery opened at eight, everything was exactly right.

Master Bouts unbolted the door and went out to pull back the shutters. There was a line down the street, waiting. Everyone had come to see the new girl, the stranger with the shorn hair and trousers, the stealer of buns. The old ladies looked at Bee with suspicious eyes as she wrapped their loaves in jute paper and tied them with twine. The baker took their money and gave them their change, for Bee had no practice with counting.

But, she thought, surely the old ladies believed it was because she couldn't be trusted. Still, she squared her shoulders and met each glare wide eyed, forcing herself to smile sweetly when the customers held out their hands for their purchases and wishing them a good day when they spun on their heels and marched out, still curious. It was very taxing.

Near sunset, the boy from the day before came. He was dirty again, but this time his hands were clean.

"Still here, I see," he observed, and Bee gave him her practiced smile as she handed him a loaf of bread. "And in a dress!"

"At least my clothes are clean," she retorted before she could stop herself.

"Mistress Bee," the baker rebuked her gently. "Willem is a customer."

"Oh, that's all right," the boy said cheerfully. "I could use a wash, I'm sure. Bee, is it? I'm Wil, apprentice to my da, the blacksmith. It's filthy work, blacksmithing. Not what I'd pick to do, but . . ."

"Sorry," Bee muttered, a bit ashamed at her assumptions about him.

"And how are you liking the bakery?" Wil asked, unbothered by her rudeness. "I've heard some reports of your work already. Very good, people are saying. Even Mistress de Vos said she felt quite lighthearted when she ate a slice of that oat bread for lunch."

"Mistress de Vos, lighthearted?" the baker said. "Well, that *is* a triumph. Bee, I do believe you have the makings of a baker!"

A baker! She'd never in all her days considered doing such a thing. She had never thought beyond simply surviving. Her whole life had been spent scrabbling and scrambling. Since the end of winter she'd not even known where the next meal would come from, much less what she'd be doing a week, a month, a year ahead. To be a baker—to sleep in that soft bed off the sweet-scented kitchen, to plunge her hands into butter and sugar and flour, to eat a Bouts Bun every day . . . it was almost too much. She wasn't sure what to do with such a feeling.

She turned away from Wil and Master Bouts and hunched her shoulders. "I don't know that I'll stay," she said in a low voice. "I have . . . other things I need to do." She didn't wait to see Wil's confusion or Master Bouts's disappointed expression but pushed through the door that led to the kitchen behind the shop, desperate to get away before an emotion that she couldn't name took her over completely.

CHAPTER 3

Bee could hear Master Bouts shut up the shop, pulling the latch to lock the door before he came back into the kitchen. She sat at the long table, her head in her hands. He took a seat himself, his weight making the reed stool groan.

"No need to stay if you don't like the work, girl," he said matter-of-factly.

Bee raised her head. "I do like the work."

"Then . . . ?"

"Why do you want me here?" she burst out. "I don't understand."

Master Bouts stood. "Tea?" he inquired, and without waiting for an answer he turned his back and put the kettle on. He stood waiting for it to sing, tapping his fingertips together as he considered his response.

"I hadn't thought it through," he admitted after a time. "My last apprentice left—got a better offer from Mistress

De Kooi, on Caneel Street. And I just had a hunch you might be well suited to the job."

"Don't you have any family to help you out?" Bee pressed on. It was hard to believe she was suited to any job.

The kettle whistled, and Master Bouts poured the hot water into the pot. Then he brought it to the table and sat to wait while it steeped.

"I do not," he said at last. "I had a family once. A wife, a little son."

Bee wasn't sure if she should ask. But now she had to know.

"What happened?"

"It was the year of the fever. That was before you were even born, I think. It didn't hit Zeewal hard, but they'd traveled out to the coast to visit my wife's parents. They took sick, and her parents, too. All four of them, gone before I could get there." The baker's voice was even, but Bee could hear the pain in it.

"What were their names?" she asked.

"My wife was Janneke. My son we called Frits, for Frederick."

"Those are nice names."

Master Bouts said, "I had two cats for a time that I

named after them, just so I could say their names every now and then. They kept the mice down in the kitchen, but it felt wrong. So I gave the cats away."

"Yes," Bee said, nodding. "I can see why."

The cat that had slept in the corner rubbed up against Bee's leg, and she patted it, looking at Master Bouts questioningly.

"There are always mice, of course," he said. "When this one came to me later, half starved, I couldn't turn it away. But I named it Kaatje."

Master Bouts poured the tea, and Bee took a sip. It tasted like flowers.

"That's my story. Maybe not as hard as yours, because I was grown when I lost my people."

"Hard enough," Bee said. "I'm sorry." She breathed deeply, inhaling the fragrant steam from the tea. "So that's why you want me to stay—to take the place of your family?"

Master Bouts shook his head. "Certainly not, girl. No one will ever take their place. I want you to stay because I need an apprentice and you need a place of your own. You can make that place here if you'd like."

Bee turned that idea over in her mind. She wanted it so much that it frightened her. But she pushed the fear down as far as she could and said, "I would like it. I think I would. For as long as you'll have me."

"That's as long as you'll stay, Mistress Bee!" the baker said, smiling so hard his cheeks puffed up like a chipmunk's. He lifted his teacup and proclaimed, "A toast to the baker's new apprentice!"

Bee clinked her teacup against his—gently, for the porcelain was thin. And then Master Bouts said, "Toast—now there's an idea. Some toast with honey and a mess of just-picked morels sautéed in sweet butter for supper, what do you think?"

The days and weeks passed in a blur of learning and baking. Bee grew more and more delighted with her work, learning how to temper a custard so the eggs didn't curdle, how to bake a sugar cookie so the outside would hold its shape and the inside remain soft and sweet, how to make a braided loaf of bread so it looked like a girl's golden plait and tasted like sunshine and wheat. The happier she was, the happier Master Bouts's customers seemed to be.

"Mistress de Kooi's patrons are deserting Caneel Street and coming here!" the baker announced to Bee, a month into her apprenticeship. "She's mad as a trapped eel, that she is!" They celebrated by splitting the day's second Bouts Bun.

Wil, the blacksmith's apprentice, stopped in nearly every day for a loaf of bread and a bun. Bee had forgiven him for tripping her. Secretly, she was grateful to him, though she would never let him know that. He took great pleasure in teasing her; he'd decided that Bee was no name for a person, and that it must just be the first letter of her real name. So every time he came in, he addressed her by a new and awful name that started with *B*.

"And how are you today, Bernewif?" he would ask, sweeping her a low bow, then ducking as she tossed a wadded-up ball of jute paper at his blond head. Or, "What's good this morning, Mistress Balthechildis?" The day he inquired, "Do you have ginger cookies, Berta-Pieternella?" she laughed so hard she collapsed on the floor behind the counter.

"That is no real name!" she cried.

"Oh, it certainly is," Wil assured her. "My great-aunt is named Berta-Pieternella, and she deserves every syllable of it." A few days later he brought his great-aunt by the shop and introduced her, and the old lady's dour expression grew even more displeased when Bee had to run into the kitchen, red faced and shaking with giggles.

But on a Monday in July, Bee woke up in the dark at her usual time and felt her own darkness descend. She didn't know why at first. In the past weeks, she hadn't thought much about her life before the bakery; she'd hoped that was all behind her. So the shadowy feeling took her by surprise.

She rose and started to measure the flour and the salt, hoping the work would push the gloom away. But there was no escaping it. At last she realized: it was the anniversary of her mother's death—of the shipwreck that had drowned her, and nearly Bee as well. She'd only been an infant and had no memory of the wreck, but somehow on the anniversary every year, her mind went to it, and it weighed on her all day until the sun set.

Bee kneaded the dough with Master Bouts in silence, lost in her thoughts. Often her fingers went to the necklace around her neck, tracing the delicate flower engravings. She was sure it had been her mother's, though she had no proof. Her foster mother had kept the necklace in a box, wearing it herself for special occasions. Bee had not been allowed to touch it, but she took it when she left. It was the only thing she had that linked her with her real family.

Once or twice Master Bouts tried to joke with her, but she only replied in mumbles. She refused to look through the ancient cookbook with him, to practice her reading and marvel over the unfamiliar ingredients as had become their habit while the dough rose. She even refused her daily bun. She was short with the customers and turned away from Wil with a frown when he came in for his bread and bun. Master Bouts handed him a cookie to make up for Bee's rudeness.

"What's the matter with our Bertgarda?" Wil asked. Bee ignored him.

"Wrong side of the bed?" Master Bouts offered. "We all have our bad days."

Wil took a bite of the cookie. "Did you leave out the sugar?" he asked Bee. "This tastes a bit off."

"It's you who's off!" Bee flared. "My cookies are fine. Same as ever. Go on home and stop bothering me."

"So I shall," Wil said, surprised. "Sorry, Mistress Baltelda. I didn't mean to doubt your delicacies." But before he could leave, three more customers, then four, then five, came in to complain.

"I don't know what it is, exactly. I believe the custard is sour," one said, her voice trembling, holding out a raspberry tart.

"The bread tastes bitter," another reported, head hanging forlornly.

"The icing is acrid," said a third, sniffling and dabbing

at her eyes with a handkerchief. Master Bouts took back the goods, breaking off the edge of the tart to taste it himself. A look passed over his face that Bee couldn't name, and he pursed his lips. She felt a prickle of worry. Was it happening again—had her baking gone bad?

Master Bouts, Bee, and Wil went back into the kitchen and tested all the ingredients. But the sugar and honey were sweet; the flour had no weevils. The eggs were fresh and the berries ripe.

"I'll give you another for free tomorrow," Master Bouts promised each patron. "Come back in the morning." They sighed and grumbled but agreed.

Master Bouts closed the shop early and then invited Wil to join them in the kitchen for tea and supper.

"They were right," Master Bouts said, as the kettle heated. "I tried the cookies, and that raspberry tart . . . something was wrong."

"I did everything the same," Bee insisted. "It wasn't me."

Master Bouts made the tea, and they sat. "I have an idea," the baker said. "But it's a crazy one, that it is."

"What?" Bee bent her head over the teacup, letting the steam warm her face.

"How have you been feeling, working here? Have you been happy?"

"Yes," Bee said. Even on this dark day, she knew she had been happy since she'd started at the bakery.

"And today, how have you felt? Are you happy?"

"No." Bee didn't want to say more, and Master Bouts didn't ask why.

"How would you describe how you feel today, my girl?"

Bee thought about it. "Bad," she said at last. "Melancholy. Sour." That was how she always felt on the anniversary—and, she realized, on many of the days she'd spent in her foster home.

"Sour," Master Bouts repeated. "Like the custard."

Bee raised her head, but she was silent.

"Bitter, like the bread," he said. "Off, like the cookies."

Wil whistled through his teeth, and Bee stared at the baker. "What are you saying?" she demanded.

Master Bouts ran his hands through his white curls, and they stood up like a crown around his head. "It's this: When you were happy, the people who ate what you baked were happy. When you felt bad, the people who ate what you baked felt the same way. I think that you bake what you feel into your food. I think your pastries make people feel the way you do."

"That *is* crazy!" Bee exclaimed. "That's more than crazy—that's . . . magic. Only the mages have magic. I'm no mage."

"Well, there are the hedge wizards and hedge witches," Wil offered. "They have some magic."

"Hedge wizards and witches are all daft," Bee said. "I'm not like that."

"And I've heard tales," Master Bouts said. "There was a cobbler a while back—people claimed that his boots made them able to walk for miles and miles without feeling it. And a cooper . . . Master Crempe. Remember him, Wil?"

Wil nodded. "I heard any wine from his barrels tasted better than the palace's own vintage."

"Those are just stories," Bee retorted. "I've never done any kind of magic at all."

Master Bouts puffed out his round cheeks. "Well, baking has its own magic. Maybe you just . . . emphasize that magic a little."

"You know," Wil said, "when I ate that cookie, it didn't really taste odd. In fact, I'm not sure it tasted different at all, exactly. But I *felt* different tasting it."

"It was the same when I tried the tart," Master Bouts agreed. "All of a sudden, I could only think of my wife, and of Frits. For a minute I was afraid I'd start weeping. I thought it was just me, or maybe that your sadness was making me sad, Bee. But now I think it's the pastry itself."

Bee slapped her hands on the table, making the teacups jump. "That's ridiculous! It cannot be true. I don't believe it." She tried not to think of the times she'd baked for her foster family in Boomkin, and their odd reactions.

"We'll just have to test it," Master Bouts said. "You should bake something when you feel a certain way. Then we'll eat it and see if we feel the same."

"Fine," Bee snapped. "I feel very annoyed right about now. I'll make some cookies—they're fastest."

While Master Bouts and Wil watched from a safe distance, Bee quickly mixed ingredients into a batter, mumbling under her breath and banging cookie sheets in frustration. She dropped chunks of dough onto a sheet, slid them into the oven, and slammed the door shut. They sat quietly, drinking tea, for the twelve minutes that the cookies baked. No one said a word while they waited for Bee's temper to cool and for the cookies to be done. When Bee pulled them out, they were nicely browned around the edges and smelled delicious.

Wil reached for one, juggling it from hand to hand when it burned his fingers. "Ouch, ouch, ouch," he said. Pieces of cookie dropped onto the table. He took a big bite, huffing when the hot dough touched his tongue. He chewed, swallowed. They waited.

"Oh," he said after a minute.

"What?" Bee asked. She felt much better after working her annoyance away.

"I should go," Wil said, rising from the table. "I don't want to say anything I don't mean."

"Wait!" Bee jumped up to stand in front of him. "How do you feel?"

He glowered at her. "Don't ask me any stupid questions. Just get out of my way."

Bee exchanged a wide-eyed look with Master Bouts and moved aside. Wil pushed through the kitchen door into the shop. "The cursed door's locked!" he shouted. There was a loud thump as he kicked it.

Master Bouts hurried into the shop to let Wil out. A moment later he was back, and he plopped down onto his chair. "Well," he said, tapping his fingers together. "I don't think I need to try one of your cookies."

"No, please don't," Bee begged. They didn't speak again but sat in disbelief and wonder as the cookies, made with butter, sugar, flour, eggs, and a dollop of exasperation, slowly cooled on their tray.

CHAPTER 4

For the next few days, Bee tried very hard to keep her emotions under control as she worked. When she burned her finger taking a tray of cookies out of the oven, she went for a walk outside to be sure she was perfectly calm before punching down the bread dough. After Mistress de Vos insisted that Bee had given her the wrong change, she sat for a few minutes breathing deeply before she mixed up the next batch of tart crust. There were no further customer complaints about the baked goods. Both Bee and Master Bouts were greatly relieved.

A week or so later, there was a commotion at the bakery door. "Stand aside, stand aside!" Bee heard someone call out. She looked up from wrapping a lingonberry tart to see a man in a very fancy uniform entering the shop, pushing patrons out of his way.

"There's a queue," Bee said sternly, pointing to the line of customers.

"I come from the palace," the man said, ignoring her. He had a peculiar nose, upturned rather like a pig. Bee suppressed the desire to snort at him.

"Well, I don't care if you've dropped in from the heavens," she retorted. "You'll have to wait your turn."

Master Bouts came through the swinging door from the kitchen just then. "No, no, Bee," he said. "This is Master van Campen, the palace butler. What can I do for you, sir?"

"Master Joris has heard your tarts are not without merit, and he would like you to deliver some tomorrow for him to try. One raspberry, one lingonberry, if you please." It was clear from the butler's expression that the *if you please* was no more than a courtesy. Whether they pleased or not, the tarts had better be delivered.

"Yes, of course," Master Bouts said. "I'll send them before noon, so Master Joris can have them for his lunch if he desires."

The butler bowed smartly, still managing to keep his nose in the air, then turned and left the shop as abruptly as he'd entered. The customers stared after him.

"Well!" Master Bouts rubbed his hands together, delighted. "We haven't been asked to send pastries to the palace in a very long time. Master Joris usually gets his sweets from Caneel Street. This is an honor indeed!"

"Will you make the tarts?" Bee asked while helping the next customer, a young mother who was eavesdropping shamelessly. The tale would ring through Zeewal by lunchtime.

"Tarts are your specialty now. But Master Joris loves his sweets. The richer the better, I've heard. So we'll put in some Bouts Buns as well, to be sure. And maybe even a cake, if I can round up the ingredients . . . but he'll prefer your raspberry tart. There's nothing better." Master Bouts nodded proudly at her.

Bee blushed, pleased with the praise.

That evening, after the shop was closed and supper eaten, Bee and Master Bouts mixed up batter for the buns and made the tart crusts. Whenever Bee felt herself growing nervous, she stepped away from the kitchen. She wasn't sure she completely believed Master Bouts's theory, that she could bake her feelings into her pastries, but she didn't want to risk infecting Master Joris, the mage of all Aradyn, with her anxiety.

"Tell me about Master Joris," she said. She'd heard of him all her life, knew he was the kingdom's mage and responsible for the well-being of the realm. But she had never seen him or known anyone who had.

"He's been mage since the princess's great-great-great grandfather sat on the throne," Master Bouts said. "Or was it her great-great-great-great grandfather? No matter. You'd never know it—he looks no older than myself. 'Twas he who planted the tulips, you know, back when Aradyn was a happier place." Master Bouts thumped the dough and turned it. "But he's a very strange person, I've heard tell. Very reclusive. I've never met him myself. Collects things, I'm told. He's the princess's guardian, but no one ever sees them together. In fact, we very rarely see him at all, and never her."

"Princess Anika, is that right? She's about my age, isn't she?"

"No, I believe she's older than you, the poor thing."

"Poor thing?" Bee snorted. "She's a princess."

"But an orphan, all alone in that palace with none but the odd Master Joris for company."

Bee frowned at him. *She* was supposed to feel sorry for an orphan—an orphan princess at that?

Master Bouts frowned right back. "Our own difficulties shouldn't blind us to the difficulties of others."

Bee turned away. "If I wanted a lesson in kindness, I—well, I wouldn't want one," she said, annoyed. And then she took a few deep breaths to calm herself before getting back to her baking . . . just in case.

Very early Tuesday morning, when the bread was finished, Bee set to work on her raspberry tart. Master Bouts was working on the buns, humming as he rolled the dough into spirals and placed each bun on a tray. There was a knock at the front door, and Bee ran to answer it. It was Wil.

"I heard you've had a summons from the palace!" he said, looking around at the busy kitchen. "Do you need a hand?"

"*Those* hands?" Bee said, wrinkling her nose. "We don't need dirt in our pastry."

"Clean as my grandmother's parlor floor!" Wil promised, holding up his hands, which were indeed scrubbed clean. It being early in the day, he likely hadn't had time to get dirty yet.

"Well then, you can whisk the eggs." Bee handed him a whisk and a bowl of eggs, and he started to mix energetically. "No, gently! Gently! And all in the same direction. You can hammer a piece of iron into shape, but can you stir eggs without splattering them? What an oaf!"

Wil whisked in exaggerated slow motion, making Bee laugh. "You are a hard taskmaster, Mistress Bastianje, that you are!" She threatened him with a rolling pin, and he sped up a little, leading her in a dance around the kitchen as he dodged the rolling pin. Before long, the tart was in the oven.

Wil had to go off to the blacksmith shop then, for his father only allowed him a short time free in the mornings and evenings. Bee worked hard to trim a basket to hold the cake Master Bouts had baked, decorated with candied violets and ribbons of colored icing. A second basket held her tarts, perfect with their centers of quivering custard and circles of plump, ripe berries. And a third basket held six Bouts Buns. Bee had had to give hers up for the day to be sure there were enough for the palace.

"Why does he need six?" she grumbled, tying a gold bow around the three baskets, stacked one atop the other.

"He has a legendary sweet tooth," Master Bouts said. "He's almost as skinny as you, my girl, but I've heard he can down a whole cake in one sitting."

"I'm sure I could too, given the chance," Bee said.

Master Bouts chuckled. "Perhaps you can challenge him to a duel—a cake-eating duel!" Bee loved the idea of the black-robed mage—for they all wore black, she knew—sitting across the table and stuffing layer cake into his face as fast as he could while she did the same. But cake was only for special occasions, or for the wealthy. And in Zeewal, only Master Joris was truly wealthy.

"Now, put on your best dress," Master Bouts instructed.

"I only have one other dress," Bee pointed out. The second dress had appeared sometime near the end of Bee's first week at the bakery. Neither she nor Master Bouts had said a word about it.

"Is it clean?"

"Of course it is. Wait—you don't mean that I'm to bring the pastries to Master Joris, do you?"

"Certainly I do," Master Bouts said, adjusting the bow Bee had tied around the baskets so it was the same length on both sides. "I must attend to the customers."

Bee stared at him. Did he still not trust her alone in the shop? Not trust her with the money?

Master Bouts saw her expression. He was a man who paid attention, and he knew what she was thinking.

"I thought it might be entertaining for you—to see the palace, maybe to meet the mage. If you're very lucky, perhaps you can see the princess. You've never been there, after all, and I have—many times."

"You have?"

"Well, twice," Master Bouts amended. "And I only got as far as the outer courtyard then. I know for a fact they won't let me inside, but perhaps they'll let you. And if you do go in, I'm sure you will remember everything you see and tell it all to me."

"Oh," Bee said, clasping her hands. "Oh, I surely will! Every last thing!"

"But you must mind your manners and hold your tongue," Master Bouts warned. "You'll be representing the bakery—and me. I don't want to hear reports of misbehavior!"

Bee widened her eyes at him. "Misbehave—me?"

"I'm not joking, my girl," Master Bouts said, but his eyes twinkled as he waved Bee off to her room to change her clothes.

Just past noon, scrubbed and tidy, Bee started down the cobbled streets carrying the pyramid of baskets as carefully as she could. If she dropped them . . . well, she simply couldn't. She made certain every step she took was steady. She took a wide berth around pedestrians, and stayed far from the horses and carts on the roadway.

She'd explored the lanes and alleys of Zeewal over the past weeks, and she knew her way to the palace. She followed the canal until she reached the dam, and on the far side of the little lake the dam made, there it stood: a tall structure of red brick and pinkish stone. From one of the turrets, a flag showing a red tulip on a golden background snapped in the breeze. The lake water reflected the scene, so Bee could see two pink palaces — one above, one below. It didn't look like the kind of dark, threatening place where she'd imagined the strange, reclusive mage that Master Bouts had described would live.

Her arms were growing tired, so she started down the path that led to a small, gated entrance for foot travelers in the red brick wall. A guard stood stiffly before the iron gate, his lance upright, the epaulets on his uniform gleaming. He was very tall, and almost as wide across. He stared off into the distance as if Bee weren't even there.

"Who goes there?" he demanded as she approached.

"Well—me," Bee said. "Right here. Me." She waved her hand up at him.

The guard still didn't look down. "Who are you? What business do you have at the palace?"

"I'm Bee. The baker's apprentice. I'm bringing special sweets for Master Joris."

This got the guard's attention, though only his eyes moved. He peered down at Bee. "Why didn't you say so? You're late!"

Bee was outraged. "Late? It's not even noon. We've been working since sunup!"

The guard bent down a little and said, in a very low voice, "When Master Joris wants his pastry and doesn't get it, it can be very . . . unpleasant."

"Oh," Bee said. "In that case, you should let me in right away. I have some treats that should settle him down."

"Quite so." The guard straightened up again, knocked his lance on the ground twice, and stood aside. Bee walked through the iron gate and found herself in a paved courtyard with a circular drive before great iron doors. This, she imagined, must be where carriages stopped to let out lords and ladies for the parties and balls that took place in the palace. Only there was grass growing between the cobblestones, and some of them were a little catawampus, sticking up in a way that could be hazardous to horse hooves or ladies' slippers. It was clear that little time or money was spent on repairs and upkeep.

She walked up to the doors and struggled to balance her baskets while she lifted the heavy iron knocker and let it go again. It landed with a great *clank*. No one came. Bee's arms were getting terribly tired, and she nearly lost the Bouts Buns when she lifted the knocker a second time. *Clank.*

The doors swung open with a creak that was almost a wail, and Master van Campen, the pig-nosed butler, stood there with his arms crossed.

"You're late," he accused.

Bee rolled her eyes and said, "I'm here now. Please, can I put these down? They're very heavy."

"Follow me." The butler turned and, striding quickly, led the way through a hall with an enormously high ceiling painted with cherubs and fluffy clouds. Bee almost fell over trying to see it clearly. There was little else in the room—a wicker table, some faded wall hangings, long windows covered with heavy, rather dusty-looking curtains. As they passed a doorway, Bee noticed a glass cabinet that seemed to be filled with small frames, but van Campen was moving her along too fast to make out what they contained. She promised herself that she would look more closely on the way out.

Along twisting corridors and down narrow staircases they sped, Bee trying desperately to keep up and not drop the baskets. Finally they reached the kitchen. It was far older, darker, and dirtier than the bakery kitchen. The cook, a tired-looking woman with a face like a vanilla pudding and a striped kerchief around her head, sat on a stool drowsing in the heat from the hearth.

Panting, Bee laid the baskets on the marble-topped table. The cook startled upright and said, "Don't put those there. This is my kitchen!" At her words, the butler turned and walked out quickly.

"And these are my pastries," Bee said. "They're for Master Joris."

"Why didn't you say so?" The cook leaped to her feet and came around the table.

"I just did," Bee retorted, exasperated at the staff's rudeness, but trying to hold her tongue as Master Bouts had requested.

"Master Joris has been awaiting his breakfast for hours," the cook said, untying the ribbon that held the baskets together. "And when Master Joris has to wait . . . well, it is most disagreeable." First unpleasant, now disagreeable. Bee wondered exactly how disagreeably unpleasant the mage was. She was beginning to hope she didn't have the opportunity to find out.

The cook opened the top basket. "Ooooh," she said, eyeing the Bouts Buns. "Those will do very well."

"There's tarts and a cake as well," Bee said.

"Girl, give me a hand, will you? Find a plate and a fork. We'll make him up a nice tray so he forgets how hungry he's been." The cook pointed to a tall stack of dishes by the sink, and Bee ran over and took a small plate from the top of the pile. The dishes were all the same—white with an edging of tiny gilt-painted tulips—so there was no opportunity to match the plate to what it held as she liked to do. Next Bee rummaged through a drawer that held a haphazard heap of forks, knives, and spoons. She pulled out a tarnished fork. *All* the silver was tarnished.

"Is this all right?" she asked.

"We've nothing else," the cook said, shrugging.

"What about something to make it look pretty? A flower in a vase, maybe?" Bee suggested.

The cook shook her head. "Flowers are only for selling, Master Joris says. He doesn't care about pretty, unless it's one of his collections. And even then he just cares about how rare the objects are, not so much what they look like."

"His collections?"

The cook gave Bee a dark look. "You'll see them all around. Bugs, rocks, snow globes . . . he'll collect most anything. He's been known to spend a thousand coppers on one of his rocks. On a rock! It's a disgrace is what it is. Here, find a tray in that cupboard." She waved Bee toward a closet. When Bee pulled the door open, a broom handle popped out, smacking her hard on the shoulder. Directly behind that came a mop handle, which she managed to dodge, and then a pile of dust cloths fell from a shelf onto Bee's head. A cloud of dust poofed up around her, and she danced around wildly, coughing as she swatted the dust away.

"Don't be so clumsy, child!" the cook admonished her.

Bee clenched her fists, tossed the rags to the floor, and rummaged in the overflowing closet until her hand closed around a ceramic tray. She pulled it out, dusted it off with one of the dirty rags, and carried it triumphantly to the table.

"It took you long enough," the cook grumbled. She placed a Bouts Bun on the plate, then cut slices of tart and one of cake and slid them beside the bun. Then she cut another slice of each and reached for a bun.

"What are you doing?" Bee demanded.

"Taking some for me," the cook replied.

"That's not for you. It's for the mage—and the princess."

"The princess! Well, I never." The cook looked quite scandalized. "The princess doesn't eat sweets."

"Everybody eats sweets," Bee contradicted.

"I'll tell you what," the cook said craftily. "If you don't say anything about me taking my share, I'll let you bring some to the princess, and you can ask her yourself."

Bee narrowed her eyes. She didn't think the cook deserved a slice of tart, much less a Bouts Bun. But then she realized she'd just been given permission to see the princess. And no one ever saw the princess.

"That sounds fair," Bee said. She took another plate and put a slice of each treat and a bun on it. Then she said, "Where do I find the princess?"

"Bring the master his first," insisted the cook.

"Fine," Bee said. "Where is he?"

"In his study, of course."

"And where, if you would be so kind, is that?" Bee gritted her teeth.

"Do you know nothing, child?" The cook snorted, and Bee had to restrain herself from throwing the tray at her. "Up the stairs, down the first hall, fourth door on the left. Leave the tray outside the door. Three knocks, no more, no less. You don't want to find out what he does to frivolous knockers."

"And the princess? Where is she?"

"Well, that's anyone's guess," the cook said. Then she plunged a fork into the cake and took a bite. Her eyes closed in ecstasy, and Bee picked up the tray and marched out.

CHAPTER 5

The halls were dark, and Bee moved cautiously up the stairs and down the corridor. She counted off four doorways on her left. Each had a closed door with an iron outer edge and a center of smoked glass with wrought iron leaves and flowers climbing up and around it. At the fourth, she placed the tray carefully on the floor and picked up the second plate. After a moment's thought, she switched the plates, taking the one with the larger, nicer slices of tart and cake to give to the princess. Then she knocked sharply on the metal edge of the door, three times. She decided to trust the cook and not risk a fourth knock.

She was torn between curiosity and fear of the mage. Should she stay, meet him, find out what he was like? Shifting anxiously from foot to foot, she listened for a sound from behind the door. But there was only silence. A minute more, and then she turned and headed back down the hall. She had no idea where to find the princess. She passed door after closed door, each with a unique, beautiful wrought-iron decoration. At one she stopped and knocked, but there was no answer. Cobwebs hung from some of the iron curlicues on that door, and in the center of one web, a spider sat. Bee shuddered when she noticed it. She hated spiders.

The corridor twisted and turned, and other hallways branched off it. She climbed a stairway and then another, and wandered down a hall. Every so often, she stopped and knocked, but there was never an answer, never a sound from behind the doors. Eventually she found herself at the end of a passageway. A long window, streaked with dirt, rose above a window seat. Bee was exhausted, and she sank down onto the cushions, sneezing as dust rose around her. She found it very strange that the palace was so ill tended. Even her foster mother, as coarse and careless as she was, had kept a tidy home.

When the dust settled, Bee put down the plate and turned to look out the window, but it was too filthy. Everything was blurry and smeared. She rubbed a clean spot on the glass with the edge of her skirt and peered out. There seemed to be a garden below. It must have been the back or the side of the palace, for she had seen no garden in front. She could make out hedges, some roses, and an oddly tall, flowered bush that intrigued her. Then she saw movement and rubbed harder at the window.

It was a girl. It had to be the princess.

Bee snatched up the plate and ran back down the hall to the stairs, down one flight, then two. She tried to turn down the corridor in the same direction she'd taken two flights up, but the palace interior was so disorienting that Bee couldn't tell if she was moving to its back or its front. She passed a long, narrow room with a checkerboard tile floor. This room led to another, and then another—and at the far end of the third room, she could just make out what looked like shrubbery beyond the glass door. With any luck, that door would open onto the garden.

Bee turned into the first room where, despite her hurry, a trio of glass cabinets caught her eye. She paused before the first cabinet. It looked like it was filled with animals. Were they children's toys? There was a sweet-looking rabbit. A mole. A squirrel. In the second cabinet, lots of birds—a bright red one, a blue one, one with a black and red breast. A fox. But then Bee looked more closely at figures in the cabinets, and she began to realize what they really were. These were not toys. These were actual animals, dead and stuffed! Their eyes had been replaced by glass beads, and their fur and feathers were in various states of molting. The fox was patchy on one leg; the red bird had lost a few feathers on its tail. She shuddered, turned, and stepped into the next room.

This chamber was a little nicer, or so it looked at first. There were glass-topped tables scattered around it. Bee went over to one of the tables and rested the plate on it, but an instant later she snatched it up again. The glass top covered a selection of insects that lay pinned to mats underneath. Some of them were beautiful—dragonflies with vivid, iridescent wings, beetles with bright stripes or spots or long curved horns—but all were dead, the sheen of life gone from them.

Bee backed through the open doorway into the last room. Ah, this was better. The open shelves that lined the walls held dozens of glass globes. As Bee came closer, she could see that each globe showed a scene within. There was a mountainscape, a group of children skating on a pond, a horse-drawn sleigh crossing a meadow. All the scenes were snow dusted. Without quite meaning to, Bee reached out and picked up one of the globes. Gently, she tilted it upside down, then right side up again. Snow seemed to fall on the scene inside. It was beautiful. She tilted all the globes then, one after another, watching as the snow drifted down on the skaters, the skiers, the mountain peak. How she would love to have one of the globes for her very own!

Reluctantly, she set down the last of the globes. At the far end of the room was the door she'd seen from the hall. Through the glass she could make out the wavering image of a tall hedge. She pushed open the heavy door and slipped out.

The hedge was made of dense evergreen bushes, far taller than Bee, and she could see no opening. She darted along it until she came to a place where she could press through. Now she was in an evergreen corridor, the bushy branches nearly meeting over her head. It twisted and turned, much like the hallways in the palace. She walked and walked, but the corridor didn't seem to lead anywhere. She noticed a yellowed section of bush that she was sure she'd passed before. Was she walking in circles?

"Help," she said tentatively. The bushes swallowed her voice. "Help!" she said again, louder. "Help! Help! I'm lost in the bushes!"

"That's because it's a maze," a voice said. It was a girl's voice, high and musical. But there was no girl in sight.

"Where are you? You have to help me!" Bee cried.

"Walk forward," the girl said. Bee did, and came to a turn. "Are you at a turn? Then go left." Bee obeyed. "Now right. Straight for twenty paces, then right again."

Bee counted off the twenty paces, turned right, and found herself at an opening in the hedge. In front of her was the garden she'd seen from above, with a fountain tinkling in the center and rose bushes all around. And sitting on a stone bench beside the fountain was the princess.

Her back was to Bee. She had long, wavy red hair, and her dress was blue silk. Red hair was a rarity in Aradyn, so to Bee she looked exotic and unique, exactly the way a princess should. Bee moved forward, still clutching the plate of pastry. Suddenly she felt very nervous. What was the right thing to do when meeting a princess? Should she curtsy? She didn't really know how.

The princess turned. She was older than Bee had thought. She was surprisingly plain; her forehead large, her chin tiny and pointed, her mouth and eyes a smidge too big. But then she smiled at Bee, and her face was transformed.

"How do you do?" she said. "I'm Anika. Who on earth are you, and what are you doing astray in my maze? And what are those exquisite things on your plate?" Anika seemed to bubble over with questions, and Bee didn't know which to answer first. She gulped and then tried to curtsy. The tart slices slid across the plate.

The princess giggled. "That was the sorriest curtsy I've ever beheld," she said. "Take care—you don't want to drop those pastries!"

"They're—they're for you, Your Highness. Your Majesty. Your Ladyship."

The princess laughed again. "Anika will suffice. And you are . . . ?"

"Bee. I'm Bee."

"What a superlative name! Perhaps I should be A for Anika, then?"

"It's not an initial. It's short for Beatrix," Bee said, blushing.

"Oh dear. Then certainly you should be called Bee. And what have you brought me, Bee?"

Bee moved forward, and the princess patted the bench next to her.

"Sit, and divulge."

"Divulge?"

The princess smiled. "Tell me."

"It's a layer cake, and a raspberry tart, and a lingonberry tart. And a bun. I made the tarts." Carefully, Bee lowered the plate and set it on the bench, and then sat herself.

"Did you really? How remarkable to be able to make such luscious-looking comestibles!"

"It's nothing," Bee said modestly. She assumed *comestibles* must be a fancy word for pastries. Then she realized: "Oh no, I forgot to bring you a fork!"

"Why ever would I need a fork?" the princess asked. She picked up the slice of cake and took a huge bite, smearing frosting on her face and hands.

"Mglumph," she said, her eyes widening.

"Excuse me?"

The princess chewed and swallowed, then licked the frosting from her fingers and around her mouth. "Oh my. That is *superb*. It might be the loveliest cake I've ever tasted!"

"Master Bouts made it," Bee said. "But the cook said you don't like sweets."

"I never come upon the opportunity! Our cook doesn't bake at all, and when we obtain cakes from the bakeries, Uncle Joris usually finishes them off before I can procure a single morsel." The princess picked up the slice of raspberry tart and bit off the end. There was a momentary silence.

"Oh my, my, my," she said at last. "Spectacular.

Scrumptious. It tastes like . . . well, it tastes like nothing I've ever tasted before!" She ate another bite, and another. "How do you *do* this?"

Bee felt her cheeks redden. "I've been practicing."

"You're very skilled indeed," the princess said. "It doesn't just taste marvelous, it makes me feel marvelous. Like singing. Like dancing!" She jumped up from the bench and twirled in a circle, then sat again. "I cannot believe I've been deprived of such magnificence all these years."

Bee had to pick through the words the princess used to be sure she understood them all. Perhaps, she thought, it was how royalty spoke. "Well, this is the first time we've baked for Master Joris. Usually he uses another baker."

"Not anymore," Princess Anika declared, and Bee clapped her hands with glee. Master Bouts would be so pleased!

"So . . . ," Bee said, when the princess had finished the tart, "Master Joris is your uncle?"

"Not really," the princess replied softly. Her happiness seemed to vanish. "He's the kingdom's mage, and my guardian. I'm too young to rule—I'm only sixteen. And I don't have any parents."

"Nor do I," Bee said.

Princess Anika put a hand over Bee's. "I was sure there was something."

"Something?"

"Some way we were kindred spirits. I feel a true connection with you."

"You do?" Bee asked shyly.

"We shall be great companions, I can tell." Princess Anika rose from the bench and pulled Bee up. "Let's perambulate—I'll show you the garden."

"Perambulate?" Bee had no idea what the princess meant.

"Walk. And you can tell me all about being a baker."

"And you can tell me about being a princess!" Bee agreed, delighted.

"There's very little to disclose," Princess Anika said, hooking her arm through Bee's. "It's the most monotonous life in the world. I eat alone at breakfast, study with a tedious tutor all morning, walk in the garden, dine with Uncle Joris, and go to sleep. And the next day, the same." They took a turn around the fountain and then went to admire the roses.

"That is boring," Bee agreed. "Can't you do other things? Ride horses, maybe? Take dance lessons?" She tried to think of what else princesses might do.

"Uncle Joris would never permit it," the princess said with a sigh. "Sometimes I help him catalogue his collections."

"I think I saw some of his collections," Bee said. "One of them was . . . a little horrible."

Princess Anika grimaced. "Oh, the animals? They are horrible, you're right. When I was younger, I used to pretend they were alive, and I'd converse with them. Now I have a real one, though."

"A real what?" Bee asked.

"Come see!" Anika pulled Bee over to a little circle of boxwood. In its center was a basket, and in the basket, a tiny ball of spikes was curled on a pile of fancy embroidered pillows.

"A hedgehog!" Bee exclaimed. "Is it alive?"

"Of course he is!" Anika reached into the basket and ran her hand down the hedgehog's back. It uncurled a little, raised its nose from the under the protection of its tail, and blinked its beady black eyes sleepily.

"Isn't it prickly?"

"A little. You just have to be prudent when you caress him. His name is Pepin."

Bee put out her hand cautiously and touched Pepin's back, near his head. He followed the movement of her hand with his eyes. He felt very strange—bristly and soft at the same time.

"I transport him in a little pocket, see?" Anika showed

Bee a hammock-shaped pocket attached to a belt at her waist. "It's padded, so he doesn't impale me." She picked up the hedgehog and gently placed him in the pocket. He peered out at them. Bee smiled. What a peculiar pet!

"I want to show you something else," Anika said. She pulled Bee around a tall hedge. There was a swath of grass, and in the center was the plant she had seen from the window, taller than any plant Bee had ever seen. It had dark green leaves and was covered with pink flowers. Beneath it spread a carpet of fallen petals.

"Oh," Bee breathed. "It's beautiful! What is it?"

"It's a tree," Anika said proudly. "The only tree in Aradyn."

"A tree?" Bee walked up to the plant. It had a thick, rough, reddish-brown stem holding it up, and gnarled brown stalks that split off into smaller and smaller stalks, ending in leaves and flowers. She had never seen anything like it.

"What is a tree?" she asked. "Some kind of flowering bush?"

Anika shook her head, pleased that she had surprised Bee. "A tree is a *tree*. A thing unto itself. This one is a cherry tree. It has flowers now, and later it will bear fruit."

"Fruit? Like berries?"

"They're a little like berries. Sweet and delicious—oh, you could certainly bake something with them!"

Bee picked up a handful of petals from the ground and tossed them in the air, letting them rain down over her. "Why is there only one? Why have I never seen another?"

"Uncle Joris collected it. It's the only one remaining. Long ago, there used to be trees everywhere, or so he says. But he removed them."

Bee sank down on the ground beneath the tree, fingering the petals. "But why? How did he get rid of them?"

"I don't know how. Their roots took up a lot of room and consumed the goodness from the soil, he said. He needed them gone for his tulips."

"Did he have to take them all? Couldn't he have left some?"

Anika shook her head. "He is a man of extremes. And perhaps not entirely reasonable about his collections. With only a single tree remaining, it becomes immeasurably precious."

"And the tulips are his?" Bee remembered that Master Bouts had said that the mage had planted them.

"Oh yes," Anika confided. "They're all his. They're tremendously valuable, you know. Some of the bulbs are worth thousands of coppers. He sells them to other kingdoms."

Bee was quiet for a moment, taking this in. "But the tree is so beautiful," she said at last. "It's sad that it's the last one."

"I know," Anika agreed. "I love it. I like to sit under its branches when the sun is out and shining through the petals." She joined Bee on the ground, and they lay back and looked up through the leaves. Pepin crawled out from his pocket and began snuffling through the grass.

It was peaceful there, under the tree, and Bee closed her eyes, feeling drowsy. She knew she should get back. It was so nice to lie here with Anika and talk, though. She liked the princess very much. Anika wasn't at all stuck up or prissy, as Bee had feared she might be. And though she was older, she spoke to Bee as if they were equals. Maybe, Bee thought, that was because Anika hadn't had much practice talking to people.

A shadow fell across Bee's face, and she blinked her eyes open, then sat up fast, her heart leaping. A tall form stood at their feet, a man in black robes with a long, narrow face. He had a shock of dark hair with a white stripe running through it, like a skunk. His hands were clasped before him, and his thick eyebrows angled down toward his nose, making him look quite displeased.

"Uncle!" Anika exclaimed, sitting up too. She sounded

nervous, as if she'd been caught doing something she shouldn't.

"Who is this person?" he asked in a gravelly voice. His gaze on Bee felt almost hot, and she shifted uncomfortably and got to her feet. The mage walked slowly in a circle around her, surveying her closely. Bee noticed, to her astonishment, that as his heels struck the ground, small sparks flew upward.

"Who gave you permission to come into my garden?" the mage demanded.

Bee looked down. "Nobody, sir," she said. She didn't want to tell on the cook, despite the woman's rudeness. "I came out on my own. I saw the princess from a window and wanted to meet her."

"You are a very presumptuous girl," he snapped. Bee wasn't sure what he meant, but it didn't sound good. The mage turned to Anika. "Your tutor has been waiting for you," he said sternly. "You are very late. Why do you waste his time—and yours?"

"I'm sorry, Uncle," Anika said humbly. "I was talking to Bee—I forgot the time. Did you try her extraordinary pastries?"

The mage frowned. His long nose almost touched his long chin. "There was a plate of them outside my study.

This is . . . Bee, you said?"

Bee made her awkward curtsy. "Yes, milord," she said. "I'm the baker's apprentice."

"You made the sweets?"

"I made the tarts. Master Bouts baked the rest," Bee said. "I do hope you liked them."

"I liked them well enough," the mage replied curtly. "You may bring more next week. With extra buns."

"Of course," Bee said, and curtseyed again. "I should go now. I'm sorry for making the princess late."

"It won't happen again," the mage suggested. His face twisted in a peculiar smile that showed his teeth. It made Bee far more uneasy than his scowl had.

"No indeed!" Bee agreed. She backed away, knocking her head on a low-hanging branch and making a shower of petals fall onto Master Joris's hair. She almost wanted to laugh at the way he looked with his black and white hair all sprinkled with pale pink petals. But he glared at her, and the urge to laugh disappeared.

Picking up her skirts, she turned and hurried from the garden, feeling the mage's eyes still on her. She trotted through the maze, which, to her astonishment, allowed her to move in nearly a straight line from one end to the other. Then, breaking into a sprint, she wound back through the dusty, echoing palace halls and, with a gasp of relief, pulled the heavy front doors open and escaped outside.

CHAPTER 6

When Bee got back to the bakery, it was nearly closing time. She was afraid Master Bouts would be annoyed that she'd been gone so long, but he just nodded at her and handed her an apron when she came in. The customers turned to her, faces full of curiosity. Everyone, it seemed, knew where she'd been.

"What was the palace like?" Mistress Tenbrook asked eagerly, her lace cap bobbing atop her gray curls. "Was it beautiful? Full of paintings and fine furnishings?"

Bee tied on the apron and joined Master Bouts behind the counter. "Not quite," she said. "It was a little old. And surprisingly unclean."

"Really!" Mistress Tenbrook exclaimed. She and the other women looked scandalized. "Do they not have servants?"

"I only met the cook," Bee said. "And I didn't see any other servants besides the butler."

The bell above the door jingled, and Wil came in. "You're back!" he said. "Did you meet the mage? Did he like your pastries?"

Bee finished packing up an order before she answered. The customers all waited; no one wanted to leave the shop before hearing all about it.

"I did meet him," she said finally. "He was a bit . . . strange. But I'm pretty sure he liked the sweets. He wants more next week."

"What did he *say* to you?" Mistress Van Vleet demanded. "He never speaks when we see him in town. I don't know anyone who's ever even heard his voice."

"I asked him if he liked the pastries. He said . . ." Bee tried to remember his exact words. "He said, 'I like them well enough.'"

"Well enough, eh?" Master Bouts said, chuckling. "I suppose that's high praise from him."

"He liked your buns best," Bee told him. The ladies all clucked like hens, pleased that the buns were favored, pleased that their own baker was now the palace baker. Nobody asked about the princess, and Bee was glad. She didn't want to share Anika with the crowd.

But when the last of the customers had gone, satisfied with their bread and their gossip, she told Master Bouts

75

and Wil about the rest of her afternoon.

"Master Joris was horrible," she said, wiping down the counters with a damp rag. "Tall and mean. He didn't say one nice thing. And Anika seemed a little afraid of him."

"Anika?" Wil repeated. "You're on a first-name basis with the princess now, Lady Baefje? What quick work!"

Bee frowned. "She told me to call her that. I wouldn't have, otherwise."

"And what is she like, our princess Anika?"

"Oh, she's lovely!" Bee said. "So kind, and really very funny. She speaks a little oddly, with the biggest words. It's hard to understand her. She seems terribly lonely there, though. Oh, and she has a hedgehog for a pet!"

Wil's eyebrows went up. "That's a prickly pet!" he said. "And is she beautiful, as a princess should be?"

"I think she is," Bee said.

"It is a shame that Master Joris keeps her hidden away," Master Bouts said. "Sounds as if she could use some company. He never entertains, from what I've heard. Poor girl, to spend most of her life alone with nothing but a hedgehog for company."

"Well, a hedgehog, a tutor, and Master Joris," Bee corrected. "I'll try to see her again next week, when I go—if I'm the one to go."

"And who else would it be?" Master Bouts asked. "Now off with you, Wil—here's your bun. It's time for our supper."

Over cheese omelets, Bee described more of the palace and the princess to Master Bouts. The baker was amazed to hear of Master Joris's collection of dead animals and shocked by the details of the dirty kitchen and the sour old cook.

"It's no wonder the mage gets his pastries elsewhere!" he said. "You would think a palace would have the best and nicest of everything."

"You would think," Bee agreed. She wiped her plate with a heel of bread and chewed the crust thoughtfully. "Master Bouts," she said. "Have you ever seen a tree?"

"A tree!" the baker exclaimed. "Why no, that I have not. I don't believe anyone in Aradyn has ever seen one. What made you think of that?"

"There is a tree in the palace garden."

Master Bouts's eyes widened. "A real tree? What did it look like?"

"It was beautiful," Bee said. "It had a brown trunk, thick as my waist, and stems called . . ." She tried to remember. "Branches! Green leaves, like a boxwood hedge, only lighter colored and much bigger. And little pink flowers. Princess Anika said it was a cherry tree."

"Well, I never," Master Bouts said, astonished. "Was there only the one?"

"It's the last one, the princess said. She said Master Joris got rid of all the others. Do you know about this? What did he do—did he cut them down?"

Master Bouts shook his head. "I don't exactly know. They all disappeared at once, I heard. I know that long ago, there were trees here. More than a hundred years ago. All different kinds of trees. Things grew on them that bakers used, that I've always longed to use."

"What sorts of things?"

"Nuts, for one."

"Nuts?"

"Walnuts. Pecan nuts. Hazelnuts. Like in the recipes in *A Booke of Baking*."

"What do they taste like?"

"I've no idea. They're crunchy, I believe. I'd like to find out, though—that I would!"

Bee tried to guess what nuts might taste like, but it was too hard to imagine a flavor she'd never experienced. "The princess said Master Joris took away the trees so there was room for the tulips to grow."

"Yes, that's what I heard as well," Master Bouts said.

"He wanted them all gone. Still, the trees were useful, in their way, or so the old-timers tell us."

"Useful how?"

"You know how the autumn storms come?" Bee knew it well. Every fall, gales lashed the coast, traveled up the canals, damaged houses, and sank boats.

"The storms wash away the soil, and they've gotten worse. Or the soil has gotten weaker. Every year we lose more land. The trees had deep roots, they say, much deeper than a shrub's. They held the soil in place, like a mother would hold a child."

Bee nodded. "I remember the big storm two years ago. It nearly washed away the house where I lived. And the beach where the fishermen kept their boats—that was gone. Just gone."

"That was one of the worst ones," Master Bouts said, shuddering. "Another like that . . . well, I don't know how many more of those we can take."

The family Bee had lived with, the Sutphens, had said something like that after the big storm. Master Sutphen, who fished all summer and grumbled all winter, had lost his boat in the storm. He stood out in the gale, railing against the rain and the howling wind, howling himself and shaking his fist helplessly at the sky. The relentless waves swallowed the strand and the little patch of garden that Bee and Mistress Sutphen tended and almost pulled the house itself into the sea. The rest of that fall and winter, Master Sutphen and the other fishermen had built a dike, an earthen dam, to try to keep the sea back, but the next autumn a storm washed most of it away as well.

"And the storms hurt Zeewal too?" Bee asked. The town was nearly a mile from the sea.

"They race up the canal and pull the sea with them, over the banks. We had two feet of water in the streets after that gale. It took months to clean up. There's nothing to hold the water back. And when the sea retreats, it takes part of the land with it."

Bee carried the supper dishes to the sink and scrubbed them clean as Master Bouts lit his long brown pipe and puffed smoke rings. It was hard to believe that there had once been trees everywhere. She tried to picture the land with trees instead of long grasses and fields of tulips. How different it would look!

"Do you think Master Joris knows that the sea is taking the land?" she asked the baker. He blew a smoke ring through a larger smoke ring before he answered.

"I don't think he much cares. He doesn't love the land, or Aradyn's people, for that matter. He only loves the money he gets for his tulip bulbs."

Bee could believe this, after meeting the mage. He was a strange, harsh man.

"But what about the king, before he died? Why wouldn't he make Master Joris put back the trees?"

Master Bouts shrugged. "It's only in recent times that people have begun thinking that the trees might have helped. Most likely the king just didn't know. And people have forgotten the bounty trees once gave. They think the way things are now is the way they always were. Many have never even seen the king—he's been gone a long time."

"Poor Princess Anika," Bee said softly.

"She'll set things to rights, once she reaches her majority. When she's eighteen, she'll be queen, and Master Joris will just be Aradyn's mage, nothing more."

But Bee wondered—how could Anika possibly bring back what was gone?

For the next few days, Bee experimented with her baking. After seeing Anika's reaction to her tarts, she was pretty certain that Master Bouts's outlandish idea about the baking magic might be right. Bee had danced about with Wil when she made the tarts, and Anika had danced when she'd eaten them. She was less sure about the effect on Master Joris. Maybe it didn't work on mages—or maybe the fact that he didn't shout at her and chase her out of the garden was as close to dancing as he came.

The first part of the experiment took place after Bee had an argument with Mistress de Vos, who insisted she'd paid for a cake when she'd only given a single copper for a loaf of bread. Quickly Bee ran back to the kitchen and mixed up a tart crust, letting her anger flow freely as she cut the butter into the flour. Then she fed the tart to Wil. She decided it would be better to experiment on a friend than a paying customer.

"Do you like it?" she asked him innocently.

"Why do you have to ask that?" he demanded, sounding irritated. "Your tarts are always good. Don't make me tell you every time!"

Bee suppressed a giggle—and the urge to apologize for making him cranky.

Then she thought about the afternoon in the garden with Anika as she kneaded a loaf of bread. She focused on the happiness she'd felt as they'd lain beneath the cherry tree and watched Pepin wander through the flower petals, and the wonderful feeling of having found a new friend. Wil was busy that afternoon, so she buttered a slice of the bread and put it on the floor and waited to see what would happen. Kaatje the cat came to sniff at it and then nibbled a bit. A little later, a mouse poked its head from behind the big stove. Thrilled at its luck, for the kitchen was usually spotless, it dashed over to the bread and tried to carry the slice back to its mouse home. The bread was too heavy, though, so the mouse simply bit off a hunk and then disappeared with it as Bee watched.

A half hour or so later, Bee came back into the kitchen to take a batch of tarts from the oven. Kaatje sat curled up in her basket, her eyes bright. Between her paws lay the mouse. Astonished, Bee watched as the cat gently washed the mouse with its rough tongue. The mouse seemed almost to purr with pleasure as it stretched itself luxuriously. Bee hoped the happy affection she'd baked into the bread would wear off the mouse first, or it would surely be Kaatje's supper.

Her final trial was a batch of meringue cookies she made after coming across an enormous spider in the broom closet. She whipped egg whites frantically as her heart thrummed with fear. Then, feeling a bit guilty, she fed the cookies to Wil.

"Something's wrong," he said after eating them, looking around anxiously. "Do I smell smoke? What's on fire?"

"Don't worry. It's nothing. It's me," she confessed. "I've been experimenting."

Wil stared at her. "What do you mean, experimenting?"

"I wanted to see if Master Bouts was right. I baked things while I was having . . . well, feelings. And it worked. It's true."

"What feelings?" he demanded. He didn't look pleased at all.

"This last batch—it was fear. Are you especially afraid of fire?"

Wil flushed. "I suppose I am."

"That's a funny thing to be afraid of, when you're a blacksmith," Bee pointed out gently.

"I know," he said, shaking his head. "It's not very convenient. I get sick to my stomach every time." He held out his hands, and Bee noticed, for the first time, the scars on nearly every finger, the back of his hands, his wrists. "Hurts like the devil," he said. "I have nightmares sometimes about being caught in a burning building. I'd rather do almost anything than work with fire."

"Like what?" Bee asked.

Wil shook his head. "No use thinking on it," he said. "I'm a blacksmith's son, and a blacksmith I'll be."

Master Bouts pushed into the kitchen. "Ah, cookies!"

he exclaimed. "Just the pick-me-up I needed." Before Bee could stop him, he'd popped one of the meringues into his mouth. They watched as he chewed and swallowed, then turned pale and said, "Do you hear water? Is it storming? Oh no, not another flood!"

He started back out toward the shop, but Bee called out, "Wait! There's no flood! It's the cookies."

Master Bouts turned around. "The cookies?"

"I baked them with fear," Bee admitted. "And you're afraid of . . . water?"

Master Bouts shook his head hard, as if he were trying to shake out his thoughts. "Not water all on its own. Floods. Drowning, to be perfectly honest. I've nightmares about it sometimes, since that big storm. The water rises around my bed, and there's no escape . . . and then I wake all in a sweat, as wet as if I'd been truly drowned. Horrible. Horrible." He was quiet for a minute and then, realizing what had happened, said, "Ah, but it works, doesn't it, my girl? What did I tell you? You have a small magic of your own, that you do."

"You were right," Bee said. "I don't understand it, but it's true. And I certainly don't know what use it is. It means I have to be careful when I bake, or the customers will riot!" She looked at her hands, turning them palm up and then down again. It seemed very strange that those hands could make magic. Very strange—and more than a little exciting.

"It means you can control what people feel, at least somewhat," the baker pointed out. "And that is a powerful thing. You must take care not to misuse it."

Bee hadn't thought of it that way. True, it might be fun to bake a tart of confusion that would send Mistress de Vos into a tizzy, or cookies laced with jealousy that might make the Tenbrook twins fight over the butcher's boy, but it wouldn't be right. She would have to restrain her less kindly impulses.

"Well, I made today's pastries for the palace in a state of perfect calm," Bee said. "And I should take them over there now. If I'm late, no amount of calm cakes will soothe the angry mage."

She picked up the baskets she had prepared—three tarts this time, a cake, and the Bouts Buns. On her way out the door, Wil called behind her, "Ho, Mistress Boviardis, what were you so frightened by when you made those cookies?"

"Oh, it was nothing much," she said quickly.

"Not fair! You know our fears now. What was yours? Tell!"

"It was . . . spiders. I'm afraid of spiders."

"Spiders!" Wil snorted. "Those sweet little weaving bugs?"

"They're dreadful!" she cried. "Nasty eight-legged crawling things!" And she pushed through the door to the sound of Wil's and Master Bouts's hoots of laughter.

CHAPTER 7

Bee had made three more Tuesday trips to the palace. She never saw any servants except the butler and the cook. There seemed to be no maids, no footmen, nobody at all to tend the decaying palace.

At each visit she met Anika in the garden. She still hadn't mastered the maze; she had an odd suspicion that it changed with every passage. Anika had to guide her through it with shouted instructions from the other side.

Being with Anika felt the way Bee had always imagined having a sister would feel. They were sometimes awkward with each other because they were both unused to having friends, but with each visit the self-consciousness grew less. They talked about nearly everything. On some subjects, like clothes and the meanings of words, Anika had a great knowledge. Her dresses were of the finest fabrics and most current styles, though no one but Bee ever saw them. And Anika admitted that she read the dictionary when she was bored and tried to use the most interesting words she found as often as she could. When Bee pointed out that she had never heard many of those words, Anika flushed with embarrassment and said, "I don't converse with many people, you see. Besides, there are so many wonderful words. Why don't more people utilize them?"

"Well, you sound very royal," Bee assured her. "And I'm learning a prodigial amount of vocabulary!"

"Prodigious," Anika corrected, and both girls laughed.

About other things, like the people of Zeewal and their peculiar habits, Bee was the expert. Anika loved hearing about the bakery, about Master Bouts and Wil, about Kaatje the cat and the dour Mistress de Vos. There were a few topics they didn't discuss: their lost parents, Master Joris. But Bee's feeling that Anika feared the mage grew stronger, and, worried that her presence would get the princess in trouble, she took pains not to be discovered.

On this Tuesday, when Bee left the bakery, it was raining. The rain was more of a mist than an actual downpour, but Bee was glad she'd covered her baskets with a cloth. She hurried through the dampness with her head down. At the palace Master van Campen let her in with an expressionless face, and she made her way down to the kitchen, where the cook sat in exactly the same position she'd held the week before and the week before that. Bee wondered if she moved at all in the seven days between visits.

"I've come with the pastries," Bee said. "And I brought *you* something."

"Oh?" This was a change from the previous visits.

Bee unpacked the baskets. Every week they held more and better pastries than the week before; the payments sent from the palace were making Master Bouts a wealthy man, and he used the money to purchase the finest ingredients. Carefully, Bee set each sweet on its own plate. She put a little cake on a little plate and held it out to the cook. "This is for you—but only if you tell me your name."

The cook's pudding face melted into a smile. "That's a fair trade, girl! I'm Hadewig." She reached out eagerly for the cake.

"And I'm Bee," Bee said. "Shall I cut the mage's slices?"

"Yes indeed," the cook said. "He's been down here twice this morning looking for them. You're late again, you know."

Bee ignored this. "And . . . the princess? Can I see her?" She knew Anika wouldn't be in the garden on such a damp morning.

The cook raised herself from her chair and rummaged in a drawer for a tarnished fork, then took a bite of her cake. She chewed slowly, her cheeks pink with pleasure. "I don't say that you can, and I don't say that you cannot. But she'll be in the library—that's on the top floor, third door on the right. Not that you heard it from me."

"Of course not," Bee assured her. She prepared Master Joris's tray and a plate for the princess, then bade the cook goodbye. "Till next week," she said.

"Don't stay long," Hadewig warned. "The master will be checking, I've no doubt."

Bee picked up her tray and left the cook chewing in delight. Up the stairs, down the corridor, to the fourth door on the left. The door to the mage's study was very slightly open, and as she bent to leave the tray on the floor, she heard voices. Quietly, she angled herself so her ear was against the opening. Yes, that was the mage's raspy tone.

"That is correct, it's settled," she heard him say. "They'll come in a fortnight for her, and then the thing is done."

"The princess won't be happy," another voice warned. Bee thought it was Master van Campen.

"Making her happy is not my responsibility," Master

Joris replied. "It's a fine match."

"Fine for him at least," Master van Campen said. "He's fifty if he's a day. And with three children to boot."

"They need a mother," Master Joris pointed out. "She's a biddable girl, and she'll be good to them."

"And you'll be master here for good—unless King Thiedric decides the marriage entitles him to Aradyn."

"Do you think he would dare move against me?" Master Joris chuckled, and the sound made Bee shudder. It was like fingernails drawn across a slate. She heard a movement inside the room, and she jerked away from the door and fled with the princess's plate, leaving the tray lying on the floor. Back down the corridor, up the stairs, and up again, then down the hallway. Second door—or was it third? She knocked on the second, but there was no reply, so she tried the third. It opened almost before her knuckles lifted.

"Bee!" Princess Anika's face was filled with joy. "I was so hoping you could locate me. It's far too sodden for the garden today, and I dared not await you in the kitchen, as Uncle Joris kept checking for his pastries. I was fearful that you would have to depart without a visit."

Bee was panting. "Here, take this." She handed the plate to Anika. "I can't stay long," she said. "I heard something—oh, Anika! I heard something terrible."

"Something terrible? Whatever do you mean?" The princess looked perplexed, but not alarmed.

"Your uncle—the mage—he was talking . . . talking—" Bee was trembling.

"Sit down. Compose yourself. What on earth is wrong?" Anika set the plate on a small table.

"They plan to marry you off!" Bee burst out. "To an old man, some king—King Thiedric."

The color drained from Anika's face. "How do you come by this knowledge?" she demanded, her voice low.

"I heard the mage talking to Master van Campen. It was clear, what they said. It's to happen in two weeks."

"But . . . why? Why would he consider such an action?"

"To get rid of you,'" Bee said solemnly. Anika covered her mouth with her hand. "He plans to keep Aradyn for himself, I think."

Anika gasped. "No, that's not possible." She sank into a leather chair, then leaped up. "Ouch! Pepin, move!" She picked up the hedgehog, then sat again with him in her lap. "He has never mentioned marriage before. You must have misconstrued." At Bee's blank look, she said, "Misunderstood."

"I don't think I did," Bee said, shaking her head. There

was a silence. "Does your uncle have the power to make the decisions? He isn't the king, after all."

In her dismay, Anika squeezed the hedgehog a little harder than she intended. He looked quite perturbed and let out a squeak.

"Give him here," Bee suggested, and Anika, distraught, handed Pepin over.

"He is not the king, you're quite correct," the princess said. "Nor is he truly my uncle. But he is the mage, and he has been so for more than a century. He has appropriated far more sovereignty than he's entitled to. He has decided everything since my father's death. I am just a girl. I am sixteen, and I am an orphan. If this is his strategy, what can I conceivably do? Oh, Bee, must I be joined in matrimony with an old man?"

"An old man with three children," Bee said.

"Three children!" Anika wrung her hands with horror, and Bee was relieved she had rescued Pepin. "No, I won't do it. I will not."

"But what can you do?"

"Let me ruminate. Let me cogitate," Anika said. Bee worried and waited, looking around at the library for the first time. The shelves were immensely tall, running from the floor to the high ceiling of the room. They were made of a brown material that Bee had never seen before. She walked over to a shelf and ran her hand over it. It was smooth and hard and warm, not cold like metal. She could almost imagine it breathing beneath her hand. Each shelf was crammed with leatherbound volumes. There was a rail halfway up the shelves on which a ladder could be moved around so that the uppermost books could be reached. So many books! Bee didn't know so many books existed in the world. She looked at the titles on their spines, sounding out the harder words silently. *A Guide to Growing Bulbs in a Damp Climate. The Micropropagation of Tulips. Flowering Fields: A Handbook.* They all sounded dreadfully dull. It was no wonder Anika read the dictionary!

"Bee, what would you do?" Anika's voice brought Bee back to the problem at hand. She was taken aback. Did the princess truly want her advice?

"Well," Bee said cautiously, "I lived in a place that was . . . bad. And when it got worse, I ran away."

"How was it bad?"

"The master shouted and threw things. And the mistress beat me."

"Oh, Bee," Anika said. There were tears in her big blue eyes. Bee marveled that the princess could be sympathetic when her own dilemma loomed so large.

"I was all right," Bee said. "I knew I could take care of myself on my own. So I left."

"You had to," Anika said. "And I have to, as well. How did you do it? Was it difficult? Will you help me?"

"Help you run away?"

"Yes." The princess's voice was firm. "I will run away. I will not marry King Thiedric, nor anyone else not of my choosing. Will you help?"

Bee was troubled. Surely Master Bouts wouldn't think this was a good idea. But on the other hand . . . "Well, you are my princess. I will do as you please."

Anika jumped to her feet. "No, not like that! I don't ask for your aid because I am your ruler. Will you help me, as my friend?"

A warmth spread through Bee, and she made up her mind instantly. "Of course I will. We'll make a plan."

Anika threw her arms around Bee, squashing Pepin between them, and the poor hedgehog squeaked again. "Ouch!" the princess cried. "Pepin, you are a very vexing pet. But you will come as well."

"We haven't much time," Bee warned. "The mage said a fortnight."

"Then we will go soon. Tomorrow. No, the day after—

my tutor's day off. They don't guard me well, for I've never tried to abscond before. Uncle Joris has no reason to believe I would."

"How will we go, though?" Bee asked. "We have to be practical. We can't just walk off, a princess and a hedgehog and a baker's apprentice. That would attract a lot of attention."

Anika looked out the window, cleaner than most of the palace windows. "The canal," she said, pointing. "Have you a boat?"

"I'm a baker," Bee pointed out. "Bakers don't have boats."

"Can you get a boat?" Anika persisted.

Bee thought about it. "I'll have to tell Master Bouts. I'm sure he'll know someone with a boat. He knows everyone."

Anika's brow furrowed. "But will he keep it clandestine? Is he trustworthy?"

"I would trust him with my life," Bee declared. "He is the most trustworthy man there is." She said it without even thinking, but the words echoed in her heart. It was true. For the first time, she had someone she could trust utterly.

Anika looked at her with shining eyes. "Oh, you are

fortunate to know someone like that!" she exclaimed. "Then I will escape somehow—I'll fix upon how—and I'll unite with you on the other side of the dam at midnight, two days hence."

"Hush!" Bee warned, holding up a finger. There was a heavy thump of footsteps outside the library. Panic filled Anika's face, and she pointed to a little closet in the corner of the room. Bee tossed her the hedgehog, which unrolled in midair and then rolled up again before Anika caught him. Then Bee scurried over to the closet, pulled open the iron door, and wedged herself inside, bent almost double, just as the door to the library opened.

"Well, young lady," she heard the mage say. "Have you finished your morning's lessons?"

"Yes, I have, Uncle," Princess Anika replied. Bee marveled at how calm and even her voice was. "After my music lesson, we spent some time looking at the maps on the wall. It was very interesting indeed, to learn about the geography of Aradyn."

"Geography," the mage mused. "It is a valuable course of study for a ruler—or even for the wife of a ruler. To know a kingdom's reaches is to know the kingdom itself."

"I think that to know a kingdom's people is to know the kingdom," Anika said. Bee held her breath. It didn't seem wise for the princess to argue with her guardian. But perhaps she was trying to distract him.

"Well." The mage was not pleased at being contradicted. Bee heard his footsteps on the hard tile. "I see that the baker's girl has been here."

Oh no! Bee thought. She had left the plate of pastries!

"I thought I made it clear you were not to see her again."

Anika laughed, a charming, tinkly sound. "Well, Uncle, you made it clear to me, but no one told her not to come. And I am not at all sorry to have her lovely tarts!"

Master Joris made a noise that might have signaled agreement. "They have an odd delicacy, I will give her that." This description interested Bee. *An odd delicacy.* Could he have been affected in some way by her first batch of tarts, as the princess had been?

But then Bee heard Joris's footsteps pace toward her hiding place. He walked slowly, slowly. She held her breath again. Did a mage have powers to sense a hidden person? Could he smell her, or look right through the door to see her scrunched in the tiny room?

Bee didn't understand how, but the mage knew she was there. The footsteps stopped right before the closet. She closed her eyes, wishing she could somehow become invisible, but when Master Joris threw open the closet door and bent to look inside, she summoned all her courage and met his gaze with her own. His eyebrows winged up in outrage, and his black eyes narrowed.

"Come out of there this minute, you sorry wench," he commanded. "I cannot imagine what you are doing hiding in my closet, but your explanation had best satisfy me, or you'll know what it is to be truly sorry."

CHAPTER 8

Bee crept out of the closet and straightened up with difficulty, stiff from crouching. Her heart hammered in her chest, and her palms felt clammy.

"Oh, Uncle!" Anika cried. Her voice was high and playful. Bee didn't dare look at her. "You've found her—and spoiled the game!"

Master Joris turned his dark eyes to the princess. "Game?"

"We were playing hide-and-go-seek," Anika said. "I'd quite forgotten about that closet—I should never have guessed it as a hiding place!"

"You have deliberately disobeyed me." Master Joris's mouth was pinched, as if he'd tasted a sour berry.

"But Uncle, I see so few people. I didn't think it would matter, just for an hour. And she is only the baker's apprentice. I *am* sorry to have contravened your orders. But I get so lonely, you know. . . ." Anika's voice trailed off, and she gazed downward, her mouth quivering.

Master Joris looked from Anika to Bee, from Bee back to Anika. Bee tried to make her face look innocent and sorry and not very smart. She twisted her hands together and scuffed her shoe on the floor for effect.

"Out, girl," Master Joris commanded her finally. "Go to your master and tell him that his disobedient apprentice has cost him the honor of supplying the palace with sweets. We shall go back to using the bakery on Caneel Street."

Bee was about to protest, but thought better of it. "Yes, master," she mumbled, bowing. She bowed again and again as she backed out of the room, bumping first into a chair and then the table as she went. She only missed stepping on Pepin by an inch, and the animal gave her a tiny hiss of warning as she stumbled by him.

"And you, child," Master Joris said to Anika, as Bee exited backward through the door, "you shall not be lonely much longer. I will see to that!"

Bee couldn't see Anika's face, but she could imagine how the princess's heart must have fallen at the mage's words. "Courage!" she whispered, though she knew Anika couldn't hear her. Then she picked up her skirts and fled.

The rain pelted her as she sprinted along the streets

back to the bakery, which had closed for the day by the time she got back. In the kitchen, she toweled her short hair vigorously and told Master Bouts what had happened as he prepared their supper.

"You agreed to *what*?" Master Bouts stood at the stove, his face a mask of astonishment, his mouth a perfect O.

"To help the princess run away," Bee said in a small voice, hiding her face behind the towel.

"*To help the princess run away,*" Master Bouts repeated. "You are completely mad."

"I know," Bee said helplessly.

"You got us fired as the palace bakers."

"Yes."

"And you agreed to help the princess run away."

"I already said that," Bee protested. "You can't yell at me for it again."

"I haven't even begun to yell at you!" Master Bouts said. He wasn't quite yelling, but he was close. His face had grown very pink. Behind him, a pan started to smoke.

"Something's burning," Bee noted, grateful for the distraction.

Master Bouts spun around and snatched the omelet pan off the stove. He forgot to use a cloth, though, and the heat of the handle scorched his fingers. He shouted and the pan went flying. Bee watched in horror as the omelet flipped out of the pan, sailed up, up, up—and then, twice as fast, down. It missed Master Bouts's head by a breath and landed with a splat on his shoes.

For a moment there was silence in the kitchen. Then Master Bouts snorted. "My girl," he said and had to stop to chuckle. "My girl," he began again. "Oh, Bee, you will be the death of me!"

Bee was giggling just a little, more out of relief that he wasn't truly angry than anything else. But when she saw his reddened fingers she ran to pump a pan of cold water, and they sat at the table while he soothed his burned hand.

"I *had* to promise," she told him. "They are going to marry the princess off to some ancient king with three children. She's only sixteen—and she has no one!"

Master Bouts grimaced, whether in pain or sympathy Bee couldn't tell. "Yes, I do understand. Truly I do. The poor child. But Bee, how can it work? Have you a plan?"

"Not much of one," Bee admitted. "I'm to meet her in two days, at midnight. With a boat."

"A boat! Where on earth would you get a boat?"

"Well . . ." Bee let the word trail off. She gave Master Bouts a hopeful smile.

Master Bouts looked at her severely. "I see," he said. "So I am to be implicated in this grand plot. And what do you think will happen when you're found out?"

"I don't care!" Bee said, defiant. "All I know is that I've made a promise that I intend to keep."

Master Bouts ran his uninjured hand through his white hair. "Master Joris is a powerful man, Bee. I don't even know the extent of his powers—no one does. But it's certain that he would be dangerous to cross." He paused, then nodded decisively. "Still, year by year, he starves his own people to gain more wealth from his tulips. No one has taken a stand against him in all this time. It's time someone did—even if that someone must be me. I'll not let him marry that poor child to a man three times her age and more. I'll help with your plan, my girl—that I will!"

There was a knock at the kitchen door, and Wil let himself in. He took in the pan, the ruined omelet on the floor, and Master Bouts with his hand submerged in water.

"Come to my house for supper," he suggested, and Bee and Master Bouts exchanged a glance. *Yes indeed,* their eyes agreed. *Yes, Wil should be told. Yes, we should go and eat his mother's cooking.*

On the quick walk to Wil's house, which stood beside the blacksmith's shop, Bee filled him in on her visit to the palace and the planned escape.

"I have a friend with a reed boat," Wil said softly as they picked their way past puddles on the cobbled street.

Bee clapped her hands. "Will he loan it to us?"

"I'm sure he will—if I am with you to ensure its safe return."

Before Bee could protest, they were at the house, and Wil opened the door to a room overflowing with relatives. Bee had met his mother in the bakery once or twice, a wisp of a woman who looked as if she could float away on a strong breeze. But she didn't know his father, who was enormously tall and broad, all muscle and soot-blackened skin, with a fringe of singed hair the color of ash. And she'd had no idea Wil had so many brothers and sisters— two brothers, one just a year or two younger, and the other tottering about on wobbly legs, and three sisters, all younger, who seemed to take great delight in teasing Wil.

"So this is your girlfriend, Willem Weatherwax!" his sister Sanna crowed. "She's a bit young for you, don't you think?"

"Enough," Wil growled as Bee's face turned red. "They're company."

"Yes, they are—behave yourself, miss!" Mistress Weatherwax scolded her daughter, wiping her hands on her apron and coming to the door to greet them. "Hambert Bouts, it has been far too long since you've supped with us. And Bee, I am so happy to see you!" As tiny as she was, Wil's mother seemed to fill the room like a whirlwind, cuffing Sanna's ear in reproof for her rudeness while lifting the toddler away from the danger of the hearth and then shaking her visitors' hands with her free hand.

"We're sorry to intrude with no notice," Master Bouts said, "but there was an accident with our supper, and Wil took pity on us."

"You're welcome any time at all," Mistress Weatherwax assured them. "Isn't that so, Klaas?" This was directed to her husband, who sat in a very large chair before the fire, his eyes closed. He grunted in reply without opening them.

"Da gets tired of an evening," Wil explained. "Now, sit here with me, and we'll sort this out." He directed them to a window seat away from the flow of traffic in the main room.

"Supper in five minutes," Mistress Weatherwax called. "Sanna, set extra places."

"So you need a boat—and where do you plan to go?" Wil asked Bee, his voice low.

She shook her head and shrugged. "Away is all I thought. We'd decide when we got there."

"Bee, you're talking about the princess," Will said. "You can't just go away. Master Joris will find you in an instant."

Bee pursed her lips. "Does he read minds? What exactly can he do?"

Wil looked blank. "Well, I'm not quite sure. He can . . . I think he can . . ."

"When I was a child," Master Bouts cut in, "he used to create the most marvelous fireworks for the king's birthday. Remarkable, that they were. Dragons made of fire, and flowers that whirled around in circles, and once a whole city that grew out of sparks and then crumbled into ash."

"That's nice," Bee said, "but it doesn't really tell us much. What danger would we be in? What power does he have?"

Master Bouts shrugged. "I told you, no one is certain. I know each mage's job is to maintain a balance in his kingdom. To keep it healthy, and stable. But I'm not sure what that demands."

"Maintain a balance? What does that even mean?" Bee asked.

"As with baking, I believe," Master Bouts said. "If you don't balance the moist and the dry ingredients, your pastry won't turn out right. If you don't balance the sweet and the tart, it won't taste good. The land must be balanced as well."

"But Master Joris hasn't done that," Wil pointed out. "Aradyn is covered with tulip farms, always more and more of them, and there is less and less space for crops. The people are hungry. And the storms are worse, or at least doing worse damage. The land doesn't seem balanced at all."

Bee was surprised at his passion, and he seemed a little surprised as well. But his mother overheard and said, "That's my gardener. Look out back if you want to see what he's done. He practices what he preaches, that one."

"No, no," Wil protested, embarrassed, but Bee insisted. Wil led her and Master Bouts to the back door, which opened onto a kitchen garden that even in early fall was lush with herbs and vegetables—squashes of all sorts, tomatoes, beetroot, sage and dill and basil.

"It's beautiful," Bee said as Mistress Weatherwax called them back in.

"Tell that to Da," Wil said morosely. "He doesn't think a blacksmith should think about anything but metal and fire, fire and metal."

It was time for supper, and Bee had a grand time eating Mistress Weatherwax's good roast and potatoes and joining Wil's sisters in tormenting him. He pretended to be cross, but it was clear that it was all in play. Bee had never seen a family where everyone got along. When the baby passed by, Master Weatherwax scooped him up and planted a big kiss on his head, leaving a smear of ash on his beaming face. When one of the girls carried in a big platter of roasted vegetables, Mistress Weatherwax ruffled her hair and then made gentle fun of her when she fussed over her ruined braid. The teasing was nonstop, but nobody's feelings were hurt. Everyone laughed.

At the end of the evening, when Master Weatherwax was dozing over his tumbler of ale, Master Bouts and Bee bid the family good night. "I'll walk them out," Wil said, and his mother nodded.

"Come back soon," she told her guests, enfolding Bee in a hug. "You need no invitation. I know you've kept my son supplied in buns these many years, Hambert—we couldn't pay you back if we fed you roast beef every night for a twelve-month!"

Back on the street, Wil said, "So, is it decided? Shall I bring a boat, and myself, and join the expedition?"

"But your father needs you in the forge," Bee protested. "What will he do while you're gone?"

"My brother Geert loves the forge, and he's getting old enough to help," Wil said. "He'll take my place gladly. And he'll do a much better job than I!"

"He loves it, you hate it—and yet you're the one who must do it?" Bee was honestly confused.

"That's the way it is," Wil told her. "Is and always has been. The eldest son has the family business, and the others must fend for themselves."

"That's absurd!" Bee declared.

"My girl," Master Bouts said, "the rules of human behavior are absurd much more often than they're reasonable."

"Then I'm glad to give you a chance to get away for a bit," Bee said to Wil. "You provide the boat, and you may come."

"You may have saved my life, too," Wil said, grinning. "I've longed for an adventure for years. Do you know, I've never been away from Zeewal?"

Bee spent the next two days baking things that would travel well and were seasoned in very specific ways. She cooked up a batch of cookies flavored with confidence, after she made her first Bouts Bun successfully. She stayed up very late and made oatmeal bars spiced with exhaustion, and a few more Bouts Buns as well. She packed all the pastries, along with cheese and bread and sliced salami, into a leather haversack that Master Bouts gave her, being careful to keep straight which pastries were which.

The day before they were to leave, Master Bouts came into the kitchen as Bee prepared the dough for the next day's tarts. He towed behind him a man Bee had never seen before, small and dark and dressed in the dark green robes of a hedge wizard.

"Bee, this is Master Arjen, an old friend of mine."

Bee bowed, and the hedge wizard bowed back.

"I saw him on the street and invited him in to talk to us. He knows a little something about mages. More than I do, at any rate."

"Well," the hedge wizard said modestly, "I am no mage, of course. My own magic is very small, very small indeed. And my ignorance is very great." Despite his humble words, there was something self-important in his manner that irritated Bee.

"Not at all!" Master Bouts protested. "You have a fine

way with bees—the namesake of my apprentice here."

"Bees are my specialty," Master Arjen admitted. "Most people do not know how important they are. They only think, *Beware the stinger!* and swat, there goes one of nature's great wonders."

"I'm very fond of bees," Bee said, taking up the rolling pin. She knew that many hedge wizards had an area of expertise, a little corner of the world that they were responsible for. She hadn't known that the corner was ever as small as *bees*.

"Hambert, there was a promise made," Master Arjen reminded Master Bouts.

"A promise—yes, of course! Bee, fetch Master Arjen a Bouts Bun. It's his payment for telling us what he knows."

Bee gave the hedge wizard a sidelong look, but obediently she went into the shop, brought back a plate of buns, and placed it before the guest. He took a big bite of one and closed his eyes, sighing deeply. "Ah, it has been too long since I tasted one of these!" It took him an extraordinarily long time to finish, and Bee had rolled out five tart crusts and was ready to use the rolling pin on the hedge wizard by the time the bun was gone.

"So, the powers of the mage," Master Bouts prompted.

"Indeed. The powers of the mage." Master Arjen closed

his eyes again as if summoning strength.

"They are . . . ?" Master Bouts said. His voice betrayed just a little impatience.

"Yes. Well. Mages are not like the rest of you. They are not even like us hedge wizards."

"We know that!" Bee burst out. Master Bouts put a finger to his lips.

"Indeed you do. But what you do not know is that a mage is a wizard of the earth. Like the hedge wizard or hedge witch, in fact, but on a somewhat larger scale. He can control the things of the earth."

"Plants, you mean?" Master Bouts asked.

"Plants, animals. The land itself. But not water. Not the sea. The mages have no power over the sea at all. It is far mightier than they."

Bee and Master Bouts look at each other. Bee's eyes were shining.

"So," Bee said, "if a person were in a boat on a canal, could a mage do any magic to hurt him? Or stop him?"

"Not if the canal led to the sea and had sea water in it."

"Oh!" Bee clapped her hands with glee. "That's very interesting, Master Arjen. Have another bun!"

"Are you quite sure?" Master Arjen asked, then grabbed a bun from the plate before Bee could reply.

When the hedge wizard was full of bun and had taken his leave, Bee and Master Bouts began the nightly kitchen cleanup. "I think I know where we will go," Bee said as she ran a cloth over the stovetop.

"Oh?" Master Bouts stopped sweeping up flour.

"You said that a mage's job is to keep balance in the kingdom. Well, our mage isn't doing that. In fact, he's doing the opposite, from what I can tell. Isn't that right?"

"Quite so."

"There are rules for mages too, aren't there?"

Master Bouts nodded.

"And who makes the rules?"

"The mages' council," Master Bouts replied, raising one silver brow quizzically.

"Right. The mages' council. I've heard about them. They live on some island, isn't that right?" Bee asked.

"It is," Master Bouts said slowly. In the dim light from the one lamp still burning, Bee could see awareness dawning on his face.

"We will go there, Princess Anika, Wil, and I. To the island. We will tell them what Master Joris is doing. The princess will be with us, so they will have to believe us. And we will get them to remove Master Joris and give us a new mage and bring Aradyn back to the way it's supposed to be."

CHAPTER 9

After supper the next day, Bee sent the cooper's son to the palace with a big plate of Bouts Buns, baked full of exhaustion. Enclosed was a note that read:

Please accept these as a sincere token of our regret for our apprentice's misbehavior.

Humbly yours,

Hambert Bouts, Baker

"They're for the mage," she warned the boy. "Don't you take so much as a bite. Believe me, I'll know if you do." She gave him a copper and sent him off.

"What if the princess eats one?" Master Bouts asked.

"She won't get the chance," Bee said. "Master Joris is very greedy. The only reason she got to taste our treats at all was because I brought them to her specially. But I'm hoping the other servants will sneak a helping before they get to the mage. The more of them asleep, the better."

Wil came by with his own haversack after sundown.

Bee described the visit with Master Arjen and told him the plan she had devised. He approved.

"We should be safe on the water, then, away from Master Joris's power," he said. "And I should think the mages' council would take action when you explain what Master Joris has done. At the very least, they'll investigate."

From his pack, he pulled a pair of trousers and a shirt. "These are for you, Mistress Blitekin. I remember you dressed like a boy when we first met, and I thought it might be easier for you without skirts. They're Geert's—they should fit you well enough."

Bee was delighted. To wear trousers again—how she'd missed it! She changed quickly in her little room. The trousers were a bit long, so she rolled them up. To her they were perfect.

As the hours passed slowly, Wil twitched with excitement, ready to go long before it was time, and Master Bouts fussed and worried, too anxious to sit down. Bee spent a good deal of time reassuring him.

"I am a fine swimmer," she said, when he wondered out loud how safe a reed boat on the sea would be. "I grew up by the sea and spent summers paddling in it." It wasn't quite a lie. She could swim and had spent much of her childhood by the water, but she was allowed to swim only when the chores were finished, and the chores were very rarely finished.

"I'm not afraid of the mages," she told the baker, when he fretted nervously about how a group of esteemed and powerful magicians would react to the demands of a twelve-year-old girl. "The worst they could do is say no." That was not at all the worst she imagined, but she didn't want to share her fearful thoughts with Master Bouts and upset him still more.

At last, it was nearly midnight, and Wil and Bee took their leave. "Perhaps I should go with you," Master Bouts said, for the fourth or fifth time.

"On a boat? On the water? You'd die of fright," Bee said matter-of-factly.

Master Bouts ran his hands through his white hair in frustration. "It shames me, my girl, but you are right."

"We fear what we fear," Bee said. "You can't help it. I know you'd come if you could." She threw her arms around the baker as far as they would reach and squeezed him tight, and he hugged her back.

"Take care of her," he said severely to Wil. "I'll expect you back safe and sound in a week or less."

"Tell her to take care of *me*!" Wil protested. "I'd put my

money on Bee against almost anyone." Master Bouts had to agree with that, and they parted with smiles, much to Bee's relief. She hated to see the baker distressed.

"The boat is tied up at the wharf at the end of Oukoop Lane," Wil told Bee as they made their way through the dark streets. There was a moon, but clouds covered it, so it gave very little light. No one was about. The people of Zeewal were early to rise and early to bed, and their lamps were out by ten.

"Good," Bee said. "We haven't too far to paddle to the palace, then."

The reed boat bobbed on its tether in the still waters of the canal. It looked sturdy, and just big enough for three. Bee sat up front in the bow, and Wil took the stern. Their paddles were thick reeds lashed together, shaped to catch and hold the water so they could pull the boat forward easily. It took them a few minutes to find a rhythm, but before long they were moving very quickly up the canal toward the palace.

"You're good at this!" Wil said in a low voice, surprised.

"I lived with a fishing family," Bee said. "I spent some time in a boat."

The canal stopped at the earthen dam that had created the lake in front of the palace. The palace loomed on the far side of the lake. It must have been a bit before midnight, because Princess Anika wasn't there yet. Or maybe she was late. Bee strained to see through the misty darkness. Was that the princess, hurrying toward them?

"I see her!" Wil hissed. Bee waved her hand, rocking the boat a bit.

Anika emerged from the gloom. She wasn't just hurrying—she was running. And someone was running behind her.

"Who is that?" Bee said. Then she saw sparks flying upward from the runner's feet. "It's Master Joris!" she cried in horror.

The mage was stumbling as he ran, and weaving a bit, almost as if he'd had too much wine to drink. He stopped once to point at the princess, who sprinted ahead of him around the lake toward the dam. Bee held her breath, sure that some dire magic would come from his finger and cut Anika down, or lift her up and spirit her away. But instead Master Joris tripped on something and fell facedown on the ground as Anika dashed the last few yards to the dam. She stood uncertainly on the embankment above the little boat, and Bee saw the mage struggle to his feet.

"Jump!" she shouted, and Wil echoed her: "Jump, Princess!"

Anika glanced behind her at the mage, standing now, and as he raised his hand toward her again, she gathered her skirts together and leaped off the earthen dam.

It wasn't very far to jump, but she landed hard in the boat, and something flew from her hand. It was Pepin, rolled into a tight ball of hedgehog terror. Bee scooped him up from the bottom of the boat, and he unrolled partway, snuffling with dismay. Anika wobbled on her feet as the boat tilted to one side, and she slid with it. Bee held on with her free hand, while Wil reached out to grab the princess before she toppled into the water. He pulled her to him and they stood swaying in the little boat face to face for a moment before Wil released her. Bee caught a glimpse of his expression as the clouds scudded away from the moon and its light shone down. He looked dazed.

"Stop right there!" The mage stood where Anika had been an instant before. In the moonlight his face was furious, and the shock of white in his black hair seemed to glow like lightning. "Return to me, Princess, and I will forgive this transgression. If you do not return, your friends will pay for your disobedience!"

Anika stood tall, rocking the boat wildly. "I owe you no obedience, Master Joris," she said in a clear voice. Bee was a little amazed that she could sound so forceful. "I owe you nothing at all—but you owe me my kingdom. Will you give it to me?"

The mage quivered in rage. Sparks flew from his fingers and rose into the air, forming themselves into shapes. A fiery eagle, its talons outstretched, flew toward them. It shrieked in a terrible, high-pitched tone, and Anika shrieked too in fear, ducking as it flapped overhead. Again the boat nearly overturned.

"Sit down, or we'll capsize!" Bee shouted.

An enormous sparkling snake wriggled down to the water's edge and hissed at them, but it could go no farther. Blazing bats swooped out of the darkness, coming close enough that they could feel the heat from their wings. Pepin squealed in distress and Anika crumpled to the bottom of the boat, covering her face with her hands. Bee set the hedgehog between her knees, and then she and Wil pulled at their paddles as hard as they could. Toads with flaming eyes leaped toward them from the shore as they passed, disappearing with a sputter when they hit the water. One landed in the boat, and the reeds started to smolder. Wil cried out, and Bee remembered his terrible fear of fire. Swiftly she knocked the toad into the water with her paddle, and the princess scooped a handful of water into the boat to cool the sizzling reeds.

And then they passed under the Lelykade Bridge, and they could no longer see the mage.

They paddled on for a time in silence. Bee could feel the boat quaking from Anika's shivers, but she said nothing. At last the shaking stopped. Anika uncovered her face and sat up straight.

"I didn't know there would be another accompanying us," she said to Bee, struggling to keep the quiver out of her voice.

Bee turned on her reed seat. "That's Wil Weatherwax, the son of the blacksmith. It's his friend's boat." The hedgehog's quills poked uncomfortably into her legs as she rowed, and she handed him back to Anika.

"I see," Anika said, stroking Pepin. "Then I thank you, sir, for your aid in my time of direst need."

"I—I am glad to be of help, Your Highness," Wil stammered.

"Really," Bee said, "can't we be less formal? We're in this together, after all. If we sink, we all go down as one."

"Quite so," the princess replied. "Then you must call me Anika, Master Weatherwax."

"And you must call me Wil, Your . . . Anika."

They paddled quietly as the dark clouds blew away,

and one by one the stars came out. Then Wil said, "Do you think Master Joris will send someone after us, Anika?"

"He may try, but they are all asleep. It's very strange. Even the guard could not be roused. He snored at his post as I tiptoed out. Uncle Joris was incensed!"

"Ha!" Wil snorted. "That's our Bee's handiwork!"

"Whatever do you mean?"

Wil explained Bee's special baking skills to the princess, and Anika drew in a sharp breath.

"Why, Bee! Is that why I felt such rapture when I first ate your tarts?"

"Well . . . yes," Bee said uncertainly. Perhaps Anika didn't like the idea of having her emotions swayed by pastry.

"And today you baked in . . . sleepiness? Is that why the servants slumbered?"

"I didn't know if it would work for certain," Bee admitted.

"You're magic! And so very clever!" Anika marveled. "Even Uncle Joris was affected. He dozed off after dinner, and then when he pursued me—that must be why he stumbled so. I do wish I had a skill like that!"

"You're a princess," Wil pointed out. "You don't really need a skill."

"What a foolish thing to say," Anika chided him. "A

good ruler needs all manner of expertise."

Bee couldn't see Wil's face, but she could imagine how embarrassed he must feel at the rebuke. "Sorry," he muttered. "Of course you're right."

"But I have none of those proficiencies," Anika went on. "I've had no chance to learn them, with Master Joris in charge of my education. I see now that he taught me very little that would be beneficial to me as a queen."

"You still have time to learn," Bee said.

"And maybe you can learn to be a bit more agreeable while you're at it," Wil added under his breath.

"Wil!" Bee protested. First names or not, that was no way to speak to a princess. But Wil didn't apologize this time. Quiet descended on the boat once more.

"Where exactly are we going?" Anika asked after a time.

"The Island of the Mages," Bee answered. She described the hedge wizard's visit and her own plan, and Anika clapped her hands, pleased.

"It's a marvelous idea!" she exclaimed. "Of course the mages' council will disapprove of Master Joris's behavior, and his scheme for me. Oh Bee, you are a wonder!"

Bee flushed in pleasure. No one had ever called her a wonder before.

The slight current in the canal moved in the same

direction as the boat—toward the sea. Still, paddling was hard. Bee began to rest after every few pulls on the paddle. Her arms and shoulders throbbed, despite the muscle she'd built from kneading dough and rolling out crusts.

"Let me paddle for a time," Anika said, noticing her frequent stops.

"No, no, I'm fine," Bee protested, but Anika edged toward the bow.

"I can take a turn," the princess insisted. "Rest your arms." The girls exchanged places carefully, and Anika plunged her paddle deep in the canal and tried to push it backward. An arc of water flew up behind her, spraying Wil from head to foot.

"Watch out!" he sputtered, and Bee clapped a hand over her mouth to hold back a hoot of laughter. Anika was horrified.

"I'm so sorry!" she said again and again. "Really, it was quite unintended! Oh, I'm so very maladroit!" She pulled a kerchief from her bodice and passed it to Bee.

"That's what you get for being rude to a princess," Bee teased, handing Wil the silken square.

"Oh Bee, don't say that!" Anika was so upset she was nearly in tears. "It wasn't on purpose, I assure you."

Wil mopped his face and hair as well as he could with the tiny kerchief and shook his head. "A fitting revenge, I suppose," he said in a mock-serious tone. "I'll be more careful with my words next time!" Bee giggled, and Anika, turning in her seat to try to see their expressions, realized they were making fun of her. For a moment she didn't seem sure how to react, but then she started to laugh too.

"Next time, I'll soak you even more," she vowed, and she dug her paddle into the water again.

"Not so deep!" Bee warned. A short lesson on paddling followed, and soon the little skiff was skimming over the water.

Bee almost dozed, resting in the bottom of the boat with Pepin in her lap, but a loud *splash* off to her right roused her. There was a louder one to her left, and whatever had fallen in the water doused her with spray. Then, all at once, splashes surrounded them, and something crashed against Bee's temple, so hard that the night sky spun before her eyes.

"It's rocks!" Wil called. "Cover your heads—the rocks are throwing themselves at us!"

Dizzy with the impact from the rock, Bee couldn't make sense of Wil's words. Then she understood. "Master Joris can control the land!" she cried. "He has power over the earth—the rocks too!" She wrapped her arms around her head as the stones whizzed by. Most landed harmlessly in the canal, but a few clattered into the boat. One struck Wil on the back, and he let out a pained grunt. They floated slowly down the canal, unable to paddle until the land they passed grew less rocky, and the attack gradually stopped.

"Is everyone all right?" Bee asked, when several minutes had passed without a flying stone.

"I'm fine," Anika answered, straightening up on her seat.

"I have a bruise I can boast of," Wil replied. "How many can say they've been to war with an army of rocks?" Bee put a hand to her forehead, feeling the warm trickle of blood on her face. There was a bump there the size of a Bouts Bun.

Soon after, Bee could tell that they were getting close to the sea. The current lapped back toward the boat, and little wavelets started to break against it. Her arms rested, Bee took over at the bow again. The canal had grown much wider and the paddling was harder now.

They passed a group of ships, their shadowy forms looming tall in the darkness, waiting to unload cargo for the towns and villages of Aradyn. And then, suddenly, it was clear that they were no longer within the protection of the canal banks. They had reached the open water. Instead of knocking against little waves, the boat climbed up swells and then dipped into the ocean valleys between. Bee gripped the reed seat with her knees and paddled fiercely. She didn't dare look behind her to see if Anika was all right for fear she would tip them.

Finally they were far enough from the shore that the waves subsided. Bee and Wil rested their paddles so they could take a moment to catch their breath.

"That was harder than I thought," Wil admitted.

"It's always choppy near the shore," Bee said.

"You could have mentioned that."

"I didn't want to scare you," Bee said in mock disdain, and Wil laughed. But there was no sound from Anika. Bee turned and saw, in the dim moonlight, the wide, frightened eyes of the princess looking up at her.

"It's all right," Bee said soothingly. "It was just a little rough water. It should be better now."

"No, it won't," Anika countered, her voice panicky. She held the hedgehog up high. "I'm sitting in a puddle of water, and it's rising. This boat is leaking!"

CHAPTER 10

Bee could feel the cold touch of the seawater soaking through her shoes. *Oh, my beautiful shoes—they'll be ruined!* she thought foolishly, before common sense took over. They were on the open sea in a boat made of reeds, and it was going to sink. More than her shoes would be ruined soon enough.

"We have to head back," Wil said, his tone calm. "It seems this boat wasn't meant for the open ocean. Let's turn toward land." But when they looked, there was no way to tell which direction land lay. In the dark, the sea, sky, and horizon all looked the same.

"How long do you think it is until dawn?" Bee asked.

"Not too long," Wil replied. "We've been paddling for a couple of hours at least. If we can keep afloat until first light, we can at least head toward land. Can you swim, Princess—Anika?"

"Not a bit," Anika said. "It is another of those skills I was never taught. But I'm pretty sure Pepin can, though he doesn't seem to like the water overmuch." Her voice trembled just a little.

"I'm a strong swimmer," Bee said. "I can help you stay afloat if need be."

A few minutes later, Anika said, "The water is up to my hips. Is there anything I can utilize to bail?" Pepin was muttering something in his hedgehog language, and he didn't sound pleased at all.

"I cleaned out the boat before we started," Wil said. "I'm afraid I threw out anything that might've been useful to make room for us."

"Then I'll bail with my hands," Anika said.

"We all three should," Bee agreed. "There's no point to paddling." They scooped water as fast as they could, but the boat rode so low now that the waves broke over the sides. Every time the water sprayed him, Pepin hissed.

"He has a great variety of sounds," Wil observed, trying to keep his tone light.

"That is his angry noise," Anika said.

"And what's his terrified noise?" Bee asked. Talking helped to keep the panic at bay.

"Oh, he screams. He can be exceedingly strident."

"You mean loud? Like this?" Bee asked. She threw back her head and shouted, "Help us! We're sinking!" as loudly as she could.

"He has fewer words, but that is close enough!" the princess said, and called, "Help! We beg for succor!"

"Help! Help!" all three cried over and over, with no real hope that anyone would answer.

Bee had no idea how long they bailed and shouted. The princess and her pet had subsided into silence, and her own voice was just a crowlike rasp. The boat was nearly submerged. Anika knelt on the bottom instead of sitting, and still the water came to her waist. The sea lapped against the reed seats where Bee and Wil sat. Bee was about to kick off her shoes and suggest they swim when she saw a flicker of light on the horizon.

"Did you see that?" she croaked.

"It's a light," Wil said. "On a boat!"

Energized, they started to shout again. Bee and Wil waved their paddles and howled as the light seemed to come closer. Still, the skiff sank faster than the light approached.

"Wil," Bee called, "do you have a knife?"

Wil passed a pocket knife wordlessly to Anika, who handed it to Bee. She sawed feverishly at the ties that held her reed seat to the sides of the boat, and at last it was free. She gave the knife back to Wil.

"Do the same with your seat!" she told him. "They're light; they'll float better than the boat." Quickly Wil detached his seat. Bee shrugged off her haversack and placed it on her seat. Wil did the same with his pack. Just then, as the waterlogged reeds grew too heavy to float, the boat dropped beneath the three weary sailors and sank out of sight.

Quickly Bee yanked off her shoes, which were pulling her down. She swam over to Anika, who was kicking desperately in the waves while holding the hedgehog above her head. "Give him here," she said, taking Pepin from the princess. The hedgehog's clawed feet scrabbled in the air. "Now lie back," she instructed Anika. "As if you were lying on your bed. I'll support your head, and that will keep you afloat."

Anika did as she was told, but her skirts were sodden and dragged at her. Bee had to use all her strength to keep Pepin, the princess, and herself above water. She looked around to see if the ship's light was still visible, but all was darkness.

"Wil!" she called. A wave broke in her face, and she got a mouthful of water. Coughing and retching, she cried out, "Wil!" again. Where was he?

"I'm here," he said, treading water at her shoulder, one hand on each of the two reed seats. "I'm all right. Hold on to the seat. Let me help the princess, you keep the hedgehog."

Bee transferred her grip on Anika to Wil. He murmured something to her, and Bee saw Anika relax against him. Relieved, Bee lay back in the water, grasping one end of the buoyant reed seat that held her sack, and floated. Wil held the second seat with one hand and Anika with the other.

Bee placed Pepin on her chest, the way she'd seen mother sea otters do with their babies. They rested on the gentle swells. But every third or fourth wave broke over Bee's face, and she had to cough and sputter and tread water to regain her equilibrium. She was tiring quickly.

Gradually, the sky began to lighten. It was as if a dark curtain were lifting, setting the stage for day. Bee blinked and realized that she had fallen asleep, floating on the sea. How long had she slept? It couldn't have been more than a few minutes. She checked to make sure she still held Pepin. Yes, her grip on him hadn't loosened. She kicked her legs to move herself in a circle, so she could see where Anika and Wil were. And then she screamed.

Directly behind her, looming as tall as the biggest building in Zeewal, was the hull of a ship, and it was bearing right down on her.

Bee took a gasping breath and dove as deep as she could. The hedgehog slipped out of her hand and she grabbed for him and cried out underwater, despair trailing from her in a stream of bubbles. It was no use. Pepin was gone.

Above, the dark shadow of the ship passed over her. It moved so slowly, like a ship in a dream. Bee's breath was spent. She floated far beneath the surface, her arms and legs splayed out, the rays of the just-risen sun bouncing off her hands so it looked as if her fingers were shooting out flames, as Master Joris's had done. She had no strength left. She blinked her eyes against the stinging salt water.

Something grabbed her by her cropped hair and yanked, pulling upward. Oh, it hurt! She tried to scream, but her lungs were empty, and instead she inhaled the ocean. Up and up she went, but as she moved toward light, darkness took her.

And then she was coughing as if she would heave her lungs from her chest. Water spewed from her like a fountain. The sun was bright again. She lay on a ship's deck, flat on her back. Sails snapped above her in the stiff breeze.

"Aye, this one's alive," she heard a man say. "And most likely'll stay so."

Bee closed her eyes. She never wanted to open them again. The princess was drowned, and it was her fault. And Wil was drowned as well. She could never go back to Zeewal. She could never see Master Bouts again. Her heart hurt more than her lungs, more than her throbbing head.

"The others is doing better," another voice said. "Excepting the girl keeps crying for something. Peppers, I think she wants. Mayhap she's lost her mind."

The others? They were alive?

"Peppers?" said the first voice. "Does she fear the scurvy then? I could do with some peppers. And some beefsteak, come to think of it. And a seven-layer cake, now that'd be a treat."

"Pepin?" Bee croaked. She opened her eyes.

Four boots stood beside her, worn brown leather boots. Soldiers? Sailors? She looked upward, saw that the boots were folded down at the calf, wide trousers tucked into them. Black coats that nipped in at the waist, with gold buttons at the front and on the sleeves. Sword belts slung on their hips. White linen blouses, long, dark flowing hair. Three-cornered hats. One wore a long, pointed beard, the other was clean shaven. No, the other was smooth-skinned, with deep-set brown eyes, a mouth like the red tulips that grew in the fields closest to Zeewal. It was a woman.

"Pepin," Bee managed again. The woman narrowed her eyes.

"What is pepin?" She had a strong accent.

"He's a hedgehog."

"A 'edge'og? What is that?"

"It's an animal. A pet. Spiky, rolls into a ball," Bee said weakly.

"Like this?" A third sailor joined the other two, tossing something in the air and catching it again. "Found this creature floating on its back, happy as you please. Is it edible?"

Bee sat up too quickly, triggering another coughing attack. "Pet," she gasped. "Not to eat. Princess's pet." She held out her hands, and the man tossed Pepin to her. The hedgehog was rolled so tightly she couldn't tell which end was front and which was back.

"Princess," the woman repeated. "The girl we 'ave pluck from the sea, she is princess?"

"Princess Anika," Bee said. Then she wondered if it was wise to tell who Anika was.

"I see," the woman said. "And you be who?"

"Bee."

"Yes, be who? This is what I am asking."

"That's my name. Bee. Beatrix."

The woman peered more closely at Bee, and then she grinned. "You are female, to be sure! Girl in trousers, girl with short hair! I like!"

Bee sat up straight, trying to preserve what little dignity she had left. "Yes, I'm a girl." She tried to speak with self-confidence, but she ruined the effect with a hugely messy saltwater sneeze. The sailors fell about on the deck laughing.

The woman wiped her eyes with her lacy sleeve, and said, "Very glad to make acquaintance, Bee-girl! As you are, I too am a female. I am Captain Zafira Zay, and I am commanding this ship."

A woman, and a captain! Bee had never heard of such a thing. She stared at Captain Zay with astonishment, and the captain doffed her feathered tricorn hat and gave a little bow.

"Bee!" Anika came flying down the ship's deck, her soaked skirts leaving a wet trail behind her. She threw herself into Bee's arms, hugging her so hard Bee could barely breathe. "We thought you were drowned!"

"I thought *you* were drowned," Bee replied.

"And none of us is drowned at all—except . . ." Anika's voice trailed off, and she hung her head in sorrow. But then Pepin squeaked, and Anika looked up to see Bee holding the hedgehog out to her.

The princess burst into tears. "Not even—not even Pepin is drowned," she managed between sobs. "Oh, I thought I had lost you all. I thought I was lost myself. I did not want to perish as my father did!"

Wil, as wet as washed laundry, joined them, and he patted Anika gently on the shoulder. "It's all right," he said. "These kind sailors have rescued us. We were very lucky."

"Sailors indeed!" Captain Zay snorted, offended. "'Ave you never 'eard of myself, you great yellow-haired mooncalf of a boy?"

Wil gazed at the captain, nonplussed. "No, ma'am," he said. "I don't believe I have."

"Then you are very lacking in education, you ignorant whelp," the captain said, crossing her arms in indignation. "You are rescued by the 'and of Zafira Zay, captain of the ship *Egbertina-Henriette*. We are no mere sailors, my friends. Look there." She pointed upward, and Bee saw the flag flying at the top of the tallest mast. It was a skull and crossbones, the white bones vivid against a bright pink field.

Captain Zay stood erect, her expression proud. "Our ship is a pirate ship. And we are tulip pirates."

CHAPTER 11

At Captain Zay's orders, Bee, Wil, and Anika were taken belowdecks and given dry clothing. They changed quickly, and then one of the sailors—one of the *pirates*—brought them into the captain's quarters.

The cabin was spacious and luxuriously appointed. There were thick carpets on the floor and woven hangings on the walls. A bronze chandelier swung gently from the ceiling as the ship rose and fell with the waves. A painted screen hid the captain's bed. In one corner, a table was set, and a silver tray holding a pot and porcelain cups had been placed in its center. The pot steamed gently, giving off a scent that Bee had never smelled before.

The captain sat in a cushioned chair, and three more chairs were drawn up to the table. They were made of the same glossy substance as the bookcases in Master Joris's study. Bee passed her hand across the arm of one. Like the bookshelf, it was both hard and soft, as warm as a living thing.

"What are they made of?" she asked.

The captain stared at her, puzzled. Then she smiled. "I 'ave forget," she said. "You in Aradyn do not know wood. It is of the tree. This chairs is of the mahogany tree. Very dark wood."

"It's beautiful," Bee said, rubbing the wood.

"All the trees is different wood, different color, different 'ardness. In other kingdoms, they make many a thing of the wood. A building, a table, a bed—all of the wood. This very ship is of the wood, the oak tree wood."

"But we have no wood," Anika said. "We have no trees. It is because of Master Joris."

Captain Zay rubbed her chin, as a man might rub his beard. "You are Princess Anika. Welcome on my ship." She stood and gave a deep bow to Anika, sweeping off her triangular hat. Anika inclined her head slightly, and the two exchanged an appraising look. They were as different as dusk and dawn: the pirate with her tanned face, dark, dancing eyes, and long black curls, and Anika, ivory skinned and red haired.

"Yes, I am she," Anika said, taking a seat. The others sat as well.

"Not so much princess in pirate clothes," Captain Zay observed.

Bee thought Captain Zay was wrong. Anika held herself with great dignity, even in an oversized linen shirt and trousers, with her hair tangled and salty. She was every inch a princess.

"We are fugitives from Master Joris, who wishes to marry me off to a king several times my age," Anika said.

"Oho!" Captain Zay cried, her eyes bright with interest. "And which of kings would this be?"

"King Thiedric."

Captain Zay slapped the tabletop with her hands. "Thiedric! This is old man indeed! And cranky, with breath so bad, like a dungpile. Marrying such a man, a beautiful girl like you, this is very wrong, to be sure." She reached out and touched Anika's red hair, still wet from the sea. "And yet . . ."

"Yet?" Wil said, frowning. It was clear he thought the captain was disrespectful.

"Yet Master Joris is from where our fortune is made."

"You steal his tulips?" Bee asked.

"They 'ave very great value, Bee-girl. 'Ere, you look at this one." The captain went to the opposite corner of the room, picked up a clay pot, and placed it on the table. It held a tulip in bloom—but not a tulip like one Bee had ever seen. This one was more like a flame than a flower.

Its petals were fringed, and it was striped with orange and yellow. It seemed almost to flicker in the sunlight that came through the porthole.

"Oh," Anika breathed. "A Flaming Parrot tulip."

"That is quite so, Princess!" Captain Zay said, beaming. "You know of the exotical tulips, then?"

"Master Joris brings them to the palace sometimes, the strangest, most beautiful ones."

"The mage breed them, the exoticals, and then 'e sell the bulbs for a great many coppers. 'E is shipping them to other kingdoms. But we find the ships full of bulbs, and then we take them and sell them our ownself. It is very full of profit, our work, and also very dangerous."

"But surely it is unethical to steal," Anika said. Bee looked down at the floor, remembering the Bouts Bun she'd stolen from the bakery on her first day in Zeewal.

"Indeed, so it is!" the captain agreed. "And yet, this is our business. Master Joris, 'e steal from the people of Aradyn, and I, I steal from 'im. Look, another one." She placed another pot on the table. This one held the most elegant tulip Bee could imagine. So dark it was almost velvet black, it had silver stripes and silver tips on its petals.

"The Havran tulip," Anika said. Wil reached out to feel it.

144

"No!" Captain Zay thundered, making Bee jump. "'Keep those 'ands off, Mooncalf. This flower, it is worth as much as my whole ship completely. No grubby fingers." Wil drew back quickly.

"You see that you make for me a large dilemma," the captain said. "I am not wishing for Master Joris to look for my ship, and now this is all the more likely. What shall I do with you? Shall you be walking the gangplank? Or shall I put you off on the island most near?" The captain rested her chin on her clasped hands, as if she were thinking deeply. Bee and Anika exchanged a worried glance. Was she joking? It was very hard to tell.

"'Tis too tricky of a decision for this moment. I decide later." Captain Zay laughed at their anxious expressions. "For now, you are guests. You 'ave some coffee?" She looked around at them, waiting. For a moment no one moved, unsure of what she wanted, and then Bee jumped up to pour.

The dark liquid in the cups gave off a rich, unfamiliar aroma. Bee tasted it. It was bitter and complex, completely new to her. Anika made a face, but Wil gulped his.

"What is this?" Bee asked, taking another sip.

"Coffee, you know. Coffee?" The others shook their heads. "No, but of course you do not know! It is from tree as well, from coffee tree. Very good, warming. It only need a cake to go with. Alas, no cake on the *Egbertina-Henriette*."

Bee jumped up again. "Did someone find my haversack? I have cake! Or cookies, at any rate."

Captain Zay clapped her hands smartly, and the cabin door opened at once. "Find 'aversack," she commanded the pirate who peered in. A moment later, he reappeared with the two leather sacks in hand. Water dripped from them onto the carpet.

"Oh, they may be ruined," Bee said mournfully. She rummaged through her sack and pulled out a packet of cookies, well wrapped. "No, the inner ones are dry!" She moved her coffee cup and laid the cookies, round balls of sugar, flour, and rum, on the saucer. Had these been baked with enthusiasm or with wariness? She hoped it was the former.

Captain Zay took two and popped them into her mouth, chewing ferociously. Her expression changed immediately from dubious to blissful. "Oh, Bee-girl, you 'ave bake these?"

"Yes."

"They are quite full of delicious. They are so full of delicious that I will not throw you back in the sea if you make more of these for me."

"If you have an oven, and flour, and sugar and rum, I will make as many as you want," Bee said.

"This things we 'ave," Captain Zay declared. "You will be baker for the *Egbertina-Henriette,* and we will take you where you need to go."

Now Bee remembered: the cookies were baked full of helpfulness. She'd made them just after Master Bouts had knocked over a barrel of flour and she had volunteered to clean it up.

"We want to go to the Island of the Mages," Bee said.

"And whyfore is that?" the captain asked.

Bee made a quick decision. The captain relied on Master Joris's tulips for her thievery and might not take kindly to any move that could risk that. "We want to find out if he has the right to marry off the princess," she said. It was not a lie; just not the entire truth. "The mages will know this."

"I see," Captain Zay said. To Bee, she didn't sound entirely convinced, but she added, "Then go to the galley, Bee-girl, and see the cook. 'E will be giving you what you need. And take the Mooncalf with you."

"The Mooncalf stays with Princess Anika," Wil said firmly. "I am her guard."

147

"You are not even 'aving a sword!" Captain Zay protested. "'Ow you will guard this princess?"

"With my life," Wil replied. Bee looked at him, surprised, and he flushed. Anika smiled.

"I see," Captain Zay said again, amused now. "This is the best kind of guard, to be sure. You stay then, Master Mooncalf!"

The pirate at the door took Bee down the short, steep flight of stairs belowdecks to the galley. It was a long, narrow room lined with cabinets, with a stove at one end. The cook, Limmo, was a skinny fellow with legs so bowed it looked as if he were astride a horse even when standing. At first, he didn't seem at all pleased to be sharing his space with Bee, but when she explained that she only baked, and would help him chop and peel and slice when needed, he gave her a great gap-toothed grin and bowed low, snatching off the kerchief that covered his few strands of hair.

"In that case, I'm glad to have a helper, Mistress Bee!" he exclaimed. "And the crew will be wild to eat some sweets. What ingredients do you need? Let's see." He rummaged in the cabinets, pulling out packets and jars. "I have flour and sugar and salt, cinnamon, nutmeg. A little bit of chocolate. Hmmm . . . walnuts, hazelnuts. Do

148

you use lemons? We use them to keep away the scurvy, but we've a barrel of the things, so you're welcome to them." He plopped a yellow globe on the counter.

Bee picked up the lemon, turning it over and over. This was the ingredient in the meringue pie in *A Booke of Baking*. She sniffed it. There was a faint, sweet-sour, pungent odor. She did the same with the other unfamiliar items, her eyes widening at the scents of cinnamon and nutmeg and chocolate. The walnuts were unshelled, and she held them up and shook them, trying to figure out what they were.

"Oh, aye, you're from Aradyn!" Limmo chortled with glee. "I'd plumb forgot—you folks don't know a thing about foodstuffs from trees."

Trees held all this bounty? Oh, what she could do with these ingredients! Bee slipped on the apron Limmo handed her and got to work, mixing, tasting, adjusting here and there. Limmo showed her how to open the walnuts, and she ground them up for her batter. There were no cake pans, but a huge cast-iron skillet worked well enough.

She baked with enormous pleasure, though the galley stove wasn't used to pastry and singed the edges of the cake she pulled out an hour later. But she cut off the burned pieces and then mixed the dark, bitter chocolate with sugar to make an icing, which she sampled so freely that she felt a little queasy afterward. She had never tasted anything as wonderful as chocolate. She cut the cake into layers and iced each layer with chocolate. The finished cake wasn't her prettiest, but it rose high and proud, and the smell of it pulled pirates to the galley, eager for their supper.

"It ain't suppertime yet, you feckless oafs," Limmo told them. "Come back later!"

As Bee peeled potatoes and chopped onions, the long night caught up with her. When she almost cut off her finger dozing as she sliced the carrots, Limmo sent her off to sleep. In the room he directed her to, she could see Anika and Wil already sleeping in hammocks hung from the ceiling, and she tried to crawl into one of the dozen or more empty ones. It wasn't easy. The hammock rolled and dumped her onto the floor with a crash, and Wil's bleary eyes peered over the side of his.

"Lay yourself down carefully in the center," he instructed her. "And then don't move." In an instant he was asleep again, and Bee tried again, slowly and cautiously this time, positioning herself with care. It wasn't the most comfortable of beds, but the rocking of the hammock as the ship rose and fell was like the rocking of a half-remembered cradle, and it put her right to sleep.

They woke to an earsplitting ruckus: Limmo hammering on a pot cover to call the pirates to supper. Boots clattered down the narrow hallway outside the bunk room, and Bee, Anika, and Wil rolled themselves out of the hammocks and stood, momentarily confused about where they were.

"Pirates," Bee recalled. "We're on a pirate ship. And I baked a cake. Wait till you taste it!"

They followed the others into another room belowdecks, this one with a long wooden table scarred with the carved names and rough artwork of generations of sailors. Benches lined the table. When the pirates saw the three of them, they pushed away from the table and stood, snatching off their caps and tricorn hats. Bee realized at once that it was Anika they were standing for. Anika inclined her head regally, motioning for them to sit. The men made room, and Anika, Bee, and Wil took seats too.

"They have very good manners for pirates," Wil whispered.

"Except for these," Bee noted, pointing to the carvings,

which they were now close enough to see in detail. Anika blushed and even Wil's eyebrows went up at a couple of them.

"Captain Zay wanted me to dine with her in her cabin, but I wouldn't," Anika confided. "She said, 'This princess shall not be dining with the rabble.'" Anika mimicked the captain's accent perfectly, and Bee giggled. "But I disclosed that I thought the rabble would be much more enjoyable. And so it is!"

They looked around at the motley crew. Bee counted ten—no, eleven. One wore an eye patch, some had gaps where teeth were missing, and most of the rest had faces as scarred as the table. Their skin was of all possible colors, from the coffee brown of one pirate who looked, even seated, a full foot taller than any of the others, to the pasty white of another who was crowned with a halo of wild orange curls that matched the freckles on nearly every inch of his skin. They had black eyes and brown, green and blue and amber, like a cat. One looked at least sixty years old, white haired and white bearded, while the youngest could have been Bee's age. One by one, they introduced themselves, and most of their names and accents were as strange and different as their faces. They were Filmon and Haleem, Thoralf and Jacinto. There was

Quigley, the pirate who had pulled them from the water. After that, Bee lost track.

Limmo's stew was passed down the table, and Bee ate it with great gulps. She was starving, and it was very good. Then Limmo brought out the cake. Shiny brown and fragrant, it sat in the center of the table with a single slice removed, already sent up to the captain. The pirates stared at it in awe.

"You slice it, Bee," Limmo commanded, passing her a jeweled knife. Bee cut thin, even slivers, not wanting to offend any of the pirates with a piece that was smaller than another's. The men waited until Princess Anika took a taste, and then they dove in. After the first bite, there was a loud and general groan of pleasure.

"What is that glorious flavor in the icing?" Anika asked, licking her fingers.

"It's called chocolate. It's from a tree," Bee told her.

"They never have tasted chocolate afore, nor any food that grows from a tree!" Limmo told the others, and they stared with disbelief.

A blond pirate, whose name was Rijkie, said, "I hail from Aradyn as well. The mage keeps the bounty of trees from the people. He controls all the trade, he does. He's a greedy old duffer, that one. Only wants the coppers.

I never tasted an apple in all my life till I signed on with the *Egg-Hen*."

"The *Egg-Hen*?" Bee said, confused.

"The *Egbertina-Henriette*. Our old captain called the ship after his mother, and Captain Zay never changed it when she took it over. But that name's a sight too long to say!" Then Rijkie stuffed another bite of cake into his mouth, and the others followed suit.

The cake was gone in minutes, and some of the pirates picked up their tin plates and licked them to get every last bit of icing. Bee couldn't tell for sure if the pirates' reaction was to the pleasure she'd baked into the cake or to the taste of the cake itself, but she was gratified by their delight.

As Bee and Limmo collected the dishes for washing, a pirate—one who'd worked while the others ate, it seemed—came dashing into the dining room. "Ahoy!" he cried. "Cargo ship in sight—man your posts!"

In an instant, the pirates had clapped hats on their heads, sprung to their feet, and were out the door. Curious, Bee, Wil, and Anika followed them up onto the deck of the ship. There, all was wild activity, but purposeful: every man had his task and set himself to it. The sails were trimmed, the ship turned, and swiftly they were headed toward the darkening horizon, where Bee could just make out the sails of another ship.

Captain Zay came out from her cabin, holding a spyglass. She trained it on the distant ship, her feet wide apart for balance on the pitching deck, while the pirates waited. Then she lowered the spyglass.

"'Tis one of Joris's ship, most certain," she declared. "I see the flag of Aradyn, the *Tulip Gules on a Field D'or.* Pirates, get ready. Be sure your blades is sharp, your last wills and testaments is signed, and your courage is big!" A cheer went up from the men on deck.

"What—what's happening?" Bee asked the nearest pirate. "What does she mean?"

The dark-haired pirate with an eye patch and a scar that ran from beneath the patch down to his chin—Jacinto?—grinned at her and unsheathed his sword. He swiped it from right to left, and Bee jumped away from the flashing blade. "Best get out of the way, little baker. That's a tulip ship we're heading for. The *Egg-Hen* is going into battle!"

CHAPTER 12

"Belowdecks, Princess!" Captain Zay commanded as the *Egg-Hen* sped closer and closer to the other ship. Now Bee could make out the flag, the same red tulip on a gold field that flew on the palace in Zeewal.

Anika took Bee's arm and whispered, "I'm not going below. We'll just stay out of the way. I want to observe!"

Bee wasn't completely sure she wanted to observe. She'd seen the sharpness of the blade that Jacinto had unsheathed, and she shuddered to think what such a blade could do to human flesh. But she backed away with Anika to a spot behind the mast, out of the captain's view. She motioned to Wil to join them, but he shook his head.

"I'll fight too!" he said. "Captain Zay, have you an extra sword?"

The captain looked him over, sizing him up. "'Ave you been using a sword before?" she asked skeptically.

"I'm a blacksmith. I make swords for the palace guards.

Of course I've used one!"

"Quigley!" the captain shouted. "Give this boy a sword!" To Wil she said, with a wink, "More is merrier, Mooncalf. Only make sure you are not getting yourself killed!"

When the captain had turned away again, Anika reached out from behind the mast to grab Wil's sleeve. "Wil, no!" she protested. "You cannot fight. There's no army, no soldiers in Zeewal—how can you know how to use a sword?"

"My brother and I swordfight all the time with the blades we fashion," Wil said. "I've always longed to try it for true."

"That's only playacting! Please don't try to fight," Anika begged. "You'll be maimed, or killed."

Quigley, the freckled pirate, ran up with a sword belt, and Wil buckled it on. With his pirate clothes and sword, Bee thought he looked quite dashing, and in Anika's face she could see admiration and dismay battling each other.

"Wil, those are our own people, the merchants of Zeewal, on that ship!" Anika protested.

"Nay, Princess," said Quigley. "They are mercenaries, hired to guard the tulips. The merchants, they stay safe in their homes."

Wil looked at Anika gravely. "If you forbid me as my ruler, I'm bound to obey," he said. "But I want this, Princess." Anika blushed. Bee noticed that she blushed in a very charming way, her color rising pink on the apples of her cheeks. It was a little annoying; Bee herself turned splotchy and a little sweaty when she was embarrassed.

"I'm just Anika to you," the princess said in a low voice. "Of course I would not forbid you."

"You need a tricorn hat," Bee told Wil.

"Alas," he said, unsheathing his sword and then slipping it back in, "I shall have to be a hatless pirate. Imagine the tales of the swashbuckling Hatless Pirate— they will go down in history!"

"If the Hatless Pirate survives," Bee pointed out. "And if you don't survive, I won't either. Your mother will kill me."

"All the more reason for me to stay alive, then," Wil said. He picked up Anika's limp hand and kissed it, ruffled Bee's hair, and joined the pirates at the ship's railing as the *Egg-Hen* approached the tulip ship. Only Haleem, the enormously tall first mate, would stay on board to hold the ship steady.

Anika looked at her hand, blankly at first. Then a new flush rose in her cheeks. "Well," she said.

"Don't you have any big words for that?" Bee said. "Gallant, maybe? Or heroic? Or . . . foolish?"

Anika's eyes shone. "Courteous," she said. "Genteel. Valiant." Her expression changed to alarm as she turned to watch the pirates. "Oh, Bee," she gasped.

They were very close to the merchant ship now, maybe twenty feet distant, and Bee could see the sailors on it scurrying about, trying to prepare for what they surely knew would happen. Without warning, two of the pirates threw a thick rope with a hook on its end across to the other ship. It landed perfectly, locking tightly onto the tulip ship's railing. The sailors rushed to it with knives, trying to hack it free, but in an instant the pirates were sliding across, hand over hand, from the *Egg-Hen* to the tulip ship. As each pirate swung himself over onto the deck, he unsheathed his sword and took a threatening stance. Wil was the fifth man over; Bee could tell that his grip on the sword was a little uncertain. Why was he doing this? Wasn't life dangerous enough?

"It will be the end of him," she said, fuming. Anika grasped her hand so tightly Bee thought her fingers would break.

"Oh, Bee!" she said again. Among the dozen sailors rushing around the deck of the tulip ship, two had pulled out swords of their own, and now there was fighting. They could hear the sound of blades clanking together and the shouts of the men. It was hard to tell the pirates apart—no, there was Wil, hatless among the tricorns. He was very quick on his feet, but one of the sailors must have noticed his awkwardness with a blade and headed straight for him.

Terrified, Bee and Anika watched as the sailor battled Wil to the ship's railing. The blades flashed as Wil bent backward over the rail, his sword raised against the oncoming steel that threatened to slice down onto his neck.

"No!" Anika screamed.

Then, without warning, Captain Zay swooped between the two combatants. There was a shout, louder than the others, and the sailor fell to the deck, out of view among the scrambling men. After that, it was only moments until the merchant crew was overcome. The pirates herded the hapless sailors into a corner of the deck, leaving them with three guards. Then they descended into the bowels of the ship.

They emerged laden with sealed wicker baskets. A second line was thrown from the cargo ship to the *Egg-Hen,* doubled over so it could act as a pulley. Each basket was secured to the line between the ships, and the pirates on the *Egg-Hen* reeled it in. It didn't take long before the deck was littered with baskets, and the men were sliding back between the ships onto the pirate ship.

Captain Zay, who'd been the second one onto the tulip ship, ordered the lines cut, and then the pirate ship was free, speeding away from the emptied vessel, where the sailors stood open mouthed, shaking their fists. She waved merrily in return.

"Until we are met again, gentlemens!" she cried.

As the pirates bundled the baskets of tulip bulbs into the hold, Anika ran up to Wil. His face was pasty, and he stood with his hand on his sword while the others rushed around him.

"Are you all right, Wil?" she asked.

He blinked, seeming to wake from a dream. "I think so—yes, I'm fine," he said. "That was—well, it was not what I expected."

"You are not injured, are you?"

"No, not at all. I barely unsheathed my sword. But when those sailors pulled theirs out—my heart has never beat so hard! I thought it might spring right out of my chest. And Captain Zay—she cut one of the sailors. If she hadn't . . . " He closed his eyes, shuddering.

"Was there blood?" Bee asked with great interest.

"Of course there was!" Wil sounded rather cross. "He bled all over the place. I stepped in it." He looked down at his boots. There was a smear of something on one of them. Suddenly he clapped his hand to his mouth and ran to the ship's railing. Bee and Anika turned away as he deposited his supper in the sea.

"The adventures of the gallant Hatless Pirate," Bee scoffed, and Anika smacked her arm lightly.

"Be courteous," she chided. "I am sure I would have done the same."

Bee shook her head. Sometimes it was hard to remember that others had lived lives more protected than she. Wil may have seen his share of burns at the forge, but he probably hadn't seen people bleed. On her long journey from Boomkin, Bee had come across a group of bandits robbing a merchant, and she'd hidden behind a hedge, almost afraid to breathe, as the chief bandit sliced off the tip of the merchant's finger to force him to reveal the secret compartment in his trunk that held his coppers. *That* had been a lot of blood.

Wil looked abashed when he came back to them, but his color was returning. "I think my days of swashbuckling may be over," he said. "But I should help carry the baskets down."

"You were very bold," Anika told him. "Though I still think it is wrong to steal the bulbs."

"The bulbs themselves are wrong," Bee pointed out to Anika. "Your people should be growing crops—they should be growing trees. That way, they would benefit. Now, only Master Joris grows rich."

Anika sighed. "You are right. If I am queen—"

"When," Bee said. "Not if."

Anika looked at her, and a smile grew on her face, opening it like a flower. "*When* I am queen," she said, "everything will be different."

Days passed amiably on the pirate ship as they sailed toward the Island of the Mages. Bee baked cookies and cakes; she couldn't make tarts with the pots and pans Limmo had in the kitchen, but the pirates were heartily appreciative of the confections she turned out. It took some experimentation, but she managed a batch of Bouts Buns—different from the originals, for she had to use some of the pirates' beer to make the dough rise, and she spiced them with cinnamon to mask the beery taste. Still, they were good enough that the pirates lifted her onto their shoulders and paraded her through the ship, nearly bashing out her brains on the low ceiling belowdecks. After that, Captain Zay demanded a bun each day with her coffee.

While Bee was busy at the oven, Anika and Wil spent time together. Bee would see them as she passed from the galley to the captain's cabin, bringing her an afternoon snack. They sat close together on the deck, talking seriously or playing with Pepin. Sometimes Wil held Anika's hand.

Curious, Bee pulled Wil aside one evening and asked him, "Are you falling in love with Anika?"

He glared at her. "Don't be ridiculous. She's a princess, and I am a blacksmith. Of course I'm not in love with her!" But he flushed red to the tips of his ears and swatted at Bee as she dodged away from him.

They played cards nightly with the pirates, learning euchre, primero, and knock rummy—as well as some colorful new language. The pirates bet with coins; Bee, Anika, and Wil used the rum balls Bee baked as their stake. It took a while before the pirates were comfortable beating the princess in their games, but she grew so wildly competitive that it wasn't long before they were accusing her of card counting and mocking her for her inability to bluff. Captain Zay was often part of the games, and she played with great enthusiasm, tossing her hat in the air and threatening to keelhaul the pirates whose hands beat hers—which was most of them, most of the time. She was an exceptionally bad player.

One afternoon, a tall, craggy island came into view. "There it is—the Island of the Mages," Haleem told Bee. He passed her the spyglass so she could see it more clearly. Really, it was a mountain, with barren high cliffs rising from the sea. At the very top of the island, there was a building from which sprang towers and turrets and crenellations in a wild architecture, all made from the same dark rock that formed the forbidding bluffs.

"How can we land?" Bee asked.

"There's a pier on the far side," Haleem said. "We can send a skiff there safely."

Bee took a deep breath. "I wonder if they can see us yet."

"See you!" Haleem laughed in his low, rich voice. "They are mages—they don't need to see you. They've probably known you were on your way since you first decided it." Bee scowled at him. She didn't like that idea at all. Her thoughts were her own, and she preferred to keep them to herself.

"Their magic doesn't work over water," she told Haleem, remembering what the hedge wizard had said. "And even if they did know—they aren't dangerous, are they?" She hoped that not all mages were like Master Joris.

"I suppose they could be if they wanted," Haleem said. "I met the mage of Tabira once, though, and he was really quite nice. He had a passion for birds, as I recall. Gave me a parrot. Now that parrot, *he* was dangerous! He hated everyone. Used to curse a blue streak, and nearly put my eye out more than once. I had to give him away myself—to a merchant who tried to cheat me at the market. Ha!" Bee grinned, imagining the deceitful merchant as he discovered the truth about his new pet.

That day Bee baked some Bouts Buns with truth-telling in them, saying deliberately to Limmo as she stirred the batter, "Your stew is very good, but the potatoes are lumpy, and your bread is hard as nails." He was quite annoyed until she showed him how to mix up a quick bread that didn't need hours to rise and would be soft and tasty every time. When her hands were still dusted with the flour from this helpfulness, she baked a quick batch of cookies. If Master Joris was any indication, the mages on the island would be only slightly affected by her treats, but even a little bit of honesty and goodwill could be useful. She packed up the buns and cookies and stuffed them into her haversack. Then it was time to go.

The entire pirate crew came out to see them off. "We shall be coming back this way tomorrow, after selling our ill-gotten bulbs," Captain Zay told them. "If you are standing on the pier just like that, we pick you up. If not standing, we go on. We cannot be waiting for you. Tomorrow, at"—she squinted into the sun, which was partway down the sky—"quarter-past three. No later."

"We'll be there," Wil promised.

"And you shall guard this princess well—with your life, Master Mooncalf!"

Anika reached up and gave Captain Zay a soft kiss on her cheek, and the pirates cheered as the captain's eyebrow went up as far as it was possible for an eyebrow to go. "Thank you," Anika said softly. "You've saved us. You've saved me."

"Balderdash," the captain said. But she was clearly very pleased.

Wil, and then Anika, climbed down the rope ladder into the skiff, with Rijkie ready to row them to the long pier that jutted out beyond the rocky shoreline. Bee was suddenly whirled around by a yank on her haversack. Captain Zay gripped the leather in her fist. "Not yet for you, Bee-girl. I am quite forgetting!"

"Forgetting what?"

"Where is my bun for the day?"

Bee sighed. She knew she'd never get away without

giving the captain her Bouts Bun. She pulled the pack around and rummaged inside for one of the buns she'd baked for the mages. "I'm sorry, Captain," she said. "Here you are."

Captain Zay took the bun gleefully and released her hold on Bee's haversack. As Bee climbed over the railing and down the ladder into the skiff, she smiled to herself, wondering who would have the harder task: she, Wil, and Anika facing the Council of Mages, or the pirate crew dealing with Captain Zay after she'd eaten a Bouts Bun baked full of truthfulness.

CHAPTER 13

As soon as the three travelers bid goodbye to Rijkie and stepped out of the boat, a figure appeared at the other end of the long dock. Bee could tell from the green robe that he was a hedge wizard. They walked toward him, and he bowed. He had sharp gray eyes in a friendly, open face, and straw-colored hair peeked from beneath his hood.

"Welcome!" he said. "The masters saw you coming, and they've sent me to greet you."

"The masters?" Bee repeated. "Do you mean the mages?"

"That's right. They are my masters; I am their servant, Bartholomew." The hedge wizard tucked his hands into his wide sleeves in the way that hedge wizards did, and bowed again.

"I'm Bee. This is Wil. And this is Princess Anika of Aradyn."

"At your service, Your Highness," Bartholomew said, bowing a third time.

Anika put on her regal voice. "We have business with the mages," she said. "Will they convene with us?"

"Of course they will—though they are not much for business," Bartholomew replied. "Please, do follow me. I will show you where you will be lodged, and you can have a bite to eat there if you wish, and a rest. Then I will take you to them."

They followed the hedge wizard off the pier and then up a steep flight of stone stairs that wound around and around the mountainside. Before long, the three of them were panting, though Bartholomew wasn't at all breathless. The ground was rocky, and between the rocks flowers in strange colors and shapes grew. Even stranger insects buzzed among them. Bee saw a butterfly with what looked almost like a human head flitting among the blossoms. There were flowers with petals the color of the sea, green and deep blue and turquoise. Flowers that were gray with black bordered petals, and others that were different shades of brown, from tan to the color of coffee. They weren't pretty, exactly, but they were interesting to look at.

"What kind of flowers are these?" Wil asked, fascinated. He reached out to touch one of the brown ones and pulled back sharply. "Ouch!"

"Yes, do be careful, young man. It has spines. One of our mages, Master Kajetan, likes to experiment with plants. I wouldn't say he is entirely successful, but he entertains himself."

"And the bugs?" Anika said, peering at an enormous spider that had woven a sparkling pink web. Bee drew back in horror.

"That's Master Scipio's project, Your Highness. I don't really see the point myself, but it keeps him busy."

They had no breath left for questions as they continued up and up the stairs. Bee felt a little dizzy looking down; they were so far above the sea by now that the rocks below looked like pebbles. At last they reached a tall stone wall with a gate that Bartholomew pushed open.

"No guard?" Bee panted.

"Here?" Bartholomew smiled. "Who would we guard against? Nobody comes here. You are the first visitors we've had in . . . well, I couldn't even say. A very long time."

They passed into a courtyard paved with gray bricks

and stood gazing up at the structure. Bee wasn't sure what to call it. "Is it . . . a palace?"

"It's the Council House," Bartholomew said.

"It's rather vast for a house," Anika pointed out.

Bartholomew shrugged. "The mages live here and work here, and we do too—their servants, the hedge wizards and witches. It's where the old ones go."

"You're not that old," Bee said.

"I'm the youngest," Bartholomew acknowledged. "But I chose to come here . . . for my own reasons." Bee met his eyes and saw a sorrow there, one that was familiar to her. She had seen that same look in Anika's eyes, and in her own once a year when she looked in the mirror. He had lost someone, she was sure. That was why he was there and not puttering around one of the island kingdoms doing his small magic.

They pushed open the door and entered the Council House, passing an elderly hedge witch flapping a feather duster ineffectually over the furnishings in the entrance hall. It was an impressive room, tall and gloomy with long windows shaded by velvet hangings. The furniture was dark wood—Bee recognized it now—and there were intricately stitched tapestries on the wall showing strange, wondrous scenes. She walked up to one that

172

showed a school of children, all wearing tall pointed hats, sitting in an enormous dining hall. In another, a boy battled with a figure that, from one angle, looked like a dragon and from another, looked like a ghostly version of himself. She exchanged a wide-eyed look with Wil.

"This way, this way," Bartholomew urged them. The hedge witch, her gray braid nearly long enough to trip her, didn't even look up from her dusting. They followed Bartholomew down one dim hall and up a twisting staircase, then along another hall and another. Their footsteps echoed on the stone floor. Finally he pushed open a creaking door. "You ladies can rest here, and the gentleman next door. I'll come back for you in the morning. The mages have gone to bed."

"But it is barely dusk!" Bee protested.

"They are old, and they retire early."

"You must get bored," Wil said.

The hedge wizard smiled, a little wearily. "It is not a life of great stimulation, that's true. Now, you should have all you need in the rooms. If you want food or anything else, just say so. Loudly. They can be a little hard of hearing."

"Who can?" Bee asked.

"Everyone here," Bartholomew replied. Before Bee could say anything else, he bowed and left, and the three stood in the center of the room, gazing about. The ceiling was nearly as high as the one in the entrance hall, and under it was a huge canopied bed with maroon velvet bed hangings. The other furniture was equally massive and dark. It was the gloomiest room Bee could imagine.

"Cozy," Bee murmured.

"I hope my room is just as welcoming," Wil said. He opened a door behind the bed. "Oh, it is."

The girls ran over to the door and saw a chamber just like theirs, with dark green rather than maroon hangings. The furnishings were identical, from the gigantic bed to the oversized wardrobe to the ornate, tarnished silver mirror. "Well, at least they're unsoiled," Anika said doubtfully, turning back. She walked over to a table that held a pitcher and basin, but they were empty.

"Bartholomew told us to ask for what we need," Bee reminded her.

Anika raised an eyebrow, then said, tentatively, "May we have some water?" Nothing happened.

"Water!" Bee said loudly, and suddenly a little cloud appeared over the basin. A crackle of thunder came from it, and both girls backed away. A tiny bolt of lightning shot out of the cloud, hitting the table and singeing it. A finger of smoke rose up. Then the cloud began to rain onto the table. Quickly Bee ran forward and pushed the basin under the cloud, and swiftly the basin filled with water, overflowing onto the table and then the floor. "Stop!" Bee shouted, and as quickly as it had come, the cloud rolled away and disappeared.

Wil stood watching from the doorway, his mouth hanging open. "That was a lot of trouble for a bowl of water," he observed.

Bee shook her head. "These mages . . . ," she began, but she didn't know what else to say. Gray flowers, butterflies with human heads, a rain cloud in a bedroom—this was proving to be a very peculiar place. She dipped a finger in the water. "It feels like water," she said, and splashed some on her face. After a moment's hesitation Anika did the same.

Wil came over and washed his hands in the basin. "I wonder what would happen if we called for food?"

"We'd be crushed by a cast-iron stove descending from the ceiling, no doubt!" Bee said, and they laughed, a little uneasily.

They spent a strange and restless night. They didn't dare ask for food, and they didn't want to eat the sweets in Bee's backpack. Bee stretched out on the bed, which was more comfortable than it looked, and Wil sat in an enormous cushioned chair that made him look very small. Anika paced the room anxiously until Bee and Wil begged her to stop, and then she collapsed next to Bee. Pepin lay between them, his nose twitching in slumber. They dozed off and on all night, their sleep interrupted by dreams that woke them in a panic but disappeared immediately from memory. Odd noises sounded outside the window. At one point Bee could have sworn there was a bird in the room, flapping near the ceiling, but if there was, it wasn't visible. At last Bee opened her eyes to see light outside the window. There was a knock at the door and Bartholomew poked his head in.

"I trust the accommodations were to your liking?" he said. His face was expressionless, but his eyes were bright and amused. Bee decided she rather liked him.

"Can we call on the mages now?" Anika asked, smoothing her dress. "We've journeyed a very long way."

"Yes, I know—and the mages know as well. They're in the council chamber awaiting you."

Anika stuck Pepin in her pocket and took Bee's hand in her cold hand. They collected Wil and followed Bartholomew down and around an endless series of hallways, even more labyrinthine than the palace in Zeewal. Each hall was identical to the last. Only the paintings on the walls were different, though all were portraits of mages in black robes, with long silver hair and eyes that seemed to follow them wherever they went.

Finally they stopped before a dark wooden door. Bartholomew knocked. There was no answer. He knocked again, harder. From the other side came a deep voice.

"Enter."

Bartholomew scuttled back down the hall as the door opened, seemingly on its own, to reveal a long, dim chamber holding only a table that appeared to stretch on and on. Though it was day, candles flickered at intervals down the table, barely lighting the space. The table was lined with tall, carved chairs, and each chair held a mage. They looked like the portraits in the hallways, all white- or gray-haired, the men bearded. Bee counted them quickly. Thirteen men, seven women. Twenty pairs of piercing eyes turned toward them, and involuntarily Bee took a step back. But Anika moved forward, pulling Bee with her, and bowed her head, saying, "I am Princess Anika of Aradyn, and I have come to beseech you for your assistance."

Forty eyes stared without blinking.

Finally the mage seated at the far end of the table, whom they could barely make out in the gloom, spoke in a cracked, ancient voice. "Welcome. I am Master Nicon. What aid do you seek?"

Anika's damp, icy hand clutched Bee's more tightly. "I am the ward of Master Joris. My father, King Crispin, drowned in a shipwreck twelve years ago. Now Master Joris wants to marry me to an elderly king and seize for his own the kingdom I should rule."

The forty eyes all blinked at once. Then there was silence.

Master Nicon cleared his throat. "And what do you want from us?"

Anika took a deep breath. "Master Joris has done great damage to Aradyn. He's eradicated all the trees and planted the land with tulips. He appropriates the money from the tulip trade for himself. The land is in peril, and the people grow hungry and destitute. I want him removed."

Bee gasped. The words sounded outrageous when Anika said them out loud, especially in this place, with all the mages staring at them.

"Remove him!" said Master Nicon, his beard waggling. "However could we do that? Aradyn is his kingdom. Each mage has a kingdom, and each kingdom has a mage. It has ever been thus."

Wil spoke then. "But he is destroying Aradyn. No one

else has the power to stop him. We are asking you to do it."

An ancient mage with a high, piercing voice, said, "I recall Joris. He was difficult, even long ago when I was the mage of Lyng. Wasn't it he who . . . who . . . oh dear. No, I've forgotten the story."

The fourth mage on the left, a woman with watery eyes and a lisp, said, "It is wrong that Joris abuses his land. The land is our responsibility, our main and true duty. He should be removed. Once before, it was done. I remember it. Back in the time of King Idris."

"No," another mage protested, "that was just a story. That was not a true thing."

Suddenly all the mages were talking at once, arguing and speaking over one another. "It was true, Porcius!" Bee heard, and "You are confused, as always, Clymene," and "Don't speak to me that way, I am your elder!" The candles flickered wildly as they wheezed and panted with agitation, and Bee, Wil, and Anika looked at one another in alarm.

"What is wrong with them?" Bee whispered.

The mages' voices trailed off into silence, broken only by the mumbling of the sixth mage down on the right and another mage's intermittent coughing.

"Can you remove Master Joris?" Anika asked again. "Will you give me succor?"

The mage Clymene, her white hair standing out like a halo around her head, said, "Missy, we cannot remove a mage. We are mages ourselves. It would be like . . . like cannibalism!"

Again the mages erupted. "You are an idiot, Clymene!" one of them cried. Another looked around, confused, and said, "Who is a cannibal? Are you saying one of us is a cannibal?" A third got shakily to her feet and asked, "Is it time for supper yet?"

Master Nicon hammered on the thick wood with a trembling fist. "Mages, come to order! Stop this bickering right now. Behave yourselves!" Gradually the others subsided.

"Come closer, little Princess," he said to Anika. Anika still clutched Bee's hand, so the two walked forward together, Wil trailing behind them. The other mages turned their heads to watch their progression down the room. Now they could see Master Nicon more clearly. He looked, if it were possible, even older than the others. His eyes were bleary and faded, his skin like parchment that had been crushed and crumpled and badly straightened out again. They stopped in front of him, and he looked at them for a long minute.

"There is really nothing we can do for you," he said at last. "I do not know why you came to us."

"You are the Council of Mages!" Bee burst out. "You have the power to do what you want!"

Master Nicon let out a bark of laughter that turned into a frenzy of coughing. When he stopped, he sat and wheezed while he caught his breath again. "Look at us," he said, motioning to the others seated at the table. "We are older than you can imagine. We do not sit here and make rules to govern the world, or magic to improve it. Other mages have taken our places in our kingdoms to do what needs to be done to keep the world in balance . . . or not, as you have noted. We are here because we are of no use anymore. Our magic is only strong enough to change a flower's color, or fill a basin with water. I am sorry, little Princess. I would like to help you. It is long since I have been of any real use. But there is nothing I or any of us can do for Aradyn."

Anika looked at Bee, and the tears in her eyes reflected the dancing candlelight. "Thank you," she murmured. She bowed her head to the table at large, and then she, Bee, and Wil turned and started out of the room.

But Bee couldn't bear to see Anika so distressed.

She turned back, pulling off her haversack. "Masters, I know you can't help, but I've brought you something as a thank you for seeing us. I am a baker, and these are my specialties." As she took the cookies from their wrappings, Bartholomew appeared at her side, holding a plate. A murmuring went up from the mages. In the eyes of the ones closest to her, she could see a glimmer of interest.

"There's enough for all," she said, passing the plate up the table. Then she unwrapped a Bouts Bun and brought it to Master Nicon. "I only have one of these left," she said to him. "I think you should have it."

Master Nicon stretched out a trembling hand and took the bun, turning it about and looking closely at it. Satisfied, he tasted it, and his watery eyes widened. "You have a singular talent, child," he said. Then his brow creased. Bee held her breath. She had no idea if the helpfulness in the cookies or the truthfulness in the bun would affect the mages at all—or, if it did, what would result.

For a moment there was only the sound of pleased chewing and swallowing. One mage choked a little on his cookie and had to be pounded on the back. Then Master Porcius said, "Are you quite sure there is nothing we could do for them?" Bee's heart lifted. The helpfulness was working!

"Yes," Mistress Clymene said, "surely we could . . ." But her voice trailed off. She had no ideas.

Master Nicon shook his head. "We cannot keep them here, and we cannot go back with them. And our powers, such as they are, do not work over water, as you know."

There was a general sigh of dismay at the table, and all the candles flickered wildly. It was clear from the expression on Master Nicon's face that he spoke the truth, whether as an effect of the Bouts Bun or not Bee couldn't say. Her shoulders slumped, and she turned away again.

As they reached the door, they heard Master Nicon's deep, shaky voice. "Wait, little Princess. There is one thing I can tell you."

Anika spun around, her face brightening. "Yes? What is it?"

The old mage had risen and was making his doddering way down the room toward them. "Did you say that your father was King Crispin? That he drowned in a shipwreck? Or am I confusing you with someone else?"

"That was me," Anika said, baffled. "That is what I said."

"And this was . . . twelve years ago?"

"Yes. I was four years old."

"Ah, I thought as much. Well, my dear, it did not happen as you say," Master Nicon said. "I do not remember how I know it, but this I know: King Crispin, your father, is still very much alive."

CHAPTER 14

Anika gave a little gasping cry, and Wil rushed to support her as her knees buckled. "What—what do you mean?" she asked, her voice wavering. "My father is alive?"

Master Nicon looked astounded at his own words. He wobbled as if he too would fall to the ground. Bartholomew put an arm around him, and the old mage leaned against the hedge wizard. "What did you put in the bun, girl?" Master Nicon accused Bee.

Bee blanched. The mage looked angry, his thick gray brows drawn together in a *V* shape.

"Truth," she admitted in a small voice. "It had truth in it."

Master Nicon stared at her. Then his face relaxed, and he smiled, his nose and chin nearly meeting. "A singular talent indeed," he said. "So you are part mage, girl. I did not see that."

"I am—what?" Bee was stunned.

"Only mages and hedge wizards have magic, and baking truth into a bun is magic, without a doubt. Did you not know?"

Bee shook her head, speechless.

"But my father!" Anika cried. "Divulge, please, how do you know he is alive? Where is he?"

Master Nicon thought for a long moment. His expression changed, and changed, and changed again, as if eons were passing over it, and Bee thought he must be recalling all the years he had lived in order to find the memory. But nothing seemed to register. Finally he shrugged. "I do not know how I know. Or I do not remember. And I do not know where he is. Only that he lives." A chorus of voices rose up behind him as the other mages passed what had been said down the table.

"Then we must find him," Anika said. "Oh, to see my father again!"

"He could be anywhere," Wil said. "How can we know where even to start looking?"

"I don't know," Anika replied. "But we will locate him. We will!"

"I wish you luck, little Princess," Master Nicon said. "I am sorry we cannot help you."

Anika took his trembling hands in hers. "But you *have* helped. If my father lives, I shall not have to marry. If he lives, we can compel Master Joris to depart! Thank you— oh, thank you, Masters!"

Up and down the table, Bee heard, "Look, she holds his hands!", "She is thanking us!", "Why is she saying thank you?", "What has happened?", and, from one of the mages, "Are there more cookies?"

They took their leave then, to a chorus of quavering farewells and good lucks. Back in their gloomy rooms, they collected their haversacks and waited for Bartholomew to lead them back down the endless winding steps to the long pier where the pirates would meet them. A fog had rolled in; they couldn't see more than a few dozen feet in front of them. The damp air was chilly, and Bee shivered. Would the pirates be able to find the island in this gloom?

Even in the cool dampness, Anika's cheeks were flushed with heat, her eyes bright with excitement. "I can hardly believe it," she said. "Do you think it is true, Bee? Do you think he is alive in actuality?"

"I don't know," Bee said honestly. "I'm sure Master Nicon isn't lying . . . but he is very old. He could misremember." There was something about Anika's elation that pricked at her in a very uncomfortable way. Of course it would be the most wonderful thing in the world if her father were alive. Of course it would! But . . . it was what they had in common. They were both orphans. If Anika's father, the king, came back to her, she would truly be the princess of Aradyn. How could they remain friends?

Bee felt as if the fog were inside her brain. She shook her head hard, then said, "Do you think it's almost time for the *Egg-Hen* to come?"

Wil squinted at the sky. "There's no way to tell. I'm sure it's afternoon, but it could be one o'clock or five o'clock. This fog . . ."

"It's a little after three," Bartholomew said. His tone was so sure that no one questioned him.

"They should be here momentarily then," Anika said. "Oh, I do hope Captain Zay will assist us!"

"Assist us?" Bee repeated.

"To find Papa. Perhaps she's heard something about him. She journeys far and wide, doesn't she? I never thought to inquire—I never thought he might still be alive!"

"Surely she will help," Wil said. "It seems like the sort of adventure she'd enjoy."

This was true enough. Something a little dangerous, a little suspicious—it sounded just like the captain to Bee.

And now their quest had changed. They were no longer in search of a way to stop the mage of Aradyn and save Anika from an unwanted marriage. Now they were in search of a long-lost king who might or might not be alive. Bee sighed, thinking of her kitchen in Zeewal, the dough rising and the tarts unbaked. It might be a very long time indeed before she plunged her hands into fresh flour and butter again. She missed Master Bouts, Kaatje, the sweet smell of sugared pastry, her own soft bed.

"Look!" Wil called, peering into the fog. "I think I see something—are those sails?"

The others strained to see. Yes, there in the distance— it was definitely a ship.

"It's moving fast," Bee observed.

"Dear me. It's being followed," Bartholomew said. And all at once they could see that was true. Behind the ship came another, and another. In a few minutes they could see the flags on them. The one in front was the *Egg-Hen*, with her bright pink skull and crossbones. The two behind her flew the gold and red tulip flags of Aradyn.

"They're chasing the pirates," Wil said. "The *Egg-Hen* is being pursued—they won't be able to stop for us!"

"They can't leave us here," Bee cried. "We have to get on that ship, or we'll be stranded!"

"Follow me," Bartholomew commanded. "There's a spot on the far side of the island where the rocks jut out. We can jump."

"Jump?" Bee repeated blankly.

"How will the pirates know what we're doing?" Wil asked, a hint of desperation in his voice.

"They're getting close," Bartholomew said. "Can you see any of them? Are they looking at us?"

Wisps of fog veiled the ships, and Bee couldn't make out any figures on the decks at all. Then, suddenly, a strong breeze blew across her face. It gusted, then steadied, and quickly it began to blow away the fog. There! The ship was clearly visible now, and on the deck she could see the tall figure that was Haleem. He stood, his legs spread out, the spyglass in his hand.

"It's Haleem! He's looking right at us!"

"Signal him that we're going up and around to the left. If we're lucky, they'll follow."

Wil signaled to Haleem, waving wildly to point up, then leftward. With a shifting of sails, the ship stopped its forward thrust and swerved abruptly.

"Run!" Bartholomew urged, and they sprinted up the stone steps again, crushing the gray and brown flowers beneath their feet. Almost immediately they were gasping for breath, their legs trembling, but they kept going as fast as they could. About a quarter of the way up, Bartholomew plunged off the steps and into an outlandish landscape of twisted plants and thick mosses that seemed to grab at their feet as they ran.

"This is Master Kajetan's Garden of Errors," Bartholomew puffed. "Where he puts his mistakes." Then he had no more breath to spare.

They ran around the mountain, slipping on the steep slope and brushing away moths that flapped like herons and huge flies with multifaceted emerald eyes that stared and blinked at them as they passed. The breeze turned into a wind, and they could see dark clouds rolling across the water. Finally Bartholomew halted. There, as he had said, a finger of rock jutted out over the sea. Wil walked cautiously out, testing it. He looked down, the wind lifting his blond hair on end.

"It's not so very far," he said weakly.

"Is the ship there?" Bee asked.

"I can see it," Wil replied. "It's coming closer. It looks like the others have lost a little speed."

Then Bee remembered.

"But Anika can't swim! We can't jump, she'll drown!"

"I can float for a few minutes, I am certain," Anika said. But she didn't sound certain.

"And what about Pepin?"

Anika pulled the hedgehog out of her pocket. He unrolled partway in her hand. A dragonfly with wings striped in pink and purple flew by, and Pepin lunged upward and snapped his jaws closed over it, swallowing it in a quick gulp.

"If that doesn't kill him, nothing will," Wil said. Anika glared at him, and he looked apologetic.

"He will be fine," Anika insisted. "I'll hold him above the water."

Bartholomew ran back into the garden and uprooted a thick plant. He brought it to Anika. "This should keep you afloat," he said. "Hold on to it tightly."

Bee reached out to touch the plant. It was porous and springy, unlike any shrub or bush she'd ever seen. It reminded her of the sponges that sometimes washed up on the beach near her old home. Perhaps, she thought, it was a cross between a plant and a sponge. That seemed like something that would grow in Master Kajetan's Garden of Errors.

Bee joined Wil at the edge of the rock. It was a very

long way down. There didn't seem to be any rocks below, though. Maybe they could survive if they jumped.

"We have to try to land near the ship, so they have time to pick us up," Wil said. Bee could tell he was trying very hard to sound calm and reasonable. "And we'll have to leave our packs. They'll drag us down." He shrugged off his haversack, and Bee did the same.

"I'll go first," Bartholomew announced. The others gaped at him.

"You?" Bee and Anika said together.

"Do you have any idea how long I've waited for a chance to get off this cursed island? Eons, it seems. You are not leaving without me. I'd rather drown or be broken on the rocks than spend another hour in this . . . this old-age home for fading magicians." Bartholomew's expression was resolute. It was clear he meant it.

"An old-mage home," Bee offered. The others were silent for a moment. Then Wil snickered.

Bartholomew gave a sudden whoop and shouted, "Farewell, Master Nicon's Old-Mage Home for Elderly Enchanters!" Without warning he launched himself off the rock. Anika screamed and clutched at Wil, and they watched in horror as the hedge wizard plummeted, his robes flapping wildly about him so he looked like a giant green-winged bird. There was a splash, and a moment later Bartholomew's head appeared above the waves. The *Egg-Hen* sped toward him.

"My turn!" Anika said in a trembling voice. Before Wil or Bee could speak, she cried, "Adieu, Master Nicon's Old-Mage Home for Nonagenarian Necromancers!" She took a running leap off the edge, her sponge-plant clutched in one hand, her other hand protectively over the pocket where Pepin nestled. She hit the water cleanly and popped to the surface near Bartholomew. Bartholomew swam to her and held her up, waving to Bee and Wil.

"You go, Mistress Boltiarda," Wil said, trying to sound unafraid. Bee shook her head.

"You," she told him. She needed another moment to gather her courage for the jump.

There was no time to argue. He vaulted off the rock, bellowing, "Cheerio, Master Nicon's Old-Mage Home for Wizened Warlocks!"

It was Bee's turn. The tulip ships were approaching now, pushed by the wind that whipped around her. She had to jump. She couldn't think about how far down it was. She couldn't. Then, out of the corner of her eye, she saw another of the gigantic spiders that roamed around the Island of the Mages. It scuttled over the rock toward her, and she backed away. Her foot landed on empty air, and her arms windmilled wildly as she tried to regain her balance. As she tilted off the rock, she shouted, as loudly as she could, "Goodbye, Master Nicon's Old-Mage Home for Shriveled Sorcerers!"

And then she fell.

CHAPTER 15

Bee hit the water hard, knocking the breath out of her. Her flat landing was painful, but it kept her from sinking far. Wil grabbed her and pulled her to the surface as growing waves broke over them. The approaching clouds held a storm. The *Egg-Hen* was close now, and Haleem and Rijkie tossed ropes to them. At the end of each rope was a knotted loop. Wil helped Bee slip a loop over her head, securing it under her arms. Bartholomew did the same with Anika.

On board, the pirates pulled and pulled at the ropes, hauling Bee and Anika up the side of the ship. The girls tumbled over the railing and lay sprawled on the deck, as soaked and breathless as they had been when the pirates first rescued them. Wil and Bartholomew joined them moments later.

"I see that 'edge'og is still with us!" called Captain Zay from behind the great wheel that steered the ship. "Bee-girl, why is it we are always fishing you out of the sea?" Then she barked orders to the men, and the *Egg-Hen* changed course quickly as the tulip ships approached.

Bee, Anika, and Wil led Bartholomew down into the hold, where they changed into dry clothes that Rijkie found for them. Then they joined the others on deck as the ship weaved and skipped over the waves, which grew higher with every gust of wind. The sky had darkened, and the clouds began to spit out rain.

"The first of the autumn storms, worse luck!" Haleem shouted, his words snatched by the wind.

"No, best of luck for us!" the captain called back. "We are always sailing in all kind of weathers, while these sorry seamen only know the quiet waters. Look, the winds is pushing them away! They cannot catch the *Egbertina-Henriette*!"

And it was true. The *Egg-Hen* tacked back and forth to move forward, while the other ships, sailing straight into the wind, were thrust back by its force. Lightning flashed and thunder cracked as the distance between the ships grew. All at once, the skies opened as if a giant had suddenly tossed a huge bucket of water from the clouds. It wasn't so much a rainfall as a waterfall. Bee was soaked to the skin again, and Anika shivered uncontrollably, her lips turning blue.

"Into the hold!" Haleem shouted at them as the ship keeled sharply to one side. Bee slid across the slippery deck almost to the railing before Bartholomew, anchored with a hand clutching the mast, grabbed her. They all clasped hands and made their way, crawling, back down the stairs.

Below, it was dry, but the creaking of the ship as the waves battered it was almost as loud as the wind and rain above had been. Bee stumbled about, crashing into walls, to find blankets so they could warm themselves. Then they huddled in a corner of the sleeping room, blankets pulled over their heads, trying not to slide from one side of the hold to the other as the ship listed first to port, then to starboard. Above them, the hammocks swung wildly. They all began to feel dizzy and queasy.

It seemed like hours—perhaps it was—before the storm began to quiet and the *Egg-Hen* was no longer tossed about on the waves like a child's skipping stone. Bee poked her head out from her blanket.

"I think it's stopping," she said.

The hatch to the deck opened, and Rijkie poked his head through. "The rain's ended," he said. "The captain wants you on deck."

Clutching their blankets, the four made their way up

the stairs and onto the storm-cleansed deck. Dusk was coming on, and a few stars showed among the scudding clouds overhead. There was no sign of the tulip ships.

"Wet again!" Captain Zay chortled at the sight of them, though she was drenched herself. The plume on her tricorn hat hung heavy with water, and she had to slap it out of her eyes as it dripped down her face. Finally she removed the hat altogether.

"A pirate is never removing her hat," she said to Bee. "Unless she want to, of course!"

"I am sure, madam, that a pirate does whatever she pleases at all times," Bartholomew said. Captain Zay narrowed her eyes at him.

"Who is this person?" she asked Bee.

"This is Bartholomew. Master Bartholomew. He's a hedge wizard."

The captain looked Bartholomew up and down. He didn't quail under her gaze, but straightened himself beneath his damp blanket.

"At your service, madam," he said.

"Oh, I am no madam, 'edge wizard. I am captain of the *Egbertina-Henriette*. Do not be forgetting that!" Her tone was severe.

"I wouldn't dream of it," Bartholomew said. His

lips twitched, but he kept his expression solemn and respectful. "This is a very fine ship, and it was excellent leadership that kept it whole in such fearsome weather."

"Indeed it was!" Captain Zay agreed, her good spirits restored. "And most excellent work from my mens as well. But we are far off the course now. We do not 'ave one slight idea of where we are."

"The stars are coming out," Bartholomew noted. "You can steer by them when the clouds are gone."

"Quite so, 'edge wizard. And in the meantime, we shall be consuming some food and some coffee and also some rum. For the warmth, to be sure."

"To be sure!" Bartholomew agreed. They followed Captain Zay into her cabin, where she rummaged in her wooden chest and pulled out dry shirts and trousers for all. One by one, they changed behind the painted screen. Bee and Anika had to roll up the trouser legs and shirt sleeves, but to be dry again was lovely.

Limmo the cook knocked and entered with a tray that held bowls of stew, and they settled themselves around the wooden table. The captain poured steaming coffee and added a liberal dose of rum to hers and Bartholomew's.

"It would be stunting your growth," she said severely to Wil, Bee, and Anika. "For the young people, very bad."

Limmo withdrew, winking at Bee, and they ate with gusto and then slowed to sip their coffee.

"No sweets," the captain said with regret. "Unless—you are 'aving some in your pack?" She looked at Bee.

"My pack is gone," Bee said. "We had to leave them when we jumped off the rock. And besides, I gave all the sweets to the mages."

"Ah—the mages!" the captain exclaimed. "Tell, tell—are they aiding you? Are they giving you magic and all sort of assisting?"

"They were no help at all," Bee replied. "They were just . . . old. And sad."

"But they told us something—something wonderful!" Anika said.

"What is this wonderful something?"

"The head mage, Master Nicon—he said that my father is alive."

Captain Zay furrowed her brow and added another dollop of rum to her coffee cup. "The king your father is alive? You said he died . . . in what way?"

"He drowned—or so I thought. So I was told. In a shipwreck."

"And there are 'ow many years since this is taking place?"

"I was only four. It was twelve years ago."

Bartholomew made a little noise. It was something between a hiccup and a gasp. Bee saw that his slate-colored eyes were as round as the buttons on Captain Zay's jacket.

"A shipwreck twelve years ago?" he said, his voice hoarse. "Where did this happen?" Bee felt a shiver run down her spine.

"It was just off the coast of Aradyn, in the north," Anika told him. "The ship, the *Waldethruda,* broke up on the rocks. I'd thought no one survived."

"I lost my family in that wreck," Bartholomew said. The others gaped at him.

"You had a family?" Wil asked. "But hedge wizards don't marry."

"Not usually," Bartholomew agreed. "But I did. I fell in love. I married, we had a child. The baby was only six months old when she and my wife perished. I remember now that the king had been on board, but in my rage and sorrow, I'd forgotten."

Captain Zay's eyes were bright with interest. "Well, well!" she said. "And this is a certain thing, that your family are perished?"

"I too thought everyone drowned," Bartholomew said. "I'd never heard otherwise until now." Bee's heart began to pound.

Captain Zay went to the cabin door and opened it. "'Aleem!" she shouted. The first mate came running. "What mens aboard been sailing for twelve years or more? Bring them to me."

Haleem saluted and disappeared, and the captain turned back. "I am only captain on this ship for three years now," she explained. "Before this time, I was pirate far, far from 'ere. So I am not knowing of your shipwrecks and such. But one of these old seadogs may be possessing knowledge more than I."

In a few minutes, Haleem came back with two of the pirates, Thoralf and Niek. Both were older, with craggy, sun-dried faces and gray beards. They stood, hands clasped, before Captain Zay.

"You mens, you were sailing these seas a dozen of years ago?" the captain demanded.

"No, Captain," Thoralf said. "I sailed then, but not around here. I was on a cargo ship out of Kori."

"I was on a cargo ship back then as well," Niek said. "'Twas an Aradysh ship."

"Ah!" Captain Zay said, pleased. "Then you will be knowing of the wreck of the *Waldethruda*?"

Niek nodded slowly, as if reluctant to speak. "Yes, I do recall it well. A terrible, strange thing, that. People talked of nothing else for months."

"Strange how?" Anika asked. Her hands were tight around her coffee cup, almost tight enough to crush the delicate china.

"Why, how it all happened. 'Twas a clear, cool day, all agreed. No weather to speak of. The captain knew his job, knew the coastline. No reason for the wreck, no reason at all. 'Twas as if the rocks just came up out of nowhere. There the ship was, and then there the rocks were. The *Waldethruda* broke up in no time."

"And the passengers?" Anika voice trembled.

"Drowned, mostly. I'm sorry, Princess. I know the king was on board. His body was never found."

"I know," Anika whispered. "But the mage said . . ." She trailed off. Bee reached out and took Anika's hand, which lay cold and limp in hers.

Niek went on. "The others, their bodies were mostly washed in to shore, the ship was that close. There was only one survivor I know of. A baby."

The listeners turned to Bartholomew, who had grown pale.

"A baby?" he managed.

"So I recall. A little girl. There were rescuers sent out from the mainland. They took her away, I don't know where.

Probably the nearest village."

Bee was beginning to feel very strange, as if the sea itself were rising in her. She thought her words might sound like they were bubbling up through water when she spoke, but they came out clearly. "What was the nearest village? Do you know?"

Niek said, "I do, because it was the next village over to my own. It was Boomkin."

"That's where I was taken," Bee said, her voice low. "When my mother died. In a shipwreck. I was a baby then. I was fostered in Boomkin."

Now all eyes were on Bee. Anika gripped her hand hard enough to make her wince. Captain Zay was so excited that she nearly levitated.

"What you are saying, Bee-girl? What you are saying?"

Bee gulped. She turned to Bartholomew, whose gray eyes met her own gray eyes, wide and startled. She couldn't bear his gaze and turned back to the captain. "I am saying . . . I don't know. I think I am saying that I am that baby. The baby that survived the shipwreck."

Anika gasped. "Can it be true?"

"But . . . ," Captain Zay said, thinking hard. "But this 'edge wizard has said that it is his daughter who was lost in the wreck."

Bee nodded.

"I am all in a state of confusement," the captain said, shaking her head. "What means this most peculiar news?"

Bartholomew stood abruptly. "I think it means— though I cannot imagine that it is so—I think it means that Bee is my daughter."

CHAPTER 16

Bee was amazed that a silence could be so loud. She could hear the creaking of the ship, the flapping of the sails, the breaths of each person in the captain's cabin. She stared at the pattern in the rug under her feet. A flower, a bird, a vine . . . a flower, a bird, a vine. The colors were bright, even in the dimming light that came through the round porthole.

"Can you truly be my daughter?" Bartholomew finally asked Bee. It came out in a croak.

Bee looked up. Captain Zay's mouth had dropped open. Bee would have sworn that it was impossible to render the captain speechless—yet there she was, unable to say a word.

"I think so," Bee said softly. "It all seems to make sense."

"Do you remember your . . . your mother?"

"No." Bee blinked away tears. "My first memories are

my foster parents. They told me that I'd been orphaned in a shipwreck. That was all I knew. That, and . . . this." She pulled out the necklace she wore around her neck and unfastened it, handing it to Bartholomew. He took it from her and turned it around and around. His hands were shaking. He gave it to Anika, and she pried at it with her fingernails. To Bee's shock, the gold disc clicked open. As often as Bee had looked at it, run her fingers over it, held it tightly as she tried to imagine her mother's face, the disc had never come open. It had never occurred to her that it could. She'd never seen a locket before.

Anika passed it back to Bartholomew. "Look," Bartholomew said, showing the inside of the locket to Bee. "That is your mother."

Bee peered at the tiny frame. The paper that nestled inside was old and faded, but she could make out a woman's smiling face.

"It was a miniature," Bartholomew said. "We had a passing painter do it. As tiny as could be, but a good likeness, I thought. I'd bought the locket at a fair. I could never forget it—the flowers engraved on it are lilies, for your mother, Lis. She put the painting in this locket and placed it round your neck, so she would always be close to your heart."

Gently, Bee traced the tiny face in the painting with her finger. Her mother. And . . .

"Oh, Bee," Anika cried. "You have found your father!" Her face was alight with joy, and Bee marveled that she could be so happy when her own father's fate was unclear.

"That explains the magic in your baking," Wil said. "You are part hedge wizard!"

"It's what Master Nicon said," Bee recalled. "That I must be part mage. Hedge wizard counts, I suppose. I thought he was just babbling." She felt like she was babbling herself. Her head was swimming. They were supposed to find Anika's father, not hers. She hadn't even known her father was lost.

"My daughter," Bartholomew said again. Bee looked at him then. Tears dripped off his nose.

"Oh," she said helplessly. She held out her hands, and he clutched them. "Please don't cry. Don't, Father." The word sounded strange beyond all reckoning.

"Bee-girl, you are endless with surprise," Captain Zay said, shaking her head. "A found father, this is not an everyday something—this is to celebrate! To be sure, more rum is called for!" She took the bottle and topped off Bartholomew's cup, and he let go of one of Bee's hands to take a great gulp. It went down the wrong way, and he gasped and spluttered, spraying them all.

"I am wanting you to drink it, not bathe in it!" the captain admonished. Wil snorted with laughter, and Bee started laughing as well, and then quite suddenly burst into tears.

Anika gathered Bee in her arms, and Bee sobbed on her shoulder without even truly knowing why. She was embarrassed by her tears. She had a father, Anika had none, and she was the one who was crying? She sniffed and gulped and managed to stop. Captain Zay handed her a rather grimy handkerchief, dingy white with a border of lace and a stain of what Bee feared might be blood. She pretended to use it to wipe her face, and swiped instead with the trailing sleeve of her oversized pirate shirt.

"I am very weary," Anika said to the captain. "Perhaps we could rest for a while." The captain glanced at Bee and nodded. It was true, Bee was exhausted, too. They hadn't really slept on the Island of the Mages, and this day had been . . . well, tiring. She was grateful to Anika for saying something—for giving her a reason to leave the cabin, to get away from everyone.

She had no idea how to talk to Bartholomew. She knew they would have to speak before long, but what would she say? She felt nothing for him. *I have done just fine all my life without a father,* she imagined telling him. Or *Why, in all these years, did you never look for me?* Oh, she could never say such hurtful things! And would she have to live with him? Would he tell her what to do? Would he prevent her from working at the bakery? She couldn't face it—not yet.

Instead, she and Anika went down into the hold and climbed into hammocks. The other beds were still empty; it wasn't very late. They rocked comfortably as the ship climbed waves and then sank down into troughs.

"Bee," Anika said after a few minutes. "Are you wakeful?"

"No," Bee said.

"I won't converse if you really don't want to," Anika said. "But . . . aren't you ecstatic? Is something amiss? You've finally found your father!"

"I know," Bee said. "I know it's wonderful. But . . . it doesn't feel wonderful." She sighed. "I was used to things as they were. I have Master Bouts. He's . . . he's like a father. I don't know Bartholomew. I don't need another father." The words sounded harsh and a little awful to Bee when she said them. But they were true.

"I understand," Anika said after a time. "Honestly I do. It would be so problematic to have to become acquainted with a father who was an utter stranger. You never knew him at all." Bee heard what remained unsaid: *Not like me.* Anika had known her father. She probably remembered him, at least a little.

"But really, Bee, it could be marvelous. He seems very amiable. You could have two fathers, Master Bouts and Bartholomew. Two fathers, just think of it!"

Bee thought of it as the hammock swayed, and something about the thought made her a little bit happy. She pictured Master Bouts and Bartholomew meeting. They weren't very much alike—Master Bouts was hearty and jolly, while Bartholomew seemed somewhat formal, a touch reserved, maybe even a little stuffy. But they were both kind. They would probably like each other.

She was almost asleep when Anika whispered, "Bee?"

"Hmmm?"

"Did you not bake truth into the bun that Master Nicon devoured?"

"I did."

"Could Master Nicon have prevaricated, then?"

"Could he have . . . *what?*"

"Lied. Could he have lied about my father?"

Bee was silent. Then she said, "I'm not sure. The—the magic acts differently on mages. I don't think he could have lied, exactly. But maybe he didn't really know the truth."

"Ah," Anika said. "I hadn't thought of that." Her voice was infinitely sad. "Sleep well then, Bee."

In moments, the ship rocked them into sleep.

Bee woke because the rocking had stopped. All was quiet in the hold, but dimly she heard shouting from above. The lump in the next hammock that was Anika was still. She twirled herself out of the hammock—she was quite good at maneuvering in and out of it by now—and made her way up the stairs onto the deck.

The ship was anchored near an island that looked small, very small indeed. Bee couldn't see the whole length of it, but unless it was much longer than it was wide, it was less than a mile around. And every inch of it seemed to be covered by vegetation. Tall plants—most taller than a man, some taller than five men standing atop each other.

Wil was on the deck; she wasn't sure if he'd been to sleep or not. He looked bright eyed enough, though, so she suspected he'd slumbered and gotten up before her. He handed her a piece of hardtack—rock-hard bread that had to be chewed until the jaws ached. But it didn't spoil on long voyages, and Bee had shown Limmo how to flavor it with fennel seed, which gave it a spicy sweetness.

"Where are we?" she asked him, rubbing her eyes and gnawing at the bread.

"Nobody's quite sure," he said. "This island isn't really supposed to be here. It isn't on any map. And it's very odd looking. What are those bushes all over it?"

Bee looked again, peering closely at the plants. One had reddish-brown bark, nearly as dark as the trunk of the cherry tree in the palace garden she'd sat beneath with Anika. She clutched at Wil's arm.

"Trees," Bee breathed. "Oh Wil, they're all trees!"

"Those are trees?" Wil said. "Are you sure?"

"I've only seen one," she admitted. "But it looked like that one, with the dark stem."

"They're beautiful," he said. "And each one is different!"

There were tall trees and shorter ones, trees whose leaves were yellow and red and bronze and those with green leaves and some without leaves, with just strange little pointy needles. Their barks were deep brown and light brown, gray and white and yellowish. The slender ones dipped and bent in the wind, while the thicker, stronger ones stood firm. They seemed to be beckoning to Bee, and suddenly she had to be closer to them.

"I want to look at them," Bee said. "We should go ashore."

"Let's ask the captain," Wil suggested.

They found Captain Zay gazing through the spyglass at the island. "This is one very odd thing," she said to them, lowering the spyglass. "No persons in sight whatsoever. Only very many trees. And whyfore is this island 'ere in the first place? It is not existing on my maps."

"We should explore it," Wil said. "At the very least, it may have some fresh water that we can bring back to the ship."

"Go on that isle of strangeness?" The captain looked doubtful. "Most likely there are wolves or some other things that will eat such tasty bits as yourselves. The mens should be going, not the childs."

Wil looked offended, but Bee forestalled his protest, saying, "There might be some good things growing on those trees for me to put in pastries. Some fruits, maybe. Like the lemon I used before."

The captain thought about it.

"I could bake the minute we got back."

It was too much temptation for the captain. "Well, that is another tale, to be sure. You go, take Rijkie. And take that useless 'edge wizard. 'E almost knock 'is own self dead with a mallet, that one. No use to me at all." The captain turned away, forgetting them almost immediately in the rush of activity.

"Where's Bartholomew, then?" Wil asked Bee. She looked around. The hedge wizard sat on the other side of the ship, against the railing. Even from there she could see a red swelling on his forehead.

She ran over to him. "Bartholomew. May I call you Bartholomew, please?" It was the one thing she had been able to decide before she fell asleep. She could not call him *father*.

He looked up at her. "Of course you can. You can call me anything you wish, as long as you talk to me."

Bee was abashed. "I'm sorry I ran off last night. Really I am. I just . . . well, it was so unexpected. I didn't know what to say."

"Neither did I. Perhaps that proves we're related."

Bee smiled, and Bartholomew smiled back at her. "Good. We'll just be friends, shall we? That's as good a start as any."

"Yes," Bee said, relieved. "Friends. That will work. But—will you go to the island with us? Captain Zay thinks you should come along."

Bartholomew rose, wobbling a little. "She wants me out of the way, eh? I'm not surprised. There was a little . . . accident. I was just trying to help, but the mallet got away from me. I am not exactly handy."

"Then come!" Bee held out her hand, and after a second's hesitation, Bartholomew took it.

"Hurry up!" Wil cried. "They've lowered the dinghy!"

Anika came dashing up the steps from the hold, clutching Pepin in one hand and smoothing her sleep-tangled hair with the other. "Where are you going? Why are you disembarking without me?"

"Sorry," Bee said. "I didn't want to wake you. We're going to the island. Come with us!"

Rijkie and Haleem had placed barrels into the dinghy, in case they should find water on the island. But there was still enough room for Bee, Anika, Wil, and Bartholomew.

Rijkie manned the oars, shouldering Bartholomew aside. "Don't touch them oars—you'll kill someone," he said to the hedge wizard, who reddened and fingered the bump on his forehead. But Rijkie laughed, taking the sting from his words.

In minutes, they scraped onto sand. Wil leaped over the side and pulled the dinghy up on the shore, and the others climbed out. The beach was a narrow strip, with trees at its edge. And what trees they were! They rose high, blocking out the light. Bee ran to one with white, peeling bark that looked like parchment, and ran her hand down its rough trunk.

"A birch tree," Bartholomew said. "I've seen it in pictures."

"And this one?" Bee pointed to one that was almost triangular, with sharp needles for leaves.

"Some kind of pine tree. I don't know the different kinds."

Bee drew further into the forest. "This one?" The tree was droopy, and hanging from its branches were round globes, like miniature pumpkins.

"I believe this is an orange tree!" Bartholomew exclaimed. "How very peculiar, that all these trees should be growing together." He picked up one of the globes from the ground beneath the three. "Come, smell this, Bee," he said. He used his thumbnails to pry the thick skin open, and Bee leaned down and breathed in. It was the loveliest scent imaginable—sweeter than the lemon she'd used on the *Egg-Hen*, fresh and perfumed. It made her mouth water.

"You can eat them," Bartholomew said. "I've never tried one." He peeled away the outer skin and divided the fruit into sections, handing some to Bee, Wil, and Anika, and the two pirates, who came up behind them. Then they tasted it.

"Ohhhhh," Anika said, closing her eyes in pleasure.

Wil, Haleem, and Rijkie just nodded, juice dripping from their chins.

Bee chewed, savoring the juice as its sweetness filled her mouth. She sniffed the orange rind again. "That would go very well in a custard," she said thoughtfully.

Anika put Pepin down on the bed of leaves and fragrant pine needles that covered the ground, and he scurried deeper into the forest, munching on insects along the way. They followed, stopping now and then to marvel over a tree with a trunk as smooth as velvet, another that had spiky balls hanging from its branches, a third that was so tall they couldn't see its top in the clouds that hung low in the sky. One dropped a nut on Bartholomew's head, adding a new bump.

As Pepin tired, Anika stopped to place him back in the pocket of her trousers. Bee continued on ahead of the others, looking for trees that held treasures she could use for baking. She planned to come back with a sack so she could pick up the fruits and nuts she'd seen scattered on the forest floor. When she came to a lemon tree, she thought about plucking one of the bright yellow spheres from a branch, but she couldn't quite bring herself to do it. What if it hurt the tree? Of course, picking tomatoes didn't hurt the tomato plant, nor blackberries the blackberry bush. But these trees seemed somehow closer to human, and she determined she would only take what had fallen to the ground.

And then she came to a small clearing. The dimness of the heavily wooded forest lifted here. Grass grew in a circle where the sunlight would reach, if the clouds were not covering the sun.

Sitting in the grass, heads bowed, were two figures. One was a man, Bee could see that clearly. He had a long beard, reaching halfway to his waist. She couldn't tell if it was white or blond. His hair too was long, his clothing ragged, his feet bare.

Next to him was a woman with dark reddish-brown hair. She was very slender, and—it was the oddest thing—she almost seemed transparent, as if Bee could see through her. It was a trick of the light, Bee told herself. She stood silently, unsure of what to do.

Wil came up next to her and drew in a breath, staring at the couple in the clearing. In a moment, Bartholomew, Haleem, and Rijkie stood at her shoulder. Anika hurried up, patting her pocket to make sure Pepin was settled comfortably.

"What . . . ?" Anika said as she saw them all standing motionless. Then she looked where they were gazing. She didn't move or speak, but the air was suddenly charged, almost rippling with energy. Bee reached out a hand to her, but Anika didn't notice. She was transfixed.

"Papa?" she whispered. As tiny as the sound of the word was, it carried through the trees and across the clearing. The man turned his head. His eyes were sunken; his cheeks thin. Anika's hands flew to her mouth, holding in a scream. She wavered on her feet and then, before anyone could catch her, she crumpled to the ground in a dead faint.

CHAPTER 17

Wil was crouching over Anika in an instant, and Bee ran to help him raise her. Her eyelids fluttered open, her skin so pale that Bee could see the blood pulsing in the blue veins at her temples. In the clearing, the man and woman had sprung to their feet, but they came no closer.

"Papa," Anika murmured again. She held out her hands to the man, but he stayed where he was.

"What is that?" Haleem asked, pointing at the man's feet. Bee turned from Anika to look. Around the man's ankle was a thick circle of what looked like metal. And attached to it were rusty links that led to the nearest tree, a tall straight tree laden with dark leaves and brown nuts with bright red slashes in each.

"He's chained!" Wil exclaimed. "He's bound to the tree!" He transferred his hold on Anika to Bee, who supported the princess's wobbly weight. Then he and Haleem ran forward. As they approached, the woman seemed to waver in the air, and Bee had the strange thought that she might just disappear. But she did not.

"Help me to him," Anika said, leaning on Bee. As they came near, they could see more clearly how ravaged the man was. The bond around his ankle had chafed sores into the skin above and below, and he was little more than skin and bones. His face was weathered and deeply lined, and his eyes—his eyes were so filled with pain that Bee could hardly bear to look at them.

And then Anika was standing before him. "Papa," she said a third time. Her voice was as sorrowful as his eyes. He took her hands in his shaking ones and bent over them for a long moment.

At last he raised his head. "Daughter," he said, his voice halting. "Oh, my Anika. I had stopped imagining this moment. It has been so long—I had given up all hope of ever seeing you again. How ever did you come here?" He didn't wait for an answer but gazed at her and said, "You are taller, my dear."

Anika smiled, though her lips trembled. "It has been twelve years, Papa," she replied. "Did you presume I would stay a child?"

The king looked around at the others, and as his glance fell on them they knelt. "Your Majesty," Wil managed. No one knew what else to say.

"Can you free me from these shackles?" the king asked, motioning to the iron clasp on his ankle.

Haleem stood. "On the ship. We have tools on the ship. We'll get them. We'll be back—we'll be right back!" He grabbed Rijkie and pulled him from his knees, and they turned and ran back through the forest. Bee, Wil, and Bartholomew stayed kneeling.

"Please, rise," the king said. "This is not the place for formality."

"But Papa," Anika said, "how did you come here? I thought you were dead, all these years—drowned in the shipwreck. Have you dwelt here always? What has transpired with you?"

"I was always here, dearest daughter," he answered, stroking her hand. "All this time, fettered to a tree on this floating island. Sometimes we floated close enough to Aradyn to see the palace towers in the far distance, but never for long. We would drift away again, and not return for years."

"Oh, Papa," Anika whispered. Bee knew she was imagining the island, her father, so close to her palace home, so impossibly far away. "Did Master Joris imprison you here?"

"He did. I did not know then what he was capable of.

He can control the land, you know, and he just broke off a piece and set it afloat—with all the kingdom's trees on it. And then, later—a hundred years later—with me on it as well."

"You were not in the shipwreck?" Anika asked.

"I was," the king said. "There was a storm, but we were safe and near the coast. And then all at once there were rocks, huge boulders everywhere. Joris's doing, I know."

Bee remembered the rocks that threw themselves. Yes, that sounded like Master Joris.

"I was in the water, and the next thing I knew I was on the island with the trees. I do not know how he placed me here. "

The king sank down to sit, and the others sat as well. Even Bee knew that it was bad form to stand when the king was sitting. "I cannot stand for long—I've little strength left. Ying-tao has worked for years to keep me alive, but I never thought I would see this day." He motioned to the woman who now sat beside him, her dark hair a curtain over her face. She looked up at the sound of her name.

She was very beautiful, her skin like smooth butter, her eyes turned up at the corners. Like the king, she wore an expression of measureless sorrow that made tears prickle in Bee's own eyes.

"Thank you for helping him, Ying-tao," Anika said, releasing her father's hands and reaching for the woman's. But Ying-tao shrank back.

"She does not like the human touch," the king said. "She is a moss maiden."

"A . . . what?" Bee said. The king turned to look at her, and she bowed her head. ". . . Your Highness," she added.

"A moss maiden," he repeated. "A tree spirit. Each type of tree here has a moss maiden who belongs to it. But they have all been separated, trees from maidens, maidens from trees. In his cruelty, Joris has placed the maidens on another island."

"But why?" Anika asked.

Bartholomew answered. "A tree with its spirit has its own power. Master Joris could not have put the trees here with their moss maidens still within. Or, at least, it would have been far more difficult."

Ying-tao nodded. "We would not have allowed it," she said. Her voice was as soft as the whisper of wind through leaves. "But like the king, we did not know how far Joris would go in his greed. He wanted the land for himself, for his tulips, and so with his magic he separated us from our trees, and then he moved them. Of course we had to go with them. But he kept us apart. It has been like having a limb removed—but always there is pain, as if the limb were still there."

Bee could almost feel the maiden's anguish as she spoke. "Isn't your tree here?" she asked. "It seems as if every tree in the world is here."

"Nearly every tree," Ying-tao said. "All but mine. Mine is in the walled garden of the palace of Aradyn."

The cherry tree! Bee and Anika looked at each other, wide eyed.

"Then we must bring you back to it!" Anika said. Ying-tao looked longingly at Anika.

"There is little I wish more," she said. "But there are others to think of. Others like myself."

"Do you mean other moss maidens?" Bartholomew asked. "Where are they?"

"They are not far, and getting closer," Ying-tao said. But before she could explain herself, Haleem and Rijkie came crashing through the trees. Behind them were Thoralf and Captain Zay.

The pirates pulled up abruptly in front of the king. The look on Captain Zay's face was nothing short of astonishment. She went down on one knee, yanking Thoralf down with her, and swept off her hat.

"Your Majesty!" she cried. "I am thinking this was

one big joke of my mens upon me. A king tethered to a tree—it is absurd and in all ways ridiculous. And yet 'ere you be, altogether King Crispin as in the portraits I 'ave seen, and altogether chained. I am Zafira Zay, captain of the *Egbertina-Henriette,* and I am utterly your servant!"

King Crispin blinked in surprise at the tumble of words, but he managed to nod gravely. "Forgive me, madam, if I do not rise to greet you. I am a bit tired. But I would be very grateful if you and your men could find a way to free me from my shackles."

Haleem came forward with tools. There was a great deal of hammering and wrenching and a considerable amount of profanity. Brown and red nuts rained down, and Bee picked one up and sniffed it. Spicy and sweet, the scent made her eyes water.

"'Tis nutmeg," Thoralf told her.

Then the shackle broke, and the king was free. Unsteadily, he got to his feet. He put an arm around Anika's shoulder and took a few steps, testing the foot that had been so long ringed with iron. Then he walked in a straight line away from the tree that held his chain, until he was farther than the chain would have allowed. He turned to look at the others, and for the first time, he smiled. His face lit like a candle.

Bee noticed now that there was a circle worn in the grass

of the clearing around the tree. It must have been where King Crispin walked each day, at the end of his chain. Around in a circle for twelve years—it amazed her that he had not worn through to the very center of the earth.

"I am free," the king said in a tone of wonder.

"And now you must get your strongness back," Captain Zay announced. "You will come aboard my ship, and our baker-girl will create for you the tasty delicacies, and you will rest and eat and be once again the stout and formidable king to rule Aradyn!"

Thoralf and Rijkie cheered, but Haleem bent to whisper in the captain's ear. She pursed her lips, and the enthusiasm leaked out of her like air from a balloon.

"I forget a thing, a most important thing," she said. "When you should return to ruling, there will be an end to tulips. An end to us and to our work in relieving Joris's ships of their bounty. Then we shall all be starving and my mens' families as well. For as you can see from our hats and our swords and our ship's flag, we are each and every one of us a pirate. As king, your duty is always to be putting such as we in prison." She paused, and then concluded in a low voice, "So now I fear we must be leaving you 'ere instead."

"Captain!" Anika burst out. "You cannot do that. He

is the legitimate king—he is Aradyn's king! You must transport him back. It is the only noble thing to do."

Bee watched with fascination as honor and greed battled on the captain's face. It wasn't long, though, before her features smoothed out, and she bowed to the king. "I am mistook, most disgracefully," she said, as humbly as she could manage. "To be sure we take you back. Forgive this momentary lapse, I implore."

The king nodded. "It is difficult when one's livelihood is threatened, I am well aware," he said. "But you need not worry. You will never go to prison, not as long as I am king. There will still be some fields of tulips in Aradyn if I regain my throne. And yours will be the foremost trading ship among them all, I assure you. You will not need to steal the bulbs; you can make a fine living carrying them to faraway ports and selling them yourselves."

The pirates looked at one another, their eyes wide. It was clear they had never considered making a respectable living. Not to chase other ships, and board them, and fight with the sailors, and steal their goods? They didn't look at all convinced.

"A fine offer, to be sure," Captain Zay said dubiously. "We are full with gratitude, Your Majesty. And therefore, shall we go onward to the *Egbertina-Henriette*?"

The king, with Anika still supporting him, walked over to the moss maiden. She stood with her head bowed. It seemed to Bee that she swayed, just a little, with the breeze. "It is not quite so simple as that, madam," he said to the captain. "We have the trees, and their maidens, to consider."

Ying-tao raised her head. "You must go," she said.

"I shall not go without you and yours," he told her, and touched her hand gently. She didn't pull away from him. "You followed me onto this island, separating yourself from your own tree. I know well the heartache that caused you. All these long years, you have fed me with the bounty of the trees, and covered me with leaves to protect me from the weather. You have nursed me through illnesses and brought me water to drink and clean myself. You have been my companion and my guardian. Without you, I would have died in the first week of my captivity. I will not leave you here."

The king turned to the others. Already, he stood straighter, and his eyes seemed brighter, his voice stronger. "The other moss maidens are imprisoned on another floating island," he said. "It drifts not far from here, drawn to us by the bond between the maidens and their trees. Sometimes it is close enough to see, and the maidens keen and weep, and we can hear them. At other times, it is out of sight. But it is never far."

Captain Zay clapped her hat back on her head. "Then we shall find this wondrous isle!" she cried. "We shall find it and with our ship bring it right to you, and trees and maidens shall be as one. And then the celebration with rum will commence!"

"Can a ship tow a whole island?" Bee asked.

"I don't know," the king replied. "With a magical island such as this, anything is possible."

"We can but try," Captain Zay said, and she and her men headed back to the shore. Haleem left them a bag of food, and Bee, Bartholomew, Wil, Anika, and the king sat in a circle as Bee handed around jerky and hardtack, serving the king first and with the biggest pieces. He fell on them as if he hadn't eaten in a year. Ying-tao sat beside him, but she refused to eat. Bee wondered what moss maidens ate. Ying-tao explained that their trees must do the eating for them, getting nutrition from the sun and water and soil.

"I have been hungry long," Ying-tao said. "But perhaps I will see my tree soon, and I will eat."

As they waited, Anika sat beside her father, stroking his hand, reaching out to touch his lined face, sometimes wiping away an errant tear. At last she introduced Wil, Bartholomew, and Bee, and described their adventures. The king listened intently. "I am more grateful to you than I can say for what you have done for my daughter," he said when the story was finished. Bee felt the heat rise in her face. Oh, to be thanked by a king!

Then King Crispin turned to Bartholomew. "So we are both newfound fathers, Master Bartholomew!"

"A daughter is a wondrous thing, Your Majesty," Bartholomew replied, and the king put an arm around Anika, squeezing her.

"You speak the truth!" he agreed.

Night fell, and they curled on the ground in the chilly breeze that had stirred up and tried to sleep. Warm autumn sun woke them at daybreak, and moments later they heard someone coming through the trees. They sat up, rubbing eyes and stretching the stiffness from their limbs, to greet Haleem.

"We have done it!" he announced. "We found the island and used grappling hooks to hold it. A lucky wind came up to help us pull. It's right offshore. We can't see any of these maidens, though. And there's no place for them to hide that I can tell."

Bee sprang to her feet, and the others followed.

Ying-tao came out from among the trees and helped the king to rise. As quickly as they could, they moved through the forest to the shore. There, as Haleem had said, an island floated, not more than a few yards from where they stood. The *Egg-Hen* lay just off its shore. The island was bare and very small, with a rocky outcropping in its center.

"Could you not pull it right to this isle?" King Crispin asked Haleem.

"Nay, Your Majesty. It will come no closer. The islands seem to push each other away."

Bee looked closely at the barren island. As she watched, a figure emerged from the rocks. It was a tall woman gowned in greenish-yellow, long limbed and graceful. Another followed, this one small with bright hair the exact color of the orange Bee had tasted the day before. Then another came, and another and still another, each different in appearance and dress. They moved to the edge of the isle, gazing at the island of the trees. Bee could see the longing in their eyes as they stretched out their arms to their trees, so close and yet unreachable.

"There must be a cave below the rocks, where they have been living all this time," Bartholomew said. "But I suppose they cannot swim. Could the pirates row them across?"

"The gangplank!" Bee cried, remembering Captain Zay's threat on the first day they'd met her. "Is it long enough to reach between the islands?"

Haleem called to the ship, resting between the two islands. "Throw down the gangplank, mates!"

Four of the pirates came to the ship's railing carrying the gangplank, a long wooden board. They hoisted it and tossed it overboard, and Haleem and Rijkie swam out and pulled it so one edge was on the shore of the treed island. Then they pushed the other end around.

But it didn't reach.

Quickly the pirates took hammer and nails and everything wood they could find from the *Egg-Hen*— benches from the dining room, loose boards kept for repairs, even a chair from Captain Zay's own cabin— and cobbled them together into extra length for the gangplank. And they tried again.

The plank touched the shore of the moss maidens' island, and in seconds the maidens leaped onto it and skimmed across. They seemed to have no weight at all. The gangplank didn't even tremble under their mad rush. Bee saw the tall maiden run up to a lofty tree whose green-yellow leaves exactly matched her gown. She spread her arms wide, and it almost appeared that the tree did the same. There was a moment when both tree and maiden wavered in the sunlight, and then the moss maiden disappeared, simply vanished, into the tree's embrace.

All around them, trees and maidens reached for each other. A golden-haired maiden hugged a tree with big golden blossoms on its branches, and a maiden with bright red hair clasped one with red berries drooping from it. The tree with the papery white bark that Bee had noticed the day before attracted an older maiden, her face lined but still lovely. As they merged, her hair, pale as a sheep's fleece, fused with the bark. Bee thought she could almost see the face of the maiden in the whorls and knotholes of the tree's trunk. A tall maiden with nut-brown skin and red lips ran past, and Bee knew that she was headed for the nutmeg tree that had held King Crispin chained for so many years.

The look of joy on the maidens' faces as they met their long-lost trees after years of separation was lovely to see, and almost without thinking, Bee reached for Bartholomew's hand. He took hers without speaking, and they watched in delight until the moss maidens had all disappeared—all but Ying-tao. Her beautiful face showed gladness and sorrow in equal measure. Bee's heart ached for her.

"Now," Anika said at last, "we can return to Aradyn. We can take Master Joris to task, and Papa can regain his throne."

"But . . . the trees!" Bee protested. "We can't leave them here, on this island. We must bring them back too!"

Haleem cleared his throat and wiped his eyes. He had obviously been very moved by the reunion of maidens and trees. "Nay, we can't pull this island. It's far too heavy with all the trees. I can't see how we could get them back."

Bee and the others looked at the ship bobbing in the sea in front of them, and then turned to gaze at the trees behind them. Their branches seemed to dance in the breeze, celebrating the reunion with their maidens. The king shook his head slowly, and Bee felt her heart sink. She had no idea what to do.

CHAPTER 18

Thoralf and Haleem rowed everyone back to the ship—everyone but Ying-tao, who insisted on remaining on the island with her sisters and the trees until their return to Aradyn. On board, they explained the problem of transporting the isle of trees to Captain Zay, who pursed her lips and shrugged. She had no solution either. She called a meeting in her cabin after supper, and in the meantime, Bee went down to the galley. Her fingers itched to sink into flour and butter.

With the pocketful of nuts and spices she'd collected on the island, she whipped up a batch of cookies, studded with walnuts and flavored with cinnamon bark and the nutmeg that she grated from one of the brown and red nuts that had fallen beneath the king's tree. As she baked, she tried to open her mind and let her imagination range, and she said, over and over, "We will find a way. We *will* find a way!" The cookies would be filled with ingenuity and determination—she hoped.

After a meal of stewed meat, which the king and Anika took with the captain, Bee distributed the cookies to the grateful crew, and then took a plateful to the cabin. Wil and Bartholomew joined her there, and once again they sat around the captain's table. Now the king sat in Captain Zay's big chair, which Bee could tell annoyed her a bit. But the captain took a cookie, as did the others, and chewed with pleasure.

"So," said the captain, reaching for a second. "Now the trees all 'ave their spirits as they should. But our king is saying this is not enough and we must bring these trees to land. What way are we to be doing this thing?"

There was a long, somber pause. Then Bartholomew cleared his throat. "I might have an idea," he said.

"What?" Bee asked him, passing him another cookie. He took it and chewed pensively.

"The island is not thick, and the trees' roots are deep, some of them. Perhaps the trees could sink their roots through the island to the sea and use the roots as oars, if the moss maidens so instructed them. They could row us across the water."

"What a spectacular concept!" Anika exclaimed.

"But the seawater . . . ," Wil said. "Wouldn't the salt kill the trees?"

"The moss maidens would have to tell the trees not to drink,"

Bartholomew said. "I think it could be done."

"It's the craziest thing I ever heard," Bee said. "Bartholomew, you're a genius!"

"Only if it works," Bartholomew said modestly. He took another bite of cookie and seemed to grow more certain. Bee smiled to herself.

"When the day returns, then, 'edge wizard, we will be seeing what takes place," Captain Zay proclaimed.

They bade the captain good night and went down to the sleeping chamber. King Crispin had refused Captain Zay's half-hearted offer of her own cabin for the night. He looked at the hammocks dubiously, but with a boost from Bartholomew—after the hedge wizard begged the king's pardon—he managed to settle himself without flipping back out onto the floor. The others clambered into hammocks, and some of the pirates joined them, leaving the night crew to guard the ship.

Bee was up early, making johnnycakes infused with confidence and good cheer for all. Limmo bemoaned the lack of maple syrup for the cakes, and then had to explain to Bee how the maple trees could be tapped in spring to produce a thin syrup that tasted, he said, "like sunshine transformed into sweetness."

"Why, Limmo!" Bee said. "How very poetic!" She filed

the information away for later. If they could bring the maple trees back to Aradyn, she'd be out among them with a bucket at the first sign of spring.

Haleem rowed them back to the island after breakfast, and they met Ying-tao on the shore, where she waited anxiously. Bartholomew explained his idea to her, and she nodded slowly. "It could be done," she said. "I will tell the maidens, and they will ensure that the trees do not drink." She wafted into the forest and was soon out of sight. It wasn't long before she reappeared.

"Can the trees reach the water with their roots?" the king asked her.

"Some of them can," she said in her windlike voice. "The juniper, acacia, and eucalyptus. The black walnut and white oak and the shepherd's tree. They are ready to try. But you must get off the island, for any extra weight will make it heavier and harder to move."

Haleem said, "We'll go back to the ship then. When we set sail, have the trees . . . row? Paddle . . . ? Have the trees follow us."

Ying-tao nodded, and the rest went back to the shore, climbed into the dinghy, and rowed back to the ship. On board Captain Zay roared, "Anchors aweigh! Set sail!" A flurry of activity commenced, and before long the sails filled with wind and the ship leaped over the waves. Bee, Anika, Wil, Bartholomew, and the king stood in the stern and watched the island hopefully. It was hard to tell at first, but after a few minutes it became clear that the floating land was indeed moving. Not fast, but steadily, it followed behind the ship. The trees with the biggest, thickest leaves seemed to angle themselves so their leaves caught the wind, filling and fluttering like the *Egg-Hen*'s sails.

"Oh, Bartholomew, it's working!" Bee clapped her hands, thrilled.

It was a very odd thing, sailing along with an island gliding behind. They moved slowly to the east, checking constantly to make sure the isle of trees followed. As the afternoon drew on, though, the wind picked up, and thunderclouds began to build over the water.

"'Tis another autumn storm, I fear," Haleem told Bee as he struggled with the wheel. "'Twill be a trick not to be blown off course."

The waves grew choppy, rocking the ship, and then bigger still. The *Egg-Hen* climbed each one and fell again, the island doing the same. Seawater washed over the railings of the ship and onto the island.

The captain ordered them below, and they sloshed

across the deck and down the stairs. In the hold, the ship creaked ominously. Bee went into the kitchen, hoping to bake, but Limmo wouldn't risk an open flame with the wild rocking of the vessel, so they huddled together in the sleeping room, watching the hammocks wave above them. They could hear the crew shouting various incomprehensible things on deck—"Slack windward brace and sheet!", "Square the sail!", "Make all!", and, most fearsome, "Bail! Bail!" Up, up, up the ship climbed, and then rushed down so steeply that all five slid across the room, tangling legs and arms together as they slammed into the far wall. They had only just managed to straighten out when the *Egg-Hen* tilted downward again, and again they skidded into the other wall.

"Oh, I yearn for solid ground!" Anika moaned. She was an unnatural greenish color. She stroked Pepin, who let out little gasps and wheezes that made it clear he wasn't happy. Bee was queasy too, and the others didn't look at all healthy. As severe as the storm was, though, it passed quickly. Before darkness fell the sea had settled, and they made their shaky way up the stairs to the deck, gulping the fresh air thankfully.

The pirates were busy, swabbing away the seawater, tightening the sheets, and repairing broken lines. Bee,

Anika, and Wil ran to the stern. To their great relief, the island still floated behind them. Now, though, there was less land on it. The trees were at the edge of the soil, and their roots were visible, clutching the land as a child would grip a favorite toy that it feared losing.

"Another storm, and those trees will fall," Wil said.

"Haleem!" Bee called. "How close are we to land?"

The first mate, drenched and strained with exhaustion, shouted back, "Look yonder!" He pointed just south of due east.

There, in the distance, was a dim shape, low and dark and steady on the horizon. A haze of smoke from kitchen hearths clearly showed where Zeewal lay, and Bee could just make out the tall outline of the palace towers off to the side of the town.

It was Zeewal. Home.

CHAPTER 19

"We shall wait for the darkness," Captain Zay proclaimed. Nobody argued. The thought of landing at the mouth of the canal, where ships of all kinds clustered to offload their cargo and large crowds often gathered, was to nobody's liking. What would people think of a pirate ship and a floating island covered with trees? Master Joris would hear about it in no time, and he'd send his palace guards to investigate, Bee was sure. That is, if he didn't already know.

"Do mages see things that are happening? Or see the future?" she asked Bartholomew.

"Are you asking if Master Joris knows we are here?"

"Well, yes."

"I am not certain. They cannot see the future, but sometimes they can see things that happen elsewhere. It depends on whether or not they are looking. It takes a lot of energy to look that hard. And we are on the sea still, so my guess is that Joris is not aware of our presence."

"Good." That made Bee feel somewhat better. She went

down to the galley to help Limmo with supper. She knew the next few hours would be crucial, and she whipped up batch after batch of cookies, adding this nut and that spice, this flavoring and that feeling, until she felt she had done as much as she could. The cookies she'd baked with courage she handed out to the crew. In addition, she gave each a little packet of scones that she'd infused with love of Aradyn. That had been a challenge, since she'd felt no love for her kingdom for all the years she'd been fostered in Boomkin. But she thought of Zeewal as she baked, the tidy town with its clean streets and friendly people, and she thought longingly of Master Bouts and his broad smile and halo of white hair. She knew now that she loved the town, and she loved the baker. She hoped those feelings would translate into something more general to the pirates who ate the cookies, who might not know Zeewal or Master Bouts, but who surely knew love.

As darkness fell, the pirates lowered the dinghy, and in groups they rowed to land. Then Bee, Wil, Anika, the king, and Bartholomew rowed with Haleem to the island and called softly for Ying-tao. She came to the ragged edge of the isle to meet them.

"Ying-tao, can the trees not bring the isle closer to land?" King Crispin asked her.

"Nay, Your Majesty. The mainland repels the floating island, as the floating island repelled the moss maidens' isle."

"Like magnets with their north or south sides facing each other," Wil mused.

Bee stared at him. "What do you mean?"

"In the forge, we keep the little ones busy with magnets. Lodestones, you know?"

Bee shook her head.

"The lodestone attracts iron, so if you carry it around the forge, all the iron shavings will stick to it. Or it can stick itself to the metal tools. But if you rub lodestone on an iron pin, you can make the pin itself into a magnet. If you make two of them, they'll repel each other. You can't make them come together no matter what." Bee's blank gaze showed that she had no idea what he was talking about. He shrugged. "It's fun, if you're five years old. But . . ." His voice trailed off.

"What?" Bee prompted him.

"If I'm right about the magnets . . . well, every magnet has a north and a south. The north will attract another magnet's south, and will repel any magnet's north. If the land is repelling the island, perhaps if we turn it, north to south, it will attract instead."

247

"Turn the island?" Bee found this nearly incomprehensible.

"Exactly."

"And how do we do that?"

Wil looked at Bartholomew. "Can you do it?" he asked the hedge wizard.

"Oh, dear me," Bartholomew said anxiously. "I don't think so. I haven't that power."

"Of course you do!" Bee exclaimed. "You trained with the mages for years!" She hoped she was right.

"Well," Bartholomew mused, "I have indeed spent many years among the mages. They are old, it is true, and infirm, and have lost their vigor. But I've watched and learned. They have much to teach. And I have my own small magic."

King Crispin looked thoughtful. "Is it not true that a hedge wizard or witch can become a mage? I had heard that was how it was done. The mages age and retire. Someone must take their place."

Bartholomew flushed. "I am not saying I have the power of a mage, Your Majesty. Indeed not! But like the mages, we hedge wizards work with the land and its creatures. And what is this island but land?"

"Then you think you can do it?" the king asked.

"I can but try," Bartholomew said. "But if it goes |wrong . . . well. Your Majesty, you and the princess should stay in the dinghy. Just in case. And Bee."

"I will not!" Bee said indignantly.

"Papa and I will go," Anika said. "But Bee should stay with you, Master Bartholomew."

Bartholomew looked worried, but he nodded. "If that's what you want, Bee."

"It's what I want." Bee's voice was firm.

Wil went with the king and Anika. As he climbed into the boat, he said, "We'll be right off the island. Be careful. Keep an eye on Bartholomew!"

They rowed a little way out and then turned the dinghy. In the light of the gibbous moon, Bee could see them clearly. She waved, and Anika waved back. On the island, Bartholomew began his preparations. He bent and dug his hands down into the soil and then straightened up again, brushing off the dirt. He flapped his arms and mumbled some words. Then he traced a circle in the air, and another, and another. Bee kept her eyes on the dinghy. Slowly, it began to move to her left. No—it wasn't the dinghy that was moving. It was the island. It was rotating clockwise.

"I think it's working," Bee said.

Encouraged, Bartholomew made still more circles in the air, faster and faster. And the island revolved more quickly. In a moment the dinghy was out of sight, and Bee could see only the horizon.

"Good!" she cried. But Bartholomew was only getting started. Before Bee could advise him to stop, he whirled his whole body in a circle. The island spun with him. Faster and faster it twirled. There was the dinghy again, and then it was gone. There the horizon, there the land, there the dinghy. Bee began to feel woozy.

"Enough," she managed. The island speeded up. There was a carousel in a park in Zeewal that Bee had spent an hour watching once. She'd never ridden a carousel, and she'd wondered what would happen if it were ever to spin out of control. Now she knew. The force of the rotation made her feel as if she were about to fly off, and she grabbed a tree trunk. She couldn't look out to sea anymore; the twirling landscape would make her sick. She tried to cry out, "Stop!" but her mouth was pushed into a grimace by the intensity of the island's spin. No words could escape. Her feet lifted from the ground, and only her desperate grip on the tree kept her from being tossed into the air.

Bartholomew, in the grip of his own power, was completely oblivious to what was happening around him.

He didn't bother to hold on, and that was what ended it. The centrifugal force picked him up bodily and threw him off the island, and he landed with a great splash in the sea. The turning slowed, and finally with a sound like the gnashing of gears, it stopped.

Bee slumped to the ground. Her head still spun, and she had to gulp air wildly to keep from retching. When she could look up again, she saw that Haleem had rowed around the island and picked up Bartholomew. Quickly he maneuvered the dinghy to shore, and Wil leaped out onto the strand.

"I told you to watch him!" Wil cried, running over to Bee and helping her to stand. She breathed deeply, calming her stomach, which still roiled.

"He's a little hard to control," she managed.

"Well, he did it, I think," Wil said. "The other side of the island is facing Aradyn now. Come on." He led her through the trees to the far side of the isle. Aradyn was close now—but was it closer than before?

"The island is moving," Bee said, amazed. And so it was. Inch by inch, it crept toward the land, pulled by the same magnetic force that had pushed it away when it was turned. There were twenty feet between the two, then six feet, then three feet, and then—

"Stand back!" Wil shouted, pushing Bee backward so she stumbled. The mainland and island came together with an enormous crash, buckling the soil where they'd stood a moment before and throwing Bee and Wil to the ground. The trees around them shuddered with the impact.

The others joined Wil and Bee at the seam where island met mainland, and they stepped onto Aradyn's soil. Bartholomew, dripping and embarrassed, began to apologize, but Bee cut him off.

"I'm fine," she assured him. "You did very well. A little too well, maybe, but it worked."

Ying-tao joined them. "I will tell the trees to go," she said. "They will be so glad to be home at last."

"We need them on the coast, and along the canals," Wil said. "That's where the land is eroding."

"They will go where they are needed," Ying-tao said. She disappeared among the trees, and before long they began to shift.

"Look," Anika whispered. She pointed to a great oak, the tree nearest the mainland. When Bee stared straight at it, it didn't seem to be moving, but if she took her eyes away and then looked back, it was clear that the tree had advanced. There was a pause when the oak reached the seam between the island and Aradyn, and they held their breaths. And then—how, no one could say—the oak was on the mainland. After it came a maple tree, with brilliant red leaves, and a group of smaller trees. "Fruit trees," Bartholomew said. "Pear, I think and peach. Maybe apple?" By the time they had reached the mainland, the oak had disappeared.

"Where did it go?" Bee asked, and Bartholomew shrugged.

"Where it is needed, I suppose," he said, echoing Ying-tao's words.

"But the land is filled with tulips," Bee said. "Is there room for the trees?"

"The trees will sink their roots where they wish, and the tulips will die, or they will live." Bartholomew smiled at Bee. "One life form succeeds, another fails. It is the way of nature."

The crew and Captain Zay joined them, and they watched wordlessly as the trees left the island and moved away in the darkness. It was a strange progression, a cross between a stately dance and the march of an army. As the last tree moved in its imperceptible drift from island to mainland, Anika gripped Bee's arm.

"What is that?" she hissed. Bee turned to see a line

of flickering lights moving toward them, down the canal from Zeewal.

"Men, prepare for battle," the captain said in a low voice. The pirates spread out, moving in front of the king and Anika. They unsheathed their swords. The moon had set, and now there was only starlight to see by. Bee couldn't make out what the lights were. She imagined a legion of soldiers sent by Master Joris, a terrible magical force that would surround and destroy them.

Then Wil cried out, "Da!" He ran forward, stumbling a bit in the dimness. The person carrying the first light—for it was a person, not a magical creature—held it high, and Bee recognized the blacksmith. Behind him was Master Bouts with his own lamp, and the cooper, the tanner, the seamstress. In the glow of the lanterns, Bee could even make out Mistress de Vos, her permanent scowl firmly in place. The whole town, it appeared, had come down the canal to them.

"Wil!" Master Weatherwax put down his lantern and threw his beefy arms around his son. Mistress Weatherwax and the older children crowded around them. "We'd hoped it was you—that this strangeness had something to do with you. Oh, son, you were gone so long—we feared for your life!"

"Stand down, men," Captain Zay advised the pirates. They sheathed their swords.

"Strangeness?" Wil said, thumping his brother Geert on the back. "What strangeness?"

"The plants. Someone came running from the canal shouting that huge plants had rooted along its banks, and everyone came out to see. And it is true, son! It's remarkable. Plants far taller than any man, all along the water. Dozens of them!"

"Yes," Wil acknowledged with some pride. "They're trees. We brought them."

"In one night?" Mistress de Vos asked skeptically. "All those plants? Don't be absurd."

"It's . . . it's hard to explain," Wil said.

"Bee, my girl!" Master Bouts had finally made his way to the front of the group. He lifted Bee and twirled her around. It reminded her stomach a little too much of the spinning island, and when he set her on her feet she stumbled and sat down hard. Bartholomew knelt beside her.

"Are you all right?" His face was anxious.

"I'm fine—a little dizzy. From the island." Bartholomew grimaced, and Bee laughed as he helped her to her feet.

"And who is this?" Master Bouts asked, looking uncertainly from Bee to Bartholomew.

Bee hesitated. "This is Bartholomew—Master Bartholomew," she said. "He is a hedge wizard."

"Ah," Master Bouts said. "Very pleased to meet you. Have you aided my girl in her quest to find the mages?"

My girl. The words confused Bartholomew, and he stammered, "I—I—well, yes. I suppose I did."

"Bartholomew is my father, Master Bouts," Bee said. In the lantern's glow, she saw Master Bouts's eyes widen. Again he looked at Bee, then at Bartholomew.

"I see," he said at last. "Yes, there is a family resemblance—"

A sudden shout cut him off. "The king! Look, it is the king!" The pirates had moved aside, and now King Crispin and Anika were visible in the light from the lanterns. Though no one had seen the king for a dozen years, his people recognized him.

The crowd hushed, and those in front went down on one knee. Others followed, like a wave, until at last everyone knelt, Bee and Master Bouts and Bartholomew among them. King Crispin stood before them, illuminated by the glow of a dozen lanterns. He looked very little like a king ought to look. There was no crown on his head; he was whisper-thin, his beard ragged, his borrowed pirate clothes hanging off him. Like his daughter, though, he held himself tall and straight, and while Bee knew his leg hurt him, he didn't flinch under the gaze of the hundred or more of his subjects.

"Oh, my people," he said. His voice wavered in a way his body did not. "My people!" he repeated, more strongly. But he could not go on.

"Long live the king!" Wil shouted, and the throng took up the cry. "Long live the king!" echoed through the night until the very air rang with it. Cheering, the people got to their feet.

"Oh, Bee!" Anika clutched her arm. "They remember him—they love him!"

"Of course they do," Bartholomew said. "He's their king."

The crowd quieted, and the king was able to speak again.

"I have been imprisoned all these long years," he said. "Imprisoned with the trees of Aradyn—the trees that Master Joris removed so long ago. And now we are back, I and the trees. They will bring us great bounty, and they will secure the land that has washed away under the assault of the autumn storms."

Bee could see those listening turn to one another, confused, whispering. Then one man spoke up.

"But what of the tulip fields? My great-grandda told me that the trees went to make room for the tulips. And the tulips are our wealth."

"The tulips are Master Joris's wealth, not ours," the king replied. "The small fields that the tulip farmers of Aradyn tend will remain in their hands. We will still sell the bulbs. But Master Joris's vast fields will grow wheat and vegetables—and trees. There will be food for all."

The throng was silent, taking this in. And then there came a voice that Bee knew well.

"No, Your Majesty. You are mistaken. The fields will grow tulips, as they always have. And the people of Zeewal will prosper."

People looked around to see who had spoken. From the back of the crowd, a tall figure emerged. On either side of him, folk pressed back to make way, giving him a clear path as he strode toward King Crispin, sparks snapping behind his heels. Wil's father held his lantern high, illuminating the sharp features, the dark hair with its streak of white. Many in the gathering gasped, and one woman cried out, as Master Joris reached the king and halted, his dark robes swirling around him.

CHAPTER 20

"'Tis the mage!" A murmur arose from the crowd. King Crispin and Master Joris faced each other. The king seemed even more fragile beside the mage, who towered over him. But he spoke strongly.

"You kept me prisoner for a dozen years, Joris," he said. "But I have returned to claim my throne and protect my daughter and my kingdom. Step down." It was a clear command.

Master Joris's oily smile was visible in the lamplight, though clouds now covered the stars. "Kept you a prisoner?" he said in a tone of disbelief. "I? Why, Your Majesty, if you have been lost to us it is no fault of mine. And no one is more overjoyed than I to see you restored." Bee and Anika exchanged a glance.

"What a liar!" Bee whispered. Anika hushed her, but it was too late. Master Joris's gaze fell on her, and his caterpillar eyebrows drew together. On either side of her,

Master Bouts and Bartholomew moved close.

As if announcing Master Joris's anger, a clap of thunder sounded, so near that it was deafening. Lightning flashed, and in its brief glare the mage seemed to grow still taller and more menacing. The shadow he cast in the lamplight expanded along the ground behind him, shrouding onlookers who scrambled to get out of its way.

As he lengthened, the mage spoke. His gravelly voice was nearly as loud as the thunder, and people cowered before it. "You have brought back the trees, but they will not thrive. They will die, all of them, and their moss maidens with them. And then only my tulips will remain. My tulips. *Mine!*"

A sudden gust of wind blew dust and sand into listeners' eyes, and they covered their faces with their hands. And then the storm hit, opening the skies in a torrential downpour. Another flash of lightning lit the night, and Bee could see that the space where Master Joris had stood was empty, as if he'd never been there at all. Someone screamed, and people began pushing and shoving, trying to get back on the road that led to Zeewal.

"Where did he go?" Anika cried.

"He is probably gone back to the palace to plan his next move," King Crispin said, his arm around his daughter.

"He was ever a deliberate, crafty creature."

Wil's father called out, "Son! Gather your people and follow me!" He held his lantern high, but the wet wind blew it out, and most of the other lamps as well. The darkness was nearly absolute but for the momentary brilliant strokes of lightning. Bee could hear people shouting in the distance as the citizens of Zeewal ran wildly back toward town. Someone—was it Anika?—held one of her hands, someone else—Bartholomew?—the other. They scrambled and slipped onto the muddy road and ran with the others.

"I thought—" Bee managed as she ran, "I thought mages couldn't control the weather."

"They cannot," Bartholomew answered through gasps of breath. "It is another autumn storm—well timed!"

As they reached Zeewal, the sky began to lighten a bit in the east. Day was coming at last. People streamed through the town gates, heading for their dry homes and safety. Bee turned back to look at the road they had come up and the canal it bordered. In the gray half-light, through the pouring rain, she could see a line of trees that stretched from the town to the coast, all along the canal. The trees looked as if they had always been there. They bent in the gale's wind, but they stood stolidly as the storm surge battered the banks of the canal. The trees were holding back the water.

"Come on!" It was Wil, just ahead of them. The king flanked him, and the pirates surrounded them. "To my house!" Together they clattered down the cobblestones of the high street and turned off onto the street that held the blacksmith's shop. Wil's parents were already there. They ushered their guests inside and then slammed the door on the storm, its growls of thunder receding into the distance.

"Is Master Joris following us?" Bee gasped, peering out the diamond of glass set in the front door. She could see the last stragglers racing toward their homes, but there was no sign of the mage.

"He went," Captain Zay said. "Pfft! Just like that. Mages!" She shook her head in disapproval.

"Bring towels!" Mistress Weatherwax cried, and Wil's sister Sanna, still dripping herself, emerged with an armful of soft towels and handed them around. "Get dry clothes, children!" They ran to obey.

Anika and Bee followed Sanna into her bedchamber, and Sanna found them clean, dry dresses as Wil's other sisters watched, wide eyed. When they were dressed, Anika tried to force a comb through her tangled curls, and Sanna came forward shyly, saying, "May I help you, Your Highness?" She took the comb from Anika and began to work it carefully through her hair.

"You see the virtue of short hair," Bee said, fluffing her own spiky mop with her hands.

Anika winced as the comb pulled. "Perhaps I'll cut mine off as well," she agreed.

"Oh no, Your Highness!" Sanna protested. "Your hair is lovely. I will have it untangled in a jiffy."

They went back downstairs when they were dry and combed. The main hall was filled to bursting. Pirates stood before the fire, their wet clothes steaming. King Crispin, dressed now in the blacksmith's Sunday best, sat in Master Weatherwax's cushioned armchair. His leg was bandaged, the wrappings showing below the leg of the blacksmith's too-wide trousers. Mistress Weatherwax wove through the crowd handing out hot drinks, and the littlest Weatherwaxes sat together in a corner playing with Pepin the hedgehog, squealing with delight as he rolled and unrolled himself.

Bee saw Ying-tao for a moment amid the crush, sad that she couldn't yet reunite with her cherry tree. It would be too dangerous for the moss maiden to go to the palace where Master Joris raged and plotted.

"A toddy!" Captain Zay said, pleased, as she took a cup from Mistress Weatherwax. She gulped, then frowned.

"Sorry, Captain, but we've no rum," Mistress Weatherwax said. She didn't sound especially sorry.

"Not to worry, goodly madam! I carry my own at all times." The captain pulled out a silver flask and poured a generous amount into her mug, and then did the same for her men. Even the king held out his mug.

Master Bouts took Bee aside as she came down the stairs.

"I must get back to the bakery, Bee," he said. "The sourdough will have risen far too much already. And my dry clothes are there."

"I'll go too," Bee said immediately. Bartholomew, standing near, turned his head to listen.

"Nay, child," the baker said. "I saw the way Master Joris looked at you. Even in the dark, I could tell he wasn't pleased—and he knows well where you work. I think you'd best stay away from the shop for a little bit."

"But . . . I need to bake," Bee protested.

"You do not. You need to rest. How long since you've had a night's sleep? Stay here, where you'll be out of Joris's way. Come to me in the afternoon—but come carefully. Be sure you're not watched." Master Bouts was firm. And he was right, Bee had to admit. She was exhausted.

"All right," she said reluctantly, and saw the baker to the door.

Captain Zay stood nearby, sipping from her mug. Master Bouts bowed to her, and she inclined her head. She had removed her tricorn hat, and her dark curls spilled over her shoulders. Her color was high. Bee thought at first that her flushed cheeks were the result of the sprint through the storm—or the rum—but then she realized that Master Bouts and the captain were both a bit red in the face. They stood gazing at each other for a moment. Captain Zay's mouth opened in a little O.

"Captain, this is Master Bouts," Bee said, looking from one to the other in some confusion. "He is the inventor of the Bouts Buns that you like so much. And this is Captain Zay, who saved us from drowning . . . several times."

"Madam," Master Bouts croaked. He cleared his throat. "Much obliged to you, madam. Don't know what I would do without Bee."

Captain Zay closed her mouth and then opened it again. Bee began to smile.

"Those bun," the captain managed, then started over. "Those bun are quite the delectable taste. All praise to you, Master Baker!"

Master Bouts turned even redder and bowed again. He fumbled with the door and finally opened it, bobbing his head all the while like a portly shore bird in search of clams. As he stepped out, he looked both ways quickly, to be sure he was not observed, and then disappeared around the corner onto the high street as Bee closed the door behind him.

"I am very much liking a man that is substantial in figure," Captain Zay said thoughtfully to Bee. Then she joined the rest of the pirates near the fire, taking the best spot beside the hearth.

After a spirited argument with the Weatherwaxes, who wanted King Crispin to rest in their bedchamber, the king agreed to sleep in the boys' room. Anika saw him settled and then came back downstairs, meeting Wil on the steps. Bee noticed how he took her hands and spoke quietly to her—and Mistress Weatherwax, with her sharp eyes, saw it as well.

"Sanna, show the princess to the girls' room," she commanded. Anika protested, but there was no arguing with Wil's mother. Her word was law.

There was barely a free square foot in the Weatherwaxes' main hall. Already most of the pirates were snoring. Mistress Weatherwax handed out blankets, and Bee took one gratefully and wrapped herself it in, sliding down to the floor with a yawn. Bartholomew lowered himself next to her.

"That was your . . . employer?" he asked. "The baker?"

"Yes," Bee said. "But he is more than an employer. I had no home, and he took me in. He's taught me everything I know—how to bake, but so much more than that."

"I am so very sorry, Bee, that I never looked for you." Bartholomew's voice was pained. "I had no idea. There was never any hint that you had survived the shipwreck. If I had thought even for a moment—"

"I know," Bee said quickly. "It doesn't bear talking about. I'm just glad you're here now."

"And I am glad you had someone to care for you. He sounds like a good man," Bartholomew said.

"A very good man. The best of men. He is my friend."

"I hope he will be my friend too, in that case." Bartholomew was silent a moment. "Bee," he said then, "will you tell me what it was like—your life? Not now, but . . . sometime?"

Bee winced. She tried never to think about those years, much less talk about them. "Sometime," she agreed. She closed her eyes.

"Here, use my blanket for a pillow," Bartholomew

urged her. He wouldn't let her refuse, but folded his blanket and placed it under Bee's head. A moment later she was asleep.

In Bee's dream, the wind blew so hard that branches of huge trees were knocking together, and the trees themselves wept in pain and toppled to the ground, one after another. She woke bathed in sweat, her breath coming fast and panicky. The knocking of branches kept on even after her eyes opened, and it took her a moment to realize someone was hammering at the door. She was closest to the entryway, and she got blearily to her feet and opened the door.

It was broad daylight outside, the sky washed clean by the storm, the air fresh and autumn-crisp. Master Knockert, the tanner, stood there, his weathered face worried. Bee tried not to breathe too deeply; the tanner always smelled strongly of his trade.

"Mistress Bee," he said, "they chose me to come. And they told me you were here. Everyone said I should come to you and tell you." Then he stopped.

"Tell me what?" Bee said, impatient and annoyed at having been awakened.

"It's the trees—the trees!"

Ying-tao materialized at the doorway as if summoned

by the tanner's words.

"What about the trees?" she asked in her shimmery half whisper. "What is wrong with the trees?" The others in the room sat up, rubbing eyes and stretching stiff limbs.

"They are sick, every last one of them," Master Knockert cried. "The trees are dying!"

CHAPTER 21

"What do you mean?" Bee asked. "Did the storm knock them down?" Her dream was still fresh in her mind.

"It's not that," Master Knockert said. "I do not know what ails them. The children noticed first, early this morning. And we've all gone to look. It's true. Suddenly their leaves are falling, their branches droop. They are like humans who've been stricken with some terrible illness."

"I must go to them!" Ying-tao murmured. She slipped through the door and was gone. The tanner, fearful, followed her, leaving his ripe odor behind.

By now the pirates had crowded around Bee. Captain Zay clapped her hat on her head and pulled her sword from its scabbard.

"We shall storm that palace!" she cried. "It is an injustice to be damaging those trees when we 'ave gone to such great lengths to save them!" Her men shouted in agreement and unsheathed their own swords.

"Gentlemen—Captain!" Mistress Weatherwax spoke sternly from the stairs. "Put those weapons away. There are children here!" The little Weatherwaxes stood behind her, eyes wide with fearful excitement at the sight of the swords.

Shamefaced, the pirates sheathed their swords again. The Weatherwaxes clattered down the steps, and behind them came the king and Anika, faces creased from sleep. Bee ran to Anika and told her what the tanner had said.

"Oh, Bee!" Anika gasped, horrified.

"Your Majesty," Mistress Weatherwax said, "I will make tea. There is bread and honey. Break your fast and then we can think on what must be done." Again, no one argued. The king sat at the long table, Anika at his right, and the others crowded round, taking cups and glasses of fragrant tea and slices of buttered bread that Bee recognized as Master Bouts's own. But Bee couldn't eat. She got up from the table and stared out the diamond-shaped window in the front door as the others ate and drank their tea. Wil and Bartholomew joined her.

"Without the trees, Aradyn will crumble into the sea," Wil said. "We must find a way to save them."

The front door opened, and Ying-tao slipped through. Her usually serene face was twisted with worry. "What did you find?" Bee demanded.

"This." Ying-tao held out her hand. On her pale palm rested a bug. It was about an inch long, shiny black with white spots and white-striped wings. From its head sprouted long, hornlike projectiles. It was unmoving, clearly dead, but it still looked vicious. Sanna peered over Bee's shoulder and gave a little squeal of revulsion.

"What is it?" Bee asked, uneasy. Then she remembered. She had seen this beetle before—in Master Joris's insect collection.

"It is the hemel beetle. It eats away at trees, all kinds. It kills from the inside out. It is in all the trees—every last one."

There was a great silence in the room as everyone gazed at the beetle. Then Bartholomew spoke.

"That must be Master Joris's doing. I am sure of it. The masters on the Isle of Mages—all the mages—are well versed in insect and plant life. It is part of their charge to keep things of the earth in balance. But Master Joris perverts his duty. He is a force for chaos and destruction."

Bee was thinking hard. "The beetles eat trees?" she asked Ying-tao. The moss maiden nodded. "Just the wood part, or the leaves?"

"Any part," Ying-tao said. "They have quickly burrowed

into the trunks and branches, but they are eating the leaves as well."

Bee turned to Wil. "Do you remember when I tested my baking on you?" she asked.

"When you baked fear into your cookies? I do indeed," he replied.

"I tried it on Master Bouts's cat too that week—and on a mouse. And it worked. If it worked on those animals, maybe it would work on bugs as well—if we can get the bugs to eat baked goods." Bee wasn't sure where in the process the magic lay—the mixing of ingredients, or the baking itself. She thought it best to tempt the beetles with what had worked before.

Wil considered this. "We've nothing to lose. What should we do?"

"Pirates!" Bee called out. "You come from all over the world. Tell me—do you know of any dishes baked with leaves?"

There was a general confusion. One of the younger pirates, Filmon, spoke. "In my kingdom, there was a dish, bibingka. It was baked with banana leaves. We did not eat the leaves, though—they are too tough. They held the bibingka."

"That doesn't matter!" Bee said. "Do you know how it was made?"

"More or less," Filmon replied. "I think I can describe it."

"There are banana trees," Ying-tao said. "I have seen them."

"And what else do I need?" Bee asked Filmon.

"Coconut," he said. "I'm pretty sure there is coconut in it."

"I am all bewilderment," Captain Zay said. "What is this you are planning, Bee-girl?"

"You tell her!" Bee instructed Wil. Then to Filmon, she said. "It has sugar in it, doesn't it? What is it exactly?"

"It's like . . . like a muffin," Filmon said uncertainly. "Baked in a banana leaf."

"Good. Butter and flour and sugar, then." Bee took the ingredients and the bowl and spoon Mistress Weatherwax handed her and began to work as Wil explained to the others what happened when Bee baked. As soon as Captain Zay understood, she sent out her men in search of banana leaves and coconut.

"Bananas are yellow!" Filmon called to them as they departed. "Long. Curved, like a scimitar. Coconut, it's like a cannonball, only greenish."

When the pirates were gone, Captain Zay turned to Bee. "You are some more talented than I 'ave known, Bee-girl."

Bee stirred ingredients, her head down.

"You are putting feelings into cookies and baked goods."

Bee said nothing.

"A number of things is explained," the captain mused. "For example, when you 'ave left the ship for the mages' island, you give to me a bun."

Bee kept her attention on her mixing bowl.

"What is in this bun you give to me?" the captain asked pleasantly.

"Ummm . . . ," Bee said, mixing away. "Maybe there was a little bit of . . . truthfulness." She stared very hard at the bowl of ingredients as she stirred. The captain was quiet for so long, though, that she finally had to look up.

Captain Zay had sunk into a chair at the table, and her head was in her hands. *She's furious with me!* Bee thought in dismay. Then the captain smacked her palms on the tabletop, making Bee wince.

"Oh, oh, oh, Bee-girl," she gasped, chortling with glee, "so many offensive and tremendously ill-mannered things I 'ave said to my crew after eating that bun! And all of them utterly true!" Her laughter was so contagious that the little Weatherwaxes began to giggle without knowing why.

"What did you say?" Anika asked, her lips twitching.

The captain shook her head. "I am not nor ever 'ave been accused to be a lady, but I will not be repeating those words in front of these good folk and this royalty!" she said, wiping her eyes.

"She told us we were rogues and rapscallions and should go to the devil—but only after she keelhauled us for our dastardly incompetence," said Filmon, grinning. "And that was by far the nicest thing she said. Isn't that right, Captain?"

Even the king was hiding a smile now. The captain flushed and said, "If those words were my words, they were naught but the truth as created by a bun, and none of my fault whatsoever."

The Weatherwax children hooted with joy. They ran through the room shouting, "You go to the devil!" and "I'll keelhaul you, you dastardly!" while Bee murmured, "Sorry," to Mistress Weatherwax who shook her head, trying not to laugh.

Then Bee and Filmon stirred and tasted and stirred some more, making up a huge batch of bibingka. It took longer than Bee had hoped before the pirates began to return, laden with thick green leaves and round coconuts.

"Those trees had gone south, along with the other

tropical sorts," Haleem told her, wiping sweat from his brow. "We had to run miles to find them. They wanted a warmer place, I suppose."

The coconuts were a mystery. They were like rocks. Bee tried to cut one, then hammered it with a meat mallet.

"Give to me," Captain Zay said. She put the coconut on the floor and said, "Stand back, young people, if you place value on your body parts!" She raised her sword and brought it down with a resounding thwack, and the coconut lay in two halves. Beneath its green outer shell it was hairy and brown, and inside it was white as snow. It looked very disagreeable. Bee could hardly imagine that it would taste good, but Filmon gave her a morsel of the tender coconut flesh, and she was convinced.

Filmon showed Bee how to scrape out the coconut and drain the coconut milk, and she added the ingredients to her batter. Then Bee placed the pirates and the Weatherwax children in a line, with the pirates forming rounded cups from the banana leaves and the children filling each cup with batter. At last Bee slid the trays of muffins into Mistress Weatherwax's oven.

"We'll need more," she said, and kept mixing. As soon as one batch came out of the oven, nicely browned and smelling delicious, she popped another batch in. She forced herself to keep her mind free of worry as she worked, and the hard work of stirring the stiff batter helped.

"Take these," she said to the pirates, holding out the bibingkas. "Place one at the foot of each tree."

"Each tree?" Haleem repeated. "But there are hundreds of trees!"

"Then you'll have to work fast," Bee replied, dropping spoonfuls of batter into banana-leaf cups. "Or find someone to help you."

"What have you flavored them with?" Wil asked her, sniffing the muffins with appreciation.

"I thought of the trees as I worked," she said. "How beautiful they were. How precious, and how they are helping the land. I tried to bake in a love of the trees."

"So the beetles are to feel love for the trees?"

Bee shrugged helplessly. It sounded ridiculous. "Yes. And the desire to protect them instead of eat them, I hope. I don't know! I don't know if beetles can feel anything beyond hunger. It was the best I could do."

"Then," Wil said firmly, "it will have to be good enough."

CHAPTER 22

By the time evening fell, Bee was drained. Her hair stood in spikes, sticky with coconut milk. Her face was flour-white, her clothes streaked with dried batter. Anika, who had stayed beside her to measure and mix, was just as grubby. Mistress Weatherwax's kitchen was a disaster, with dirty pots and pans, flour and sugar everywhere. Sanna and her mother had long since given up on keeping up with the mess and had joined the others in placing the banana-leaf muffins at the base of trees.

Bee sprawled in Master Weatherwax's armchair, too tired to move. As the sun set, people began to straggle in, done with the day's work. She looked up as she noticed that those who came in were not just the pirates and the Weatherwaxes. There was the cooper and the weaver, the tavern owner and the shoemaker. Sanna came in with Mistress de Vos, the old lady's starched cap awry, her face flushed. For once the surly woman was almost smiling.

Bee struggled to her feet. "What on earth . . .?" she said.

"The whole town came out!" Sanna exclaimed, taking Bee by the waist and twirling her around. "Everyone who was there last night. And more than that. People from the outer villages came to find out what the trees were, and when we told them, they stayed to help. From miles around! And Ying-tao guided us." Yes, there was the moss maiden in the midst of the throng.

"Did we get to all the trees?" Bee asked her.

"I believe we did." Ying-tao smiled weakly. She, too, looked exhausted. "They stopped moving when they got sick, so none was farther than five miles or so away. I think we managed to find them all. Now we must wait to see if the beetles eat what you have made. And if they take to your magic."

"Where is the nearest tree?" Bee felt a sudden surge of energy.

"One has settled in the square just down the high street," Sanna said. "Ying-tao says it is an oak."

"Come on!" Bee went to the door. Anika, Bartholomew, and the little Weatherwaxes followed behind. Usually at this hour, the street would be nearly empty, everyone home for supper. But now there were people milling about everywhere. Bee could tell they were not all from Zeewal. There were fishermen and their families in their customary thick wool sweaters and high boots, and villagers from places far less prosperous than Zeewal, thin and dressed in ragged clothing. But they all stood and talked together, and their eyes were bright with excitement.

Bee and the others ran down the street to the square. In its center, where on market day booths were set up to sell goods from nearby villages and hamlets, there was now a tree, a tall oak. But it drooped, its leaves in a pile around its trunk. It looked like an old man too weary to hold his body upright.

Bee walked cautiously to the tree. At its base she could see a bibingka in its banana-leaf cup. Only the leaf wasn't green, it was black—black with polka dots. It was swarming with hemel beetles.

"They're eating it!" Bee whispered. She didn't want to startle the beetles, to send them back up the tree trunk. Other people crowded around Bee, but she held them back with outstretched arms.

"And look," Anika said, low. One of the beetles crawled off the bibingka. It started back up the tree trunk, and Bee gave a little moan. Then it turned, its hornlike antennae waving in the air. Bee held her breath as it scuttled off the tree and across the square. It was working!

"Where is it going?" someone asked.

"I thought of the *Egg-Hen* as I baked," Bee told Anika. "I thought about how we were rescued on it, and how nice the hammocks were, and how we liked it. So . . . maybe they're going there."

The beetles were swarming down the tree trunk now. They stopped for a nibble of the bibingka, and then they followed the first beetle across the square and along the high street.

"All those beetles . . . ," Anika said. "All of them descending upon the pirate ship? Oh, Captain Zay is not going to appreciate that."

"We won't tell her unless she asks, will we?"

Anika shook her head. "Indeed we will not!" Behind them, people clapped as the beetles scurried away. Already, the oak looked stronger. A child ran up and cried, "The beetles are leaving the other trees! I stepped on one, and it squished." He looked very pleased with himself.

"You've done well," Bartholomew told Bee, ruffling her sticky hair. "Now you should rest—and bathe."

"I'm going to stop by the bakery first," Bee said. "I want to tell Master Bouts what we've done. I'm sure he's never heard of bibingka!"

She and Bartholomew walked Anika and the children back to the Weatherwaxes, then turned up the high street and headed to the bakery. But something was wrong. The shades were down; the door was locked. A passerby shook her head at Bee and said, "No bread this morning!"

Worried, Bee slid the spare key out from its hiding place on a ledge atop the front door and opened the shop. The tinkling of the bell seemed to echo in the silence. There was no smell of fresh-baked bread or sweet, warm pastries.

"Master Bouts?" Bee called. She and Bartholomew walked cautiously through the shop and into the kitchen. There, bowls of dough overflowed onto the marble counters, risen all night without being punched down. There was spilled flour on the floor, shards of broken pottery underfoot. Floury footprints marched from one end of the room to the other. Kaatje paced along the marble tabletop, mewing piteously.

"Oh no," Bee moaned. "Where is Master Bouts? What's that evil creature done with him?"

Bartholomew picked up pieces of plate and chunks of dough. "Dear me. This does not look good," he said.

"Listen!" Bee said, holding up a hand. She could hear

a gentle tapping at the front door.

"It might not be safe," Bartholomew warned, but Bee ran through the shop to the front door and peered out. Skulking nearby was Master Arjen, the hedge wizard who was Master Bouts's friend. His hood was pushed back and his dark hair stood on end as if he had run his hands through it over and over. Bee's heart leaped to her throat as she opened the door and took in his frantic expression.

"Master Arjen! What's wrong?"

The hedge wizard looked both ways and then slipped into the shop. He stood flapping his hands anxiously. "Oh, Mistress Bee, it's Master Bouts! He's in terrible trouble. The mage's guard has taken him. He sent me to you before the guard hauled him away. He said to tell you what has happened—but truly I don't know what has happened! I only know he is gone."

Bee and Bartholomew stared at each other.

"I don't understand," Bee said, her lips trembling. What would the mage do to Master Bouts?

"Nor do I," Master Arjen said. "I do not know what the mage plans, and I do not care to stay to find out. I have . . . business to take care of elsewhere."

"Wait!" Bartholomew said. "We may need your help!" But Master Arjen flapped his hands in dismay one final time, and Bee could hardly blame him as he pushed back through the door and disappeared down the street, his head swiveling around like an owl's to be sure he wasn't followed.

Bartholomew spoke from behind Bee. "What is that?" He pointed to a piece of paper on the counter.

Bee snatched it up. "It's a note," she said. "It's—oh. Oh no."

Bartholomew took it from her and read aloud. *"The baker will die if you do not bring the king and his daughter to the palace by daybreak tomorrow."* It was signed with Master Joris's name in a strange, spiky hand.

"Die!" Bee cried. "He will kill Master Bouts? What shall we do?"

"We must tell the king," Bartholomew said.

"But . . . but the king will not go. Surely Master Joris plans to exile him again—and Anika as well. Or kill them! King Crispin will never agree to put Anika in danger."

"It is the king's decision to make," Bartholomew said gently.

Bee stamped her foot. "It is not. It is *my* decision. Master Bouts is *my* friend."

Bartholomew's brow furrowed. "What would you do, then?"

Bee tried to think. "If I bring Anika and the king to the palace and I don't tell them it's at Master Joris's command, the mage will free Master Bouts. But . . . he would take them instead. And maybe kill them."

"That's so," Bartholomew said gently.

"But," Bee went on, "if I choose not to send Anika and the king, Master Bouts dies."

"Bee, you cannot make that decision," Bartholomew said in distress. "That is too much to ask of one so young. Give the choice to me. I am your father. Let me take the weight of it." His expression was pleading.

Bee took a deep breath. If Bartholomew chose, it would be easier. Still dreadful, but easier. At least what happened wouldn't be her fault. But then a terrible thought entered her mind. Would Bartholomew make the choice to save the king and Anika and sacrifice Master Bouts because he wanted to be her father—her only father? Because he didn't want to share her with the baker?

Bee was shocked that she'd even thought it. She had no reason to doubt Bartholomew. But it was so hard for her to trust. And why else would he want to do this thing for her?

Bartholomew looked steadily back at her. His face was open and clear. There was nothing in his expression but love, and the pain that such a decision would cause him. She could see that he would take it on for her simply because he loved her.

"Thank you," she told him, gladness and anguish battling in her heart. "Thank you. But you know I must do it myself."

And so Bee made her choice.

CHAPTER 23

In silence, Bee poured a bowl of milk for the hungry Kaatje, and then she and Bartholomew walked back to the Weatherwaxes. Inside, the crowd had dispersed. Only the family, the king and princess, and the pirates remained. A fire burned cheerily on the hearth, and somehow the kitchen had been set to rights.

Anika ran to greet Bee when she entered, but her smile of greeting faded when she saw Bee's grim face. "What is it?" she asked. "Whatever is wrong?"

Bee looked at Bartholomew, and he nodded, taking her hand.

"I have something to show you—you and your father," Bee said. With her free hand, she held out Joris's note to Anika. The gesture felt irreversible, and Bee knew she might be condemning Master Bouts to death with it. She had chosen to allow Anika and her father to decide whether they would save the baker or not. She felt tears start in her eyes, but she forced them back.

Anika read the note, then read it again. She took far longer than she needed to for so few lines. When she looked up at Bee, it was clear that she understood everything.

"I will converse with Papa," she said. "I think I can convince him that we must go."

Bee had to be sure. "If you go, Master Joris may harm you. He may kill you."

"If we do not go, he will kill Master Bouts," Anika said. "I do not believe that Master Joris will maltreat us. You misremember that he was my guardian for a dozen years. All that time, he could have harmed me, but he did not. That must count for something—even with him." Her voice was firm and certain. How she had changed, from the protected princess who had spent most of her life in solitude, to this strong, brave girl!

"I'm sorry," Bee said miserably. Anika gave her a quick hug and shook her head.

"No need," she said, and wove through the room to speak to her father.

Mistress Weatherwax, her face pink with effort, slid an enormous earthen pot into the oven. She called out to Bee.

"Stew enough for all! Do you have strength to make some biscuits?"

Bee sighed. Her arms and shoulders ached from stirring; her mind was tired from focusing on the bibingka. But she pulled a bowl from the cupboard, took the flour and buttermilk Mistress Weatherwax handed her, and began to measure and pour. And while she did, she thought of Anika: how dear she had become, and how she wanted more than anything to keep the princess safe. From her heart to her hands to the biscuit batter, that desire to protect flowed.

The Weatherwaxes, the king and princess, the pirates, Bartholomew, and Bee ate slowly and wearily. Bee and Captain Zay sat next to each other. As the captain tasted her biscuit, she looked thoughtfully at Bee, and Bee shrugged. If it worked, it worked. She could do no more.

After supper, King Crispin stood. When the others tried to stand as well, out of respect, he motioned them to sit.

"Dear friends," he said, leaning a bit on the table to keep the weight off his injured leg. "We are so grateful to you for your generous hospitality, and for your tremendous efforts on behalf of our kingdom."

The king continued, "Master Joris, who was your

mage, has demanded my presence—that of myself and my daughter—at dawn on the morrow at the palace. And we are decided to accede to his demand."

Accede? Bee was puzzled. It was clear where Anika got her formal ways of speech. But Mistress Weatherwax knew what the king meant.

"Oh, Your Majesty, you cannot!" she protested. "Forgive me, but you should not take that child into certain danger."

Anika stood then too, drawing herself up. "I am no child, mistress," she said gently. "I am sixteen, and I am the princess of the realm. I would not countenance my father facing this peril alone, not so soon after reuniting with him."

"But—" Captain Zay burst out.

"Nay, Captain," Anika said. "It will be just we two. You have accomplished enough." The captain scowled and turned away.

Bee bit her lip. "We will make our own plan," she said in a very low voice to the captain. Immediately, Captain Zay's eyes lit up. "Later," Bee added, looking around the table to be sure no one noticed.

The king and Anika climbed the stairs to the bedchambers to get a few hours of rest before they had to meet the mage. As soon as they were gone, Wil, Bartholomew, and Bee huddled with Captain Zay.

"We can't let them go alone," Wil said.

"My mens will protect them," Captain Zay vowed. "Our swords against the mage—he will be as a mewling babe before us!"

Bee shook her head. "No swords. At least—not unless everything else fails." She remembered Wil with his sword on the pirate ship.

"Do you have something in mind?" Wil asked her.

"Only that we be there," Bee said. "Though how we get there undetected—well, I've no ideas about that."

"Leave that to me," Bartholomew said. "Rest now, child. I'll wake you well before dawn."

Bee washed herself wearily at the kitchen sink, glad finally to scrub off the bibingka batter, and went off to a corner to curl up with her blanket. Despite her sore and aching muscles, despite her worry and fear, she was asleep almost before her eyes closed.

It seemed only an instant later when Bee awoke, Bartholomew gently shaking her shoulder. "It is time," he whispered. "The king is getting ready to depart."

Bee saw Wil raise his head from his own corner of the room, and Captain Zay winked at her from her comfortable perch in the armchair. Anika and her father, cloaked and quiet, crept down the stairs a minute later, tiptoeing through the room, over and around the bodies of pirates who pretended to sleep. They opened the front door a crack, letting in damp, cold air, and then they were gone.

Captain Zay sprang up. "Prepare, men!" she commanded in a low voice, and the pirates rose noiselessly. They did not want to wake the other Weatherwaxes, still slumbering upstairs.

Bee and Bartholomew and Wil pulled on their own cloaks, and quickly they and the pirates followed the king and Anika, careful to muffle their steps on the cobblestones. At the canal, the king and princess turned onto the footpath that led to the palace, but the others hung back.

"What is your plan?" Bee hissed to Bartholomew.

"It is already in place," he said. "Look around you at the pirates."

Bee looked, but she saw no pirates, nor Wil either. Instead, the footpath was lined with bushes, and each bush was a different shape and shade of green. Or were they bushes? If she looked very closely, she could see that each shrub had a peculiarity. The prickly holly bush had a branch that dipped low, just as Captain Zay's tricorn hat feather fell over her face. The elderberry shrub had berries just the color of Wil's eyes that seemed to wink at her. She blinked, puzzled, and the pirates and Wil stood before her. She blinked again, and they were bushes. She looked down at her own hands. Blink, they were branches and leaves. Blink, hands and fingers.

"Oh," she said. "That's a good magic!"

Bartholomew beamed at her, pleased. "With luck, if we move carefully, the mage will not notice us approaching," he said.

They moved along the path, a group of mismatched shrubs that inched their way up the canal. The king and Anika hurried ahead of them. At the lake that stood before the palace, they moved clockwise around the water. Bee was surprised to see trees on the banks of the lake. They looked as firmly rooted as if they'd been there forever.

There was no guard in sight. As bushes and shrubs, they passed through the entrance one at a time, into the palace courtyard. Slowly it filled with greenery where before there had been only weedy cobblestones.

When they were all in the courtyard, Bartholomew motioned that the pirates should stay planted where they were. The others crept shrubbily to the palace entrance.

One of the big double doors was just the slightest bit open. Bee stepped forward and pushed as hard as she could with her shoulder. Wil came up behind her and gave the door a shove. Bee tumbled inside.

"Sorry!" Wil mouthed, not making a sound. Bee rubbed her shoulder, now just a shoulder again and not a branch, and scowled at him. She was the only one who had been inside the palace before, so the others followed her as she tiptoed through the maze of corridors with their closed doors and dusty furnishings. The building was utterly silent. Bee knew that the rooms held their noises close, that voices would not carry into the halls unless the doors were open. She tried various doors as she moved past them, but all seemed latched.

Then Bee came to a familiar room—the room with the glassed-in cabinets that held Master Joris's strange assortment of taxidermy. If she remembered right, the big iron doors to the garden were through the rooms that held his collections. She motioned to the others to follow her, pointing to the cabinets so Wil would be sure not to miss the stuffed oddities inside.

Only—there were no oddities inside. The glass cabinets had swung open, and the shelves were empty.

Bee heard a growl behind her, and she spun around.

There, in the corner of the room was the fox, its patchy fur bristling, its teeth bared. She screamed and pushed Wil aside as it lunged for him, and it slid across the floor, its nails scrabbling, and came to a halt against the far wall. The stuffed mole and the mouse ran out from behind a cabinet. Before Bee could knock them away, the mouse had grabbed onto her trouser leg with its little clawed feet. It sank its teeth into her calf, and she screamed again, hopping on one leg and kicking with the other, trying to get the thing off her.

"The birds!" Wil shouted. From perches atop the cabinets and above the tall windows, Master Joris's stuffed birds launched themselves, their feathers molting as they flew, their wings flapping wildly. They tried to peck at Bee's cheeks, her nose, her eyes as she flailed at them.

"Do something!" Bee implored Bartholomew. The hedge wizard caught a rabbit in midflight as it leaped at him, its hind legs kicking furiously. He held it with an outstretched arm as it struggled. Then he spoke a few words. The rabbit sagged in his grip. The other animals simply dropped to the floor. All the life left them, and they were their taxidermy selves again, but no longer in their alert poses. Just badly stuffed, limp and shedding, crumpled as in death.

"That's not his only collection," Bee said to Bartholomew, panting. She wondered if her leg was bleeding where the mouse had bitten her. Could a dead animal bite through skin?

"Dear me," Bartholomew said, dropping the lifeless rabbit with a shudder. "What next?"

Bee tried to remember. "Um . . . bugs?"

She'd barely gotten the words out when a humming, buzzing noise filled her ears. She ducked automatically as an army of flying creatures swooped into the room, diving at the humans and hedge wizard below.

"Ouch!" Wil cried, slapping something on his cheek. A red welt rose up where a wasp had stung him. Flies, bees, hornets, moths, and dragonflies careened off walls and tangled in Bee's hair as she danced frantically around the room, trying to dislodge them. Then she saw what moved across the floor. Ants. Beetles. Worms and centipedes. Grasshoppers, crickets, praying mantises. And, no longer pinned in their case, spiders.

Dozens and dozens of spiders.

Bee shrieked, trying to pull both feet up at once so the spiders wouldn't crawl on her. There were hairy ones and giant beady-eyed ones, spiders as big as her hand, and a phalanx of tiny spiders that ran at her. Her feet tangled together and she fell with a crash onto the ground and then scrambled in a frantic circle, screaming and screaming as she imagined spiders scuttling on her hands and feet, slithering up her arms and legs, wriggling onto her back and neck and in her ears and nose.

"No, no, no, no, no," she moaned, tears dropping on the floor as she tried to get away. She went limp, eyes closed, wheezing with fear. It wasn't until she felt something trickling on her forehead that she opened her eyes again. She writhed convulsively, sure it was the cold legs of a spider.

Her lashes were heavy, and she was freezing cold. Around her she could see nothing but white. It was snowing, snowing hard. It was snow that had tickled her, not spiders' legs. She peered into the distance. Was that a . . . mountain? A snow-covered peak? She stood up, checking her legs for spiders. There were no insects anywhere. There was nothing but snow.

After a few strides through the thick snow, she came up against a sort of wall. It wasn't visible. It was glass, or something like glass, and she could feel that it was curved as she ran her hands up it. She couldn't see anything at all on the other side.

"Hello?" she called, her voice tremulous. Where were

Bartholomew, and Wil? Nobody answered.

She perched, shivering, on a snowy outcropping, trying to figure out where she was. How could this mountainous snowscape exist inside the palace of Aradyn? None of it made any sense. Then she remembered the third collection she'd seen, and what the palace cook, Hadewig, had once told her.

Bugs, rocks, snow globes . . . He'll collect most anything.

It was one of Master Joris's snow globes, somehow grown as big as life. And she was trapped inside.

CHAPTER 24

Bee beat frantically against the glass sides of the sphere until her hands were sore and numb with cold. She pressed her face against the glass, trying to see the others. Were they in globes of their own? The room outside was barely recognizable. The curve of the globe made the nearest wall appear as if it were only a few inches away, while the far wall stretched into the distance for what seemed like miles.

She tried to rock the globe, to knock it over. Maybe if it fell, it would crack and she could get out. But it was firmly planted, and when she threw herself against its sides, she only bruised her shoulders as the snow deepened around her ankles.

Then she heard a series of loud thuds, as if someone were hammering at a door. Right at the spot where she had pressed her face against the globe, an object slammed into the glass from the outside. She threw herself onto the frigid floor. There was another crash, and then a louder one, just above her. A crack appeared in the glass. The next crash shattered the side of the globe, and something whizzed through a hole in the glass, an inch from Bee's head. She crawled over to the object and picked it up. It was a rock, a pinkish-silver stone the size of her fist.

The rocks kept coming, big ones and small ones, all different colors and shapes. The glass showered down over Bee, and she rolled into a ball to try to protect herself from the bombardment of shards and stone. One ricocheting rock hit her in the ribs, and she gasped with the pain of it. Then there was silence.

Bee raised her head cautiously. She could see the room again, its checkerboard tile floor littered with glass, puddles of melting snow, the carcasses of bugs and moth-eaten mammals. She picked her way to the jagged edge of the snow globe and jumped down, slipping on an icy patch. There was Bartholomew, standing at the edge of his own shattered globe. This one had a little snowy cottage in its center. Bee remembered that it had looked very sweet and homey when only a few inches high, sitting on a shelf in the next room. Here, life-sized and dripping water, it appeared considerably more menacing.

Bartholomew shook snow out of his beard and jumped

down. "Dear me. Dear me. Are you all right?" he said.

"A little bruised," Bee admitted, feeling the sore spot on her ribs as she breathed.

"Is that the last of them?"

"The last of . . . ?"

"The collections," Bartholomew said. "Master Joris's collections. It is clear his plan is to use them to stop us from proceeding, don't you agree?"

Bee tried to remember. "These are the only ones I saw," she said. "I didn't actually see the rock collection."

"Using them was his miscalculation," Bartholomew said. "The flying rocks freed us from those infernal globes."

"Where's Wil?" Bee asked suddenly.

"Dear me," Bartholomew said again, faintly. He pointed. There was another snow globe still unbroken, in the corner. It was smaller than Bee would have guessed, having experienced one from within, but still taller than she was. She could see an ice-covered pool deep inside, and sitting on the ground in front of it, hugging his knees and shivering in the snow, was Wil. Bee waved wildly, but Wil didn't notice her. To him, she would probably look as if she were miles away.

"We have to get him out!" There was a rock lying near

her feet, so Bee picked it up and lobbed it at the globe. The rock bounced harmlessly off. She tried again with a bigger rock, but the result was the same.

"Stand aside," Bartholomew said. He began moving his hands in circles, and Bee backed away quickly, remembering the spinning island. Bartholomew clapped his hands together hard, and there was a crash that rattled the walls of the room. Plaster rained down on them from the ceiling, sticking to their wet clothes and hair. A crack appeared in the glass globe, and then fissures spread out from it until the entire orb was webbed with cracks. Wil covered his head with his arms just as the whole structure came tumbling down on him.

"You really must figure out how to control your work," Bee said to Bartholomew as Wil staggered out of the sphere and jumped to the floor.

"What on earth—" Wil started, looking back at the wreck of the globe. But he couldn't figure out what to ask, and Bee had no idea how to explain.

"I'll explain later. Come this way." Bee led them through the broken glass and puddles of water to the huge iron doors, and they pushed through into the palace garden. Now, they faced the hedge maze. Bee started walking, hoping that she could remember the way she'd gone before, but within moments she was completely lost. The maze seemed to have grown taller. Its upper branches overlapped now in a canopy, so the path was not only impossibly twisty, but dark and gloomy. She could hear voices in the distance that she hoped were the king and Anika, but again and again when she tried to head toward the sound, she found herself at a dead end and had to backtrack. They were getting nowhere.

"Maybe I can straighten out the path," Bartholomew suggested.

"Please don't make the whole maze explode," Bee said. She was feeling very tired and cranky and worried about Anika. They could be trapped there for days. They could starve. She hadn't thought to bring anything to eat.

Bartholomew tried a few hand motions and mutterings. The hedge quivered, and some leaves dropped to the ground, but nothing happened.

"I'm afraid that I am not entirely predictable," Bartholomew said apologetically.

Bee sank to the ground, then gave a yelp of pain and leaped up again. "Thorns!" she cried, stooping to look. But it wasn't a thorn that had pierced her backside. It was Pepin, curled in a protective ball.

Had she crushed him? She touched him with a

tentative hand, and he unrolled and waddled off in the direction they'd come from. Bee followed quickly. "Come on!" she said to the others. "Surely he'll go to Anika."

The hedgehog didn't hesitate but led them through the maze as if he were following a map. Every turn he took was exactly the opposite of the one Bee would have chosen. In a few minutes, they emerged into the grassy clearing where Bee had first met Anika. The fountain was silent and empty. In the distance, Bee could see the cherry tree. And there was Anika, her father's arm tight around her, standing before Master Joris. The mage was facing them as they came out of the maze. His face darkened with displeasure.

"Well," Master Joris said, almost spitting the word. Anika turned quickly.

"He found you!" she cried. "Oh, worthy Pepin!" She ran to her hedgehog and stooped to pick him up. Then she looked up at Bee, Wil, and Bartholomew. "You shouldn't have come," she said, but the gladness in her face told Bee otherwise.

"No, indeed, you should not have come," Master Joris agreed. "We have almost reached an arrangement here. The king and princess have decided to leave the kingdom for a time. They will return in the future, we've resolved.

Say, a hundred years or so from now?"

Bee gave a squawk of outrage. "That's ridiculous! People don't live that long!"

The mage raised an eyebrow. "You don't say. But that's precisely the point, my dear. Or are you not as perceptive as you seem? You appear to have some bit of magic yourself, I've noticed. Such delicious pastries you make, all flavored with helpfulness and love." He managed to make the words *helpfulness* and *love* sound like curses. Bee's temper flared.

"Of course they wouldn't work on *you*," Bee said, her face growing red. "You're so full of bile and nastiness and . . . and—"

"Acrimony," Anika suggested.

"Spite," Wil said.

"Rancor," said Bartholomew. They turned to King Crispin.

"Bitterness. Vindictiveness. Malevolence," the king offered. "You are nothing but a vessel of ill will, Joris. And we were not agreeing to go away, not at all. That was entirely your fantasy. We were simply allowing you to blather on until we found a way to silence you."

Master Joris gritted his teeth. "If you will not go, then I will have to bring the baker up from the dungeons and kill him. And his little apprentice here. And this hedge wizard, and whoever this impertinent boy is. Do you think I will not do it?" The mage's voice quivered with outrage. His hands were in tight fists, and sparks flew as he stamped his foot on the ground.

"I think you will not do it," Bartholomew said.

The mage looked startled. "What did you say?"

"You will not do it. You are finished here."

Bee wondered if she'd heard him right. Was this the same hedge wizard who had smacked himself in the forehead with a mallet on board the *Egg-Hen*?

"How dare you? Why, you . . ." Master Joris was sputtering with fury. It reminded Bee of his wild anger when she and Wil had run away with Anika. He wasn't used to being crossed. He stamped his foot again, like an angry child.

But the hedge wizard did not back down. It was clear to Bee that his magical success had given him confidence.

"You have done enough harm here," Bartholomew said evenly. "You very nearly destroyed this kingdom. You deprived the Aradysh people of their king for a dozen years. And you caused the shipwreck that killed my wife—Bee's mother. You are a liar and a thief. You are a *murderer*."

Anika put a comforting arm around Bee's shoulder, but Bee barely felt it. It was a shock to hear it said, though she'd known it was true. She'd known Master Joris caused the wreck of King Crispin's ship. She'd known her mother was on board that same ship, that she drowned when it sank. It may not have been his intention, but the mage had killed Bee's mother.

"You are nothing but a hedge wizard," Master Joris hissed. "I forbid you to speak to me that way!" A third time the mage stamped his foot in wrath, and when he did the ground beneath all their feet trembled as if in an earthquake. Bee staggered, and Anika tried to steady her, but the trembling continued, and they both fell to their knees.

From the spot where Master Joris's foot had struck the earth, a crack appeared. It spread in two directions, both toward the palace and away, with the speed of a ship blown by a heavy wind. The crack in the ground became a cleft and then a crevice, and it widened with every passing second. When it came to the wall surrounding the garden, the wall itself cracked, and pieces of brickwork crumbled and fell to the ground.

Through the gap in the wall, Bee watched, openmouthed, as the crack in the earth moved ever closer to the edge of the lake. When the fissure reached the shore, it seemed at first that nothing more would happen, but a moment later there was a roar, and water poured into it, rushing back toward the garden.

"Get back!" Wil shouted, pushing Bee away from the crack, which was now nearly a yard wide. The lake water rushed toward them and then past, heading for the palace. Everyone turned to watch. The water pushed along the crack, widening it still further, curving and opening a path through the maze and flowing toward the palace. The path ran directly under the palace, and as the water surged through, the palace walls appeared to wobble just a little.

"Master Bouts!" Bee cried. The baker was trapped in the dungeons. And the cook, Hadewig, was still inside, and the butler. Bricks dropped off the tallest of the palace towers, and the towers themselves swayed as if in a heavy wind. And then, without warning, the whole building crumpled and folded in on itself with a great crash and tumble. A moment later, a dust-filled wind blew past the watchers in the garden. There was nothing left of the palace but a heap of debris that was slowly being engulfed by a rising lake of water. Bee covered her face with her hands and wept.

A muddy river now flowed through the garden, its waters churning at Bee's feet. She was on one side of the crevice with Wil and Bartholomew. Anika, her father, and Master Joris were on the other side. Master Joris looked back at the palace, his expression alarmed. Bee could tell that he had not expected his tantrum to have such a devastating effect. His uncontrollable rage had unleashed a frenzy of magic.

Anika helped her father, knocked down by the force of the quaking earth, to stand. "I think you have done enough," King Crispin said to the mage. But Master Joris recovered quickly.

"You have seen just a taste of my power," he replied loftily. "If you do not depart as we have agreed, I will do the same to all of Zeewal. I will reduce the town to rubble. I will turn you and your daughter to dust yourselves!"

"Stop him!" Bee begged Bartholomew.

Bartholomew pointed a finger at Master Joris and said incomprehensible words. Something shot out from his fingertip—a wind, or another unseen force, Bee couldn't tell. Unprepared for this sudden attack, the mage sat down hard on the ground. Quickly he stood again, and now he held something in his hand, something he'd picked up when he fell. He opened his palm and showed it to Anika.

"Pepin!" the princess cried, reaching for him.

The mage smiled at Anika, showing his teeth. Then, almost idly, he tossed the hedgehog into the air. Up the creature soared, spinning like a ball, and then down, down . . . into the muddy water of the newly formed river. Without a moment's hesitation, Anika leaped in after him.

"Stop!" Bee called out, but it was too late. *Anika couldn't swim.*

"Anika, no!" Wil shouted, and he too jumped into the brown froth. Bee stood as close to the edge as she dared, clinging to Bartholomew. Anika had disappeared under the water, and Wil dove for her, but he came up empty-handed. He dove again, staying down so long that Bee began to whimper with fear.

At last Wil surfaced with the princess, her body limp but her fist closed tightly around her hedgehog. He swam to the edge with Anika, and Bartholomew and Bee pulled as he pushed her up out of the river. She rolled onto her back and lay unmoving on the ground. Her red hair, thick with mud, framed a face as pale as risen cream. She was utterly still.

Anika wasn't breathing.

CHAPTER 25

Bee gave herself up to despair. She didn't notice the warlike cries that sounded as the pirates, no longer in their shrubby disguises, clambered through and over the broken garden wall. Unseeing, unhearing, she knelt and stroked Anika's face, mourning the dearness of the friend she'd known for so short a time. When someone shoved Bee rudely aside, tumbling her onto her back, she was utterly disoriented.

"Turn 'er!" Bee heard, but she didn't understand. She sat up and stared blankly as Haleem lifted the princess as if she were a feather and then laid her on her stomach. She blinked, uncomprehending, as Captain Zay raised her clenched hands and then brought them down hard, twice, between Anika's shoulder blades. But when Anika jerked and coughed and spewed a fountain of water onto the ground, Bee let out a cry of joy.

"My mens is often requiring resuscitation," Captain

Zay confided to King Crispin, who looked as dazed as Bee felt. "I recommend a brisk thump upon the back." Then she looked around, her gaze landing on Master Joris, who hadn't moved since tossing the hedgehog. "This one is quite wicked," she said to Haleem. "Tie 'im up."

Master Joris, realizing she referred to him, scrambled backward. He just missed stepping on Pepin, who had made his waddling way from Anika's grasp over to the wizard. The hedgehog hissed, then raised himself up and bit the mage hard on the leg.

Master Joris let out a shout and tried to shake Pepin off, but he hung on, his sharp teeth embedded in the mage's calf. Dancing wildly at the edge of the river, Master Joris tried to dislodge the hedgehog—and then his foot slipped. His arms windmilled wildly as he tried to regain his balance, but the ravine bank was now steep and slick with mud. Pepin let go and rolled away from the muddy bank to safety. The mage fell into the water with a great splash.

The current was no longer flowing strongly toward the remains of the palace, so Master Joris began swimming in the other direction as hard as he could, toward the lake and the canal. Haleem tried to grab him, but the river had become too wide.

As the mage reached the lake, he slowed down. His robes were heavy, making it hard for him to move. It was clear he was getting tired, and he aimed himself toward the shore. There were trees along this bank. Instinctively, the mage reached for their overhanging roots to pull himself up, but it seemed almost as if the roots shrank away from his grasping hands. Bee turned questioning eyes to Bartholomew. He nodded as if to say, *Watch.*

Then one tall tree—an oak, like the one in the town square—with thick, twisted roots allowed Master Joris to take hold of it. He dragged himself partway out of the water onto the slick bank and lay there panting. After a minute, he tried to stand, but the oak's roots tripped him, and he fell. As Bee watched in disbelief, the gnarled roots wound themselves around the mage's torso. Another tree—a maple, Bee thought—reached out its thinner roots and grasped his legs, and the roots of a third, with a tall, silvery trunk, seized his arms.

The mage let out a shriek of terror and tried to kick and twist free. But the roots held him tight as he struggled. Slowly they pulled him downward into the mire. In a moment he was gone, sucked into the mud of the lakeshore as if he had never existed.

Horrified, Bee turned toward Bartholomew, and he

hugged her to him. The look on Master Joris's face—oh, she would never forget that expression of malice and dread! It was too awful to think about. Her nose was running, and she hiccupped as Bartholomew patted her back awkwardly. "It will be all right," he said. "Dear me, dear me, it will be all right."

"But Master Bouts," Bee sobbed.

"I know," Bartholomew said. "I am sorry."

Suddenly, one of the pirates let out a shout. "Ship ahoy!" he yelled.

"What?" Bee said, muffled in Bartholomew's shoulder.

Another pirate took up the call. "Ship ahoy! Ship ahoy!"

Bee raised her head. The pirates all pointed toward the palace ruins, now more of a rough lake crowded with debris. Bobbing amid the rubbish was a raft of sorts, a flat vessel. A figure lay on top of it. Two others floated alongside, gripping the edges.

Bee cried out and began to run. As fast as she could, she flew along the river's edge until she could see the raft clearly. It was barely longer and wider than the form atop it, and that form was clearly Master Bouts. The two in the water were Hadewig and the butler, Master van Campen, paddling with their free arms and pushing the float toward shore.

The pirates helped pull the raft to land, and Hadewig and the butler clambered out, dripping and looking highly irritated. But Master Bouts didn't move. He lay, eyes closed, atop the raft, which Bee could see now was a wooden door. Were his lungs filled with water, as Anika's had been? But no, his round stomach rose and fell with his breath.

"Master Bouts!" Bee said.

At the sound of her voice, the baker opened his eyes. "Have we reached dry land?" he asked.

Captain Zay stepped up to the shore and bowed, the feather in her hat nearly sweeping the ground. "Ah, Master Baker!" she exclaimed. "You have survived the voyage all of a piece and have come safely in to port. Allow me the pleasure to escort you from your vessel." She held out a hand, and the baker sat up cautiously, flinching when his door-raft rocked in the water. He took Captain Zay's hand and climbed off the raft onto land, where he stood looking rather pale and shaky.

"I am a little afraid of the water," he said apologetically to everyone, and Bee launched herself into his arms, which encircled her.

"I thought you were dead," she said in a small voice.

He replied, "I very nearly was, my girl. If my cell door

had been made of iron instead of wood, I'd have drowned or been crushed by falling bricks, I am sure. But the hinges gave out, and the door popped right to the surface. Luckily I managed to climb on board." He kissed Bee on the top of her head.

"Luckily for you. There was no room for us," the butler said sourly, his piglike nose twitching with annoyance.

Master Bouts released Bee, and she saw Bartholomew looking at them. His expression was glad, his smile nearly as huge as hers. He had a big heart, her father did. Both of her fathers did.

Down the canal, a line of townspeople had begun to make their way toward the palace, drawn by the sight and sound of the palace collapsing. At the head of the line were the Weatherwaxes, Wil's parents carrying the little ones. Just behind them was a wavery figure whom Bee realized was Ying-tao. She hadn't seen the moss maiden since she'd baked the bibingka the afternoon before.

Ying-tao glided past Bee and the baker to the spot where King Crispin knelt beside his daughter at the edge of the river. Anika was sitting up now, her color back in her cheeks, her hedgehog safely curled in her damp lap. Wil sat next to her, rubbing her hands to warm them.

"Your Majesty," Ying-tao said. The king looked up and

slowly got to his feet.

"Is it time?" he said.

"It is."

"Can I not convince you to stay?" The king's voice was sorrowful, and Bee looked more closely at the two.

"You know I cannot stay," Ying-tao said simply. She leaned forward and pressed her lips against the king's cheek. He reached out for her hands, but she moved away from him, her eyes on the cherry tree that now stood on the bank of the new river. She held her arms out to the tree, and it almost seemed that the tree's branches stretched out toward her in return. There was a moment when Bee blinked, and when her eyes opened again, she saw only the tree, its curved branches reminiscent of Ying-tao's graceful figure.

The king sighed and straightened up, helping Anika to stand. As the rest of the townspeople took in the sight of the ruined palace, their eyes wide with amazement, Master Bouts turned to Bee.

"It seems that strange things have happened," the baker said. "I am sure there is a tale to be told here—but there are also buns to be baked. Did you set the dough to rise in the bakery this morning, child?"

Bee shook her head.

"No matter," said Master Bouts. "We will get a new batch ready together. Buns wait for no man, and this crowd must have their bread!"

The king, Anika, and Bartholomew stayed where they were, to try to explain to the townspeople what had happened, and Master Bouts and Bee started back toward the town and their bakery. Behind them, Captain Zay stood and watched them go, her eyes shining.

"That is a venerable baker, to be sure!" she said, shaking her head in wonder and admiration. "A man with such honorable priorities is a man truly to esteem."

CHAPTER 26

A second batch of Bouts Buns was in the oven, as the first had sold out in minutes. Bee had dared to try improving on the original recipe as she had on the *Egg-Hen*, flavoring the buns with cinnamon and nutmeg and sprinkling the top with toasted walnuts. The shop was thick with delightful smells and crowded with folk come to gossip and chatter about the goings-on up at the palace. The mage, dead and gone—and so very gruesomely! Their own king, returned! The princess, in love with the blacksmith's son! It was all as delicious as the pastries on the shelves.

"But he will not be a blacksmith," Bee pointed out to Mistress de Vos, who couldn't help snorting at the thought of a common boy and a princess together. "The king said Wil would be the first Minister of Trees." Master Weatherwax had had a few choice words to say about that, but between them, Wil and his brother Geert had almost convinced him that it was a good idea.

"Humph." Mistress de Vos rolled her eyes. "It seems to me that blacksmithy is a far more useful occupation. What does a Minister of Trees do, for goodness' sake? Why do we even need all these trees?" She shook her head in disapproval, and then said, "Aren't those buns ready yet? And don't give me any of those newfangled nuts or spices. I want my buns as they've always been."

In the last two days, Bee had already made several recipes from Master Bouts's ancient *Booke of Baking*, using the bounty from the trees. Most people were eager to try the new tastes—the citrus fruits, apples, cherries, and figs, the allspice and nutmeg, the pecans and pine nuts and almonds. But secretly, as much as it vexed her to do so, Bee had to agree with Mistress de Vos: Master Bouts's original buns were still best.

Certain things had been decided quickly. The king and Anika were staying with Wil's family, while a royal dwelling was being built along the river, between the old lake and the newly formed second lake that now lapped gently where the palace had once stood. When the new residence was finished, Bartholomew would move in with the king and princess as the mage of Aradyn, despite his inability to control his power perfectly.

"The kingdom needs a mage, and you are its most magical person," King Crispin pointed out. "And you have saved our lives more than once already. I am sure your skills will improve. We do not require more than that."

For now, the hedge wizard slept on a cot in the bakery kitchen, while Bee kept her little room in the back. Anika had tried to convince her to become the royal baker, to live in the palace when it was finished in a big, comfortable chamber down the hall from her own and bake in a brand-new kitchen with all the best equipment. But Bee refused. The cozy bedroom, with its soft bed and smell of sweet pastry and yeast, was home. The bakery kitchen was her kitchen. She would not give it up. "And I'm only an apprentice," she insisted. "It is Master Bouts who must be the royal baker, not me."

Then she turned to Bartholomew. "It's not that I'm choosing Master Bouts over you," she said.

"I know that," Bartholomew said. "Just as I am not choosing the royal family over you. It is simply how things work best for us."

Bee nodded, pleased.

"But I do hope you will dine at the palace often," Bartholomew said. "You and I can talk about your mother, perhaps, if there are things you want to know."

"I'd like that," Bee said.

"And you could bring dessert," he added. Bee grinned, for Hadewig was staying on as the palace cook. The king and Anika would need some decent pastries.

Bee took a break from her work to pack up a basket of treats for the pirates, baked with great contentment. The men had spent the last two days enjoying the local inns and taverns and were returning to their ship that evening. The king had made it clear that the tulip trade would be scaled back, so Captain Zay planned to refurbish the ship as a merchant vessel, though she insisted she was keeping her pirate flag.

"You may use it as decoration," King Crispin told her, "but you must fly the flag of Aradyn if you are to be trading for my kingdom. And if you decide to go back to piracy—as is your choice—you must be prepared for my ships to evade, intercept, and attempt to capture you."

"We will give this merchanting a try," the captain said thoughtfully. "It has the sound of being quite tedious to my mind, but my mens seem no longer partial to the exhilaration and also the menace of swordplay as once they were. I cannot understand this reluctance my ownself, but there it is, and it cannot be argued."

They were sitting in Master Bouts's kitchen when this

conversation took place, as the baker and Bee mixed and stirred, rolled and kneaded. Master Bouts stared down at his work as he said, "But, my dear captain, do you not feel any desire to settle down somewhat yourself?"

Bee held her breath, waiting for the captain's answer. It was so slow in coming that she looked up from her mixing bowl. Captain Zay's cheeks were pink, and her lashes lowered as she tapped her fingers on the table.

Finally she spoke. "Master Baker, would you leave off your art of baking for any reason whatsoever?"

"Well," Master Bouts said, stopping to think. "I suppose I would not."

"Then you should not be expecting other persons who feel keen passion for their chosen employment to be stopping the work, no?"

Master Bouts rubbed his forehead, streaking flour across it, and sighed. "I suppose I should not. But . . . it would be very nice if you were to stay."

Anika, sitting next to Wil at the long table, gave a little chirp of excitement at the statement. Captain Zay's pink cheeks flamed bright red as her men hooted and pounded on the table, spilling the rum-spiked tea from their mugs.

"I shall be returning to Zeewal anon and anon," she declared. "And when a pirate—a merchant, I rather mean to say—returns from the voyage, she brings the finest of gifts to those for whom she feels fondness, to be sure!"

The pirates cheered and toasted the captain, and Master Bouts smiled at her for a long moment before turning back to his dough.

By early evening, all was ready to carry to the ship. Master Bouts closed up the shop, and Bee, Anika, Wil and he joined the pirates as they made their way down the high street to the canal. Townspeople called out greetings as they hurried home to their suppers, and lights went on in windows as they passed. They walked by the tulip fields, the blooms long gone and some of the fields themselves plowed under for a sowing of winter wheat. Bee was glad she'd had a chance to see the carpets of tulips in flower, for by the spring the enormous fields would all be given over to trees and crops with their subtler beauty.

The *Egg-Hen* was tied up near the mouth of the canal, its long gangplank leading steeply from the shore up to the ship's railing. The pirates would have to climb its wooden slope. Haleem went first, a basket of cookies for the captain hooked over his arm. He stepped quickly onto the gangplank and began to scramble up, but as he did, the wooden plank seemed to dissolve beneath him. One minute it was whole. The next minute there was simply sawdust floating in empty air. Haleem plunged into the canal with an enormous splash while the other pirates stared, open mouthed.

"Ahoy, you louses!" Haleem shouted from the water. "Fish me out, and then tell me who played this prank, and I'll swipe his head from his body!"

Each pirate shook his head. "'Tweren't me," Filmon said, and Quigley and Limmo echoed him: "Not me!"

"Though I wish I'd a thought of it!" Thoralf added.

Haleem kicked his way to the canal bank, and the waves he raised knocked against the side of the *Egg-Hen*. It was just a little push of water, no more. But the ship began to crumble, just as the gangplank had. It held its shape for a moment, and then it collapsed onto the water's surface. The entire ship, there one instant, gone the next. Only the ship's ropes and sails and a few embroidered cushions from the captain's cabin were left bobbing on the water.

"What on earth?" Bee said in wonder. The surface of the canal appeared to be writhing, almost as if it were alive. Haleem struggled onto land, brushing frantically at his arms and legs, and Bee saw insects fall from him. He kicked them back into the canal, where they clambered onto the backs of thousands of their compatriots, all drowning together.

"The hemel beetles!" Bee gasped. She had forgotten all

about the tree-eating bugs. She vaguely recalled trying to bake her enjoyment of the *Egg-Hen's* pleasures and comforts into the bibingka, hoping that the beetles that ate it would find their way to the ship and away from Zeewal. But she hadn't considered what might happen if it worked. The beetles seemed to have devoured the entire wooden ship, leaving only its fragile outline to crumple into the water. "They've eaten the ship! Oh, it's my fault! It's all my fault!"

Captain Zay stared at the place where her ship had been. For only the second time since Bee had met her, she was utterly speechless. Zay sank to her knees and pulled off her hat, bowing her head. Bee feared she was weeping. She couldn't bear the thought of the brave pirate captain in tears, and she rushed forward to apologize, to raise her up again. But the captain got to her feet unaided, and her eyes were dry.

"A valiant vessel, to be sure!" she cried. "Men, we must salute our lost ship, the *Egbertina-Henriette,* that served us with such intrepidness and met such a noble end. She is utterly consumed by beetles, but see the way she takes the wicked bugs to her own watery grave! Sailors, bakers, I give you the *Egbertina-Henriette!*"

The pirates swept off their hats, and Bee, Wil, and

Master Bouts removed their caps. Even Anika dipped into a curtsy. "The *Egbertina-Henriette*!" they shouted.

Captain Zay jammed her hat back on her head, the feather drooping over her face. "I must be discussing with the king a new ship for our ventures. Alas, mates, we shall be spending some days or weeks ashore while we await developments. No doubt you will all suffer as I will to be away from our life on the sea."

The pirates looked at one another, grinning. They did not appear to fear the torment of spending time on land. There were plenty of taverns in Zeewal with plenty of rum to keep them occupied.

"I will communicate with Papa about the necessity for a new ship," Anika told the captain. "I am confident that he will procure a vessel for you with the utmost speed."

Captain Zay swept her a deep bow. "Princess, I would be feeling the greatest gratitude, for a landlocked sea captain is by nature a tragical thing."

"I feel terrible about the *Egg-Hen*," Bee said to the captain as they began the walk back up the canal to town. "Please, isn't there anything I can do to help?"

Captain Zay linked her arm through Master Bouts's and said, in a desolate voice, "Alas, what can make up for this greatest loss of the briny depths, the leaping fish, the wind and the sun and the freedom of the open sea?"

Heavy with guilt, Bee's head drooped.

"To be sure," the captain went on, "where can there be any comfort to me, who is left with no pirating whatsoever as well as no ship to command?"

Bee was silent.

"Only . . . ," the captain mused. "Perhaps there is some small thing I could imagine that would assist me in this most grave and troublesome time."

"Is there?" Bee said. "What do you have in mind?" She started to feel a smile pulling at her mouth. Master Bouts winked at her.

"Ah, what could 'elp a pirate—I mean a merchant captain—in such a wretched state? There is only a single item, one lone article in the entire cruel world that could be providing comfort to such as I."

"Whatever could that be?" Bee asked innocently. Behind her she could hear Wil and Anika start to snicker.

Captain Zay stopped walking and placed a hand over her heart, saying earnestly, "Why, it is only the deliciousness, the palatability, the scrumptiousness of a Bouts Bun that could bring this poor captain solace and consolment."

Bee grinned. "I think we could manage that, couldn't we, Master Bouts?"

Master Bouts patted the captain's other hand. "I believe we could."

"And perhaps," Bee added, "I will bake in some calmness and serenity to make your stay on land a bit easier for us all."

There was a momentary silence, and Bee wondered if she'd gone too far. But Captain Zay burst out laughing and clapped Bee on the back so hard she stumbled.

"Calmness and serenity? To be sure, in that case I shall require two buns at least. Lead on, Bee-girl, lead on!"

Master Bouts held out his free arm, and Bee took it. And arm in arm, they strolled together, Anika, Wil, and the pirates following close behind, up the tree-lined road toward the lights and warmth of Zeewal.

Bouts Bun Recipe

<u>Buns</u>

1 package active yeast (not fast-acting)

⅓ cup sugar

⅔ cup milk

3 ½ cups flour

¾ teaspoon salt

½ cup (1 stick) melted unsalted butter

3 eggs, lightly beaten with a fork

<u>Topping</u>

2 tablespoons melted unsalted butter

½ cup light brown sugar

1 teaspoon cinnamon (if you live in a land with trees)

½ to 1 cup raisins (depending on how much you like raisins)

Icing

1 ½ cups confectioners' sugar

3 ½ to 4 tablespoons milk

¾ teaspoon vanilla

The strained juice from 4 crushed
    raspberries OR a drop of red food coloring

Be sure you are in a happy mood before you start!

Directions

1. In a small pan, warm the 2/3 cup of milk to slightly above body temperature.

2. Pour milk into large bowl. Sprinkle yeast and the 1/3 cup of sugar over milk; stir gently with a spoon to dissolve.

3. Add 1 cup flour and stir until smooth. Add the stick of melted butter, stir. Add beaten eggs and remaining 2 ½ cups flour and salt. Stir until smooth. Use your hands to form it into a ball. It's okay if it's sticky!

4. Place into a buttered or lightly oiled bowl, cover tightly with plastic wrap, and leave overnight in the refrigerator.

5. In the morning, place the dough on a floured surface and knead for 1 to 2 minutes (sprinkle with a little extra flour if sticky) by pushing on dough with the heels of your palms, turning it, folding it over, and then pushing again.

6. Roll dough out with a rolling pin on a floured board to a rectangle about 9 x 14 inches. Flour the rolling pin if it sticks to the dough. It may be hard to roll the dough because it is elastic. Keep rolling!

7. For the topping, mix brown sugar and cinnamon together. Brush dough with melted butter; sprinkle with cinnamon-sugar and raisins.

8. Roll dough rectangle up from the longer side to make a long tube. Pinch the seam together. With a sharp knife, cut the tube into 16 pieces.

9. Place the pieces on a greased cookie sheet about 2 inches apart. Cover with towel. Let them rise until double in size, about one hour.

10 About 15 minutes before baking, preheat the oven to 350 degrees. Bake the buns for 20 to 25 minutes, until they are lightly browned.

11. When buns have cooled slightly, mix together icing ingredients. Spread or drizzle on top.

Eat and enjoy!

The author extends deepest gratitude to:

Jennifer Laughran, agent nonpareil, maker of cake pops and feather pens, occasional cheerleader, writer-wrangler, and lunch companion

Krissy Mohn, my editor, whose ideas have both sharpened and sweetened the story

Debra and Arnie Cardillo, whom I trust to find the perfect voices for Bee and Captain Zay

Shani Soloff, who straightens out both my spine and my plot development

Kathy Zahler, who came along on our very first trip to the ur-Aradyn

Ben Sicker, whose love of travel and faraway lands rivals my own (Just Add Fun!)

Severina Sicker (aka Grandfeathers), matriarch and originator of the Bouts Bun

Julius Sicker, lover of tulips, who has sampled more buns than anyone should have to

Phil Sicker, my muse, whose imagination (and red pen) are all over this book

Diane Zahler is the author of four middle-grade fairy-tale retellings: *The Thirteenth Princess, A True Princess, Princess of the Wild Swans,* and *Sleeping Beauty's Daughters.* She's made her home in Seattle, Morgantown, Ithaca, Solana Beach, Manhattan, the Bronx, Belgium, and London. She now lives with her husband and dog in an old farmhouse in the Hudson Valley. She really likes baking—and eating what she bakes.